A junior ROTC cadet a war—with himself, his enemies, and his past. But no matter how hard he throws himself into the intense demands of the military program, J.T. is unable to escape the traumas of his life. His father died in Desert Storm. His mother was killed in a car accident that J.T. may have caused. After her death, J.T. was placed in a string of bad foster homes.

Haunted by self-doubt, J.T. focuses on his latest assignment at school: whip a new group of recruits into shape so his commanding officer, Sergeant Maddox, will be proud. J.T. has to be the best cadet in Covington County so he can win a scholarship to The Citadel. The rigors of training, combined with his unresolved issues from the past, wreak havoc on J.T.'s mind. J.T.'s last hope may be his new foster dad, who is contending with his own violent past.

gigged

gigged

heath gibson

Woodbury, Minnesota

First Edition
First Printing, 2010

Cover design by Ellen Dahl
Cover image © iStockphoto.com/Hagit Berkovich

Flux, an imprint of Llewellyn Worldwide Ltd.

This is a work of fiction. Names, characters, places, and incidents are either the product of the author's imagination or are used fictitiously, and any resemblance to actual persons, living or dead, business establishments, events, or locales is entirely coincidental.

Library of Congress Cataloging-in-Publication Data
Gibson, Heath.
  Gigged / Heath Gibson.—1st ed.
     p. cm.
  Summary: Georgia high school junior J.T. relies on the discipline of the Reserve Officer Training Corps to cope with grief, life in foster care, and his physical limitations, as well as to prove himself to his mother, dead in a car crash, and his father, a soldier killed in Desert Storm.
  ISBN 978-0-7387-1901-6
  [1. United States. Army. Reserve Officers' Training Corps—Fiction. 2. Physical education and training—Fiction. 3. People with disabilities—Fiction. 4. Foster home care—Fiction. 5. High schools—Fiction. 6. Schools—Fiction. 7. Orphans—Fiction.] I. Title.
  PZ7.G339293Gig 2010
  [Fic]—dc22

                                                                    2009031361

Flux
A Division of Llewellyn Worldwide Ltd.
2143 Woodsdale Drive
Woodbury, MN 55125-2989
www.fluxnow.com

Printed in the United States of America

Acknowledgments

Regardless of what I write here, it will not even come close to paying the debt I owe the following people. I can only hope that by including them on this page, each will know how much I appreciate their role in getting *Gigged* out to the world.

A great many thanks to Kim Tanner, for reading my first attempts at fiction almost ten years ago and not tearing them apart—you gave me enough courage to continue; fellow Hollins University Children's Literature students, for raking over tons of pages in workshops; Han Nolan, for her guidance, insights, and apparent ability to see into the future; Alexandria LaFaye, for being a beast of a thesis advisor—I wouldn't have had it any other way; Tony Madaris, who truly changed the way I see myself, others, and the world around me; and Brian Farrey, my editor, for his vision and direction. And Joan Evans. For once, there are no words.

part I

preliminary maneuvers

alpha

Soldiers have to live by different rules. Train, be strong, follow orders, perform. Tough, but simple. Keeps things clear. Makes you safe. Until it's time to go to sleep.

Dreams are hell. No control. Pictures that hurt. No choice but to see.

———

My hand twists the wrench, tightening the last bolt.

Just like turning on a TV that picks up one channel, same show over and over. Stuck.

"There you go Mom, that's it," my old voice says from under the hood of the 1982 Corvette she bought because my father got killed before he had the chance.

She walks around to the front of the car and puts her arm around my shoulders. "Well, Jason, what'll we do with our Saturdays now?" She laughs.

Mom pats my left shoulder. I look down at her hand, nails unpainted, nubbed from too much biting and stained with grease. Not the hand of a bank teller.

"We haven't cranked it yet. Don't jinx it."

She stares down at the engine for a few seconds. "When you've worked as hard as we have, there ain't a jinx in the world to keep this car from cranking." She holds out the keys in front of me. "Go ahead."

I know not to grab the keys. "Nah, you do it."

She doesn't hesitate. She shrugs and says, "Alright then."

Mom steps over to the driver door, pulls her hair up into a ponytail, and plops down in the seat. She turns the key and the engine spurts a couple of times before letting out a roar that fills the garage.

I want to be happy like I was then, but I hate the sound.

She revs the engine. Every time her foot taps the gas I get more pissed off because I helped her fix it.

Mom sticks her head out the door with a smile that tells two stories—happy we finished but wishes we weren't. Didn't notice it then, but now, I can't not see it.

"Sounds great, doesn't it?"

Can't say anything back. Just stare and hurt.

Her head disappears back into the car. She lays on the horn.

bravo

Thursday, 13 Oct 05, 0618

My body jerks and my eyes snap open, staring at the ceiling in my room. But it is more of a movie screen than a ceiling, showing me old home movies. Mom jumping up and down at my little league games. Her hair covered in sludge when we blew up my science project in the kitchen. Her green eyes watching me make mac 'n' cheese because I knew she was tired from standing all day at the bank.

We were both people then.

Now she's dead. And I am a soldier.

Usually, I wake up, eyes pop open at the same time, no alarm, same position I fell asleep in, covers not even wrinkled.

Black turns to light with nothing in between. No pictures, no flashes of action or memories. Just snap, click, done—like a school photograph you don't want to take in the first place. Those are good nights.

It wasn't hard to learn to sleep that way. Just did like

a good soldier should do—trained my body and brain to do what I want. Focus. Training. Discipline. That's how things get done.

Blink a few times to make the white above me turn back into a ceiling. Don't like those pictures of when I was the weak me and Mom was around. The old me was soft, let things get to him that kept him trapped. Can't have that.

Roll out of bed and hit the floor face down, hands in position next to my chest. Got to get back in my zone. My mission zone. The mission every day is to be better than the day before—more prepared, stronger, harder. It is the only way to make something out of the short life I think I'll have.

Take a deep breath and push up off the floor, letting my chest and arms feel the weight for a second. Stare down at the wooden floor that's so old light winks through the cracks between the boards.

Drop down fast, stopping right when my chest grazes the floor. Arm barely shakes and the ever-present ache in my left leg crawls into my lower back, trying to convince me the bed is better, softer. Ignore the pain and my brain. Have to. Then push up, down, up, down. A fast, easy rhythm. My father's dog tags jingle against the floor every time I go down.

After twenty-five, the blood is pumping, filling my chest and triceps, washing away any doubts about why I do this every day. My arms want to stop, but the voice in my head won't let me.

"Come on soldier. Twenty-five more."

Like the voice. It lets me know I'm back in my zone where I'm sharp, strong, hard. Most would stop when the pain gets bad, but I never do. Can't. Because the voice is my father's, and there is no disappointing him.

Keep pushing up, down, up, down until I reach fifty. Flip over on my back and start churning out crunches. And the voice gets louder.

"NO STOPPING TILL 100! Got to earn the right to wear that uniform."

Even though my father didn't made it back from Desert Storm, and I never met him, it's the voice I want to hear, the one on the audio tape Mom played over and over until it snapped. Lieutenant Robert Tillman, U.S. Army Special Forces. No better voice to pay attention to.

Make it to 100. Gut tight and hard like a fistful of rocks.

Flip back over on my face and bust out fifty more push-ups. Tell myself, "Come on, get up," on the last five. Arms shake and muscles ache like they're pulling away from the bones. Whatever it takes to make it to the number my father wants me to reach.

One hundred more crunches. Hop up on my feet, not breathing hard enough to satisfy me. This is getting too easy.

Add more tomorrow.

Open the door and step into the hallway. The floor creaks under my feet.

"J.T? You up, son?" Mr. Coffeen calls from the kitchen. Don't answer because he knows not to call me "son." I'll never be a son again, foster or otherwise. I am a soldier.

Walk into the bathroom and shut the door. Don't turn on the light. Never turn on the light. Don't need it, don't want it. Turn on the shower and step in. I know exactly how far to turn the knob to get the right temperature. It took a while, but it's down pat now.

Wash the little bit of hair I have first, then bathe. In the pitch black grab my toothbrush and toothpaste. Don't grope or fumble. A real soldier doesn't need his eyes to do some things.

Finish and step out of the shower, grabbing the towel that always hangs on the back of the door. Dry off and run my hand over my head. Hair needs a cut. It's barely limp, not prickly like it needs to be.

Open the cabinet for my clippers. Plug them in and face the mirror. It's OK to face the mirror when the lights are off. In the dark I can't see the scar that runs from my left temple to my chin. And don't have to hear tires screeching and glass shattering.

Flip the clippers on and run them over my head, always starting on the left and working my way over. Don't use a guard to make sure I get as close to my head as possible. A soldier doesn't need hair. It just gets in the way.

Finish, hang the towel over the mirror, and turn on the light to clean up. The light burns my eyes. Blink a few times to let them adjust and turn on the sink. Swirl my hand around to force all the red hair down the drain. Then take a hand towel, dry the sink, and wipe the faucet and knobs. Never leave a mess. That's what I got from Honeywell House. Mrs. Hernandez made sure we all learned.

———————

"Could I see you a second, Jasonito?" Mrs. Hernandez stands in the doorway of the game room that's really just a room with a couch, TV, a small table, and a stack of board games. This room was probably somebody's bedroom before this house became Honeywell, the place where boys wait until someone wants them, if anyone will ever want them.

I get up off the floor. I don't sit on the couch with the other three boys who are here waiting for a family. They stare too much, so the floor is more comfortable.

Mrs. Hernandez turns when I get to the doorway. "This way."

I follow her up the stairs to the bathroom that the four of us share. She flips on the light, points at the bathtub. "You?"

An empty tube of cream and used gauze sit on edge of the tub. "Yes, ma'am."

"Why?" is all she says.

I could tell her because the doctor lied to me and said the scar wouldn't be that bad. So I sit on the tub to change the bandage on my face, away from the sink and the mirror. I just shrug my shoulders at her.

Mrs. Hernandez motions toward the tub and says, "Please."

I pick up the tube and used gauze and throw them in the trash can next to the toilet. Step toward the door, but Mrs. Hernandez stops me. "Not quite."

I look back at the edge of the tub. One drop of the cream I have to put on my face hangs on the corner. With a piece of toilet paper, I wipe it off, and then look at Mrs. Hernandez to make sure it's good enough. She smiles and nods her head. I don't smile back.

"Jasonito," she says, "some people take things being clean very seriously." She stops and looks at me for a second. "You learn to keep things clean, and you can avoid all kinds of trouble, no matter who you live with. Understand?"

"Yes, ma'am."

charlie

Hang the hand towel on the rack, turn off the light, and take the towel off the mirror. Step out of the bathroom, and that same board creaks under my foot.

Mr. Coffeen calls again. "I got breakfast in here. You eating this morning?"

Stupid question. I always eat—three times a day. No snacks, no candy. Just three meals.

All his questions is the only thing wrong with Mr. Coffeen. Otherwise, he's worthy of any respect I can give. He works hard, gives me space, and has never laid a hand on me. Guess that's why I've been with him for a year and a half now. He's not like the other foster father I had.

After Mike, Mrs. Hernandez said she'd found me a nice place.

"Jasonito, this is a good man. I've known him many years. He will protect you, keep you safe."

Don't need protection anymore, but she was right about Mr. Coffeen. He smiles a lot and pretty much lets me do whatever I want, as long I show up to work at the hardware store every afternoon. He's old, but he keeps on working anyway. He likes the work. Says it keeps him young.

Got news for him. He's not even close to staying young. But at least he works and doesn't sit around drinking Pabst, smoking joints, and watching Jerry Springer like the last guy they put me with. The weak me put up with that shit, but that me is only a memory.

"J.T.? I got breakfast in here, if you're eating," he yells again.

He didn't say, "son," so I can answer. Sometimes he forgets because he calls everyone younger than him son. But that doesn't excuse it, though.

"Sir, I'll eat as soon as I get into my uniform, sir."

"Alrighty. I just wanted to make sure."

Close the door and step to the dresser next to my closet. Take out one pair of boxers, white undershirt, and one pair of green socks. Lay them on the bed in order from left to right. The items have to make a perfect square on the bed before I can put them on. I step over to the closet and pull out my Army ROTC uniform. Hang it on the hook on the closet door and pull off the plastic from the dry cleaners. Sergeant Maddox said we could wash and iron the uniforms ourselves, but the cleaners starch it stiff and perfect.

Stand at the foot of the bed and drop the towel. Boxers, undershirt, socks. Put on the shirt, button from bottom to top. Pants, with a perfect sharp crease down the middle of the legs, go on left leg first. Tuck shirt tight and neat, keeping the buttons in line with the clasp on the pants. A perfect gig line. That's what Sergeant Maddox calls it. If that line ain't right, you get gigged. And nobody wants that.

In the top left drawer of the dresser, I get my belt, tie, and pins. Belt goes on fast and easy, buckle in line with buttons. Tie takes longer.

Put on my pins while looking at my jacket. The black-and-silver Marksmanship pin for hitting a two-inch target at fifty yards with a .22 rifle. The blue-and-red Physical Training pin for a sub-six-minute mile, 65 sit-ups in a minute, and 55 push-ups in a minute. No one else even close to that. The pins go right above the name badge that says Tillman.

Only Sergeant Maddox uses my last name. He's my commanding officer, so he can call me whatever he wants. On the shoulders go my stripes for rank, Captain. The only eleventh-grader to hold that rank, and the one cadet who will win the Evans Scholarship to The Citadel—the first goal. Then the Middle East. War. Fighting the enemy. Victory. Just like my father.

Sit on the bed and slide my feet into the glossy black shoes. Then I go to the kitchen to eat.

"Now aren't we looking smart this morning," Mr. Coffeen says when I sit down at the table in front of the plate of eggs and toast. He says the same thing every Thursday morning. And I never reply. Just start eating.

"Son…" Mr. Coffeen starts.

Stop chewing, look up, and stare hard at him. He knows not to use that word.

"Sorry, J.T. You know my old brain takes a while to catch up." He chuckles and sits down at the table. "We have a shipment of lumber coming in today, so be ready for some heavy lifting this afternoon."

"Yes, sir."

"And you might want to bring an extra shirt with you to work. Remember last time." He laughs even though it isn't funny. Wasn't then either.

Yeah, I remember. "No problem, sir."

"So what's on the agenda for school today?"

Mr. Coffeen always tries to start conversations with me, even though he knows I have nothing to say. Doesn't keep him from trying.

"Class, test third period, quiz fifth, and drill formation after school."

"So, I guess you'll be a little later today than normal."

"1530, not a minute later," I say before drinking my orange juice.

"That's fine. That lumber is not going to get up and walk away." He laughs again.

"Inspection and marching end at 1515. I'll double-time it over to make it before 1530."

"Oh, that's fine, fine."

I'm thinking, *Doesn't matter if it's fine or not. That's the way it has to be.* But before I let that thought get to me, I take a breath. Can't think about Mr. Coffeen that way. He's earned that much.

"J.T., you seen my keys laying around here anywhere?"

Without looking up from the plate, I say, "On top of the microwave, sir."

"Oh, that's right. I swear to you, I must lose track of these things at least three times a week."

He wishes it was three times a week. But I always know where they are. Every time I walk into a room I try to notice everything, try to soak up as much as I can as quickly as I can. Got to be keen and observant. Plus, it cuts down on the time Mr. Coffeen has to look for his keys.

"Well, I'm off to open the store." Mr. Coffeen grabs his keys off the microwave. "You keep those troops in line today," he says and pats my shoulder when he walks by.

I jerk forward. "Always, sir." Mr. Coffeen ignores my jerking. He knows it's something I can't help. Hate the jerking. It's like a finger when it grazes a burner on the stove. That hand is going to snatch back whether you like or not.

His shoes clap against the wood floor and stop with him shutting the front door.

One last swallow. If I wasn't a soldier, I'd look at my watch to see what time it is. But I already know exactly how long I have before I have to leave.

Get up from the table, wash the plate, fork, and glass, and place them on the drying rack. No mess. Walk back to my room and put on my jacket. On top of my dresser is my black beret. Slide it tight on my head. Sergeant Maddox would freak if he saw me wear my cover inside, but I have to be in full uniform before saluting my father.

Adjust the beret and turn toward the only picture in my room. It is a picture of my father, head to toe in desert camouflage, holding an M16, and wearing a smile stretched across his face. Stuck in the middle of a war and still had a smile like that. But he was a soldier, and that is what soldiers do. Do what you have to when you have to. Maybe Mom loved him because he was a soldier—strong, fearless, committed. She was proud of him. And I have to make her proud of me.

That's why I have this picture and the brochure from The Citadel. It reminds me of what I have to be, the standard I have to live up to. First in his class at The Citadel, officer, platoon leader. I'm on the right track. No. Have to be better. Just got to keep studying, training, taking on enemies, and winning battles. Sergeant Maddox says every day is a battle that must be won. No doubt my father would agree.

delta

Turn quickly away from the picture before I start remembering and grab my books and gym bag off the chair in my room. Pick up the house key and almost run to the front door. Two minutes off schedule. Make it up on my walk to school.

Slam the door, turn the key. Moving smooth, fast now. Sunlight bounces off my pins, pricks my eyes. Hear a car coming. Student's car. The music gives it away. Focus, analyze, conclude. All the time. Never turn it off. Clues everywhere. Just look, listen. Beware.

Hear the car slow down, almost stopping.

Bubblegum and venom voices scream over music booming out the car windows. Probably four of them. Daddies' jackals. "PICKLE!"

They sing the "L" like it is the end of their favorite song. The driver lays on the horn and covers their voices. Don't turn to see them.

———

"Mom, I don't get it."

"Don't get what, honey?" She puts the Corvette in reverse and looks over her shoulder.

"I have to wear my seat belt, but you don't." I click the buckle that's so hot from the sun I almost need an oven mitt to touch it. I look to Mom for an answer.

She keeps looking over her shoulder and pulls out of the parking spot in front of the church. "Well, I don't like it. I feel trapped."

"I don't like it either, but I still have to wear it."

Mom stops backing up, puts the car in drive, and then looks at me. "Jason, I don't want to argue after church, honey. There's just some things I can do that you can't. You'll understand when you're older. O.K.?"

It's not O.K. I don't understand. Never will. Should argue some more. But I back off. Face the windshield. "Isn't fair."

echo

The car has stopped in front of the house like they're waiting for something. The girls laugh and flip their hair. The driver says, "Need a lift, soldier?" They laugh louder, and the driver punches the gas.

They get away with no consequences just like Chris Walker does. Whatever stunt he pulls, he always slips the grip of punishment. Nobody busted him when he blew up a Coke bottle with water and dry ice in Mr. Brownlow's chemistry class, keeping them out of the lab for the rest of the week. Abel Gonzales kept his mouth shut when Chris Walker and a couple of his buddies spray painted, "No Green Card," on the side of his car. And even though almost a hundred people saw Chris Walker shove Missy Jackson on the ground after she slapped his hand off her ass at a party, everybody but Missy forgot by Monday morning. That's what money and the right last name do for you around here.

But name and money don't matter to me. They can't save you forever.

Legs churn down the sidewalk toward school, double-timing it to make up for the lost two minutes. The tail-lights of the car get brighter as the car slows to make the turn into the school parking lot half a mile ahead. Pickle. That's what they call all of us in ROTC. But I am the only Pickle Freak.

Pisses me off because none of them have the guts to put on the uniform. They just want to cause trouble.

Guess it fits the way the world works, though. Every soldier has enemies. And enemies have to be overcome—or taken out. Some will figure out they're wrong or can't win, do the right thing and surrender. And if they don't, only one choice left. Elimination.

foxtrot

Normal students belong to cliques. I have five kids dressed in Army green. They stand in the mass to the left of the main entrance of the school. For most of ROTC, Thursday is the only time they are soldiers. Every other day they fade back into the normal population and forget the green. I never forget because that means getting off track. And that would make me weak. Don't want to be weak. Need to be a soldier. So I can fight.

March toward the crowd of green figures with black berets. Sweat rolls down both temples after double-timing it for five blocks to get back on schedule—0715, exactly five minutes before the bell. Sergeant Maddox says if you're not five minutes early then you're late. Otherwise, I'd get here right when the bell rings. Normal kids are early because they want to hang out and talk to friends. Don't have friends. Don't want to talk—it's worked since the end of ninth grade when I came to North Covington. I just want to be a good soldier, so I endure the five minutes every day.

Step to the edge of the crowd and sit my bags down and wipe the sweat off my face before it drips onto my uniform. Some of these cadets kill me. They're standing around chatting, slouching with their hands in their pockets, some wrinkled like they keep their uniform tucked in the back of their sock drawer. Makes me sick.

I face away from the crowd, stand with my feet barely more than shoulder width apart, and clasp my hands behind my back. Four minutes until the bell, not too long to have to ignore the stares and snickering.

"Good morning, Captain," a voice says behind me. I know the voice.

"Good morning, Cadet Pickens." My back stiff, not turning.

He steps around in front of me. Cadet Pickens got his knee crushed in eighth grade and has some slight nerve damage in his left arm, so he walks with a slightly spastic limp that will never leave him. The first drill formation we had, Sergeant Maddox yelled at Pickens, "Good God son, you move around like a puppet on a string." That's why he sometimes calls Pickens Puppet. But that's the way he is, hard on everybody without exception or discrimination. Pickens actually likes the name, I think. "You are all equally worthless," is what Sergeant Maddox yells at the platoon to explain why nobody gets special treatment. Pickens just wants to be equally anything, no matter what it is.

"How'd I do this morning?" he asks, standing in front of me at attention, but still slightly bent toward his left, his bad leg. Without moving my head, I inspect his uniform, starting with his shoes. My eyes move up slowly, paying special attention to the belt and buttons. When I make it to his tie, I say, "Turn."

Pickens whips around, quick and sharp like he's supposed to. Have to make sure his tie is completely hidden in the back. "About face," I say, and he snaps around. I nod and say, "Good, Cadet."

Pickens smiles. He knows if he gets by me, then he'll make it through inspection this afternoon. "Captain, I guess I finally got it right, huh?"

"It looks that way."

A month ago, Pickens got gigged for sloppy uniform. It was my job to PT him for it. And I did just like Sergeant Maddox would have done. Didn't back off until it was clear mistakes can't be tolerated. Mistakes make you weak. Pickens doesn't want to be weak, so I made sure I let him know I didn't think he was. Ran him till his legs barely held him up, kept him on his face doing push-ups till he couldn't get one more off the ground, and then made him lie on his back and hold his feet straight out in front of him six inches off the ground till he almost puked.

Unfortunately, he got gigged the next two Thursdays, so he had to spend more time with me. Anybody else would have fallen on his knees and begged God to strike one of us down. Cadet Pickens is just the opposite. He never misses a chance to prove he can take it.

"Sir, thank you, sir," he says, still at attention.

"At ease," I say because I can tell how hard it is for him to stand up straight for that long. Not mercy, just courtesy.

Pickens lets his body relax.

A group of students fifteen feet away laugh and mumble something I can't hear. Ignore them because they don't matter.

Pickens pipes up. "J.T., I got up at 0500 this morning to get ready. No way was I spending another afternoon with you trying to kill me." He laughs and shakes his head. "My mom wanted me to go to my physical therapist to get straightened out after that second time. If you think I walk funny normally, you should have seen me that Friday morning. I had to check in at lunch I was hurting so bad." He stops to see if I have anything to say.

"Pickens, there's always a price to pay if you want to be better than you were the day before."

"Yeah, I know. She just doesn't get it. She wants me to quit. But I ain't no quitter. I'm harder than she thinks. And I told her only punk soldiers quit."

"Cadet Pickens, you are correct."

"Yeah, but my mom's not buying it for a second."

Pickens talks too much, especially about his mom. Makes it harder to listen to him. Only good thing about him talking is I don't have to. That's why I can tolerate him. Plus, he's too busy talking to ask questions. Don't like questions.

The bell rings, and Pickens snaps to attention. "Captain, thanks for the inspection."

Nod my head once. "No problem, Pickens. Just don't screw it up before this afternoon."

"No way, sir. No way." He doesn't move because he's waiting on me.

"Dismissed."

He lets his body fall back into its normal distorted posture and limps over to the wall to pick up his backpack. The rest of the pickle patch walk past me, some of them saying, "Good morning, Captain," as they do. The others ignore me. Fine with me. Different story at drill formation.

Watch the cadets stop at the door to remove their covers before they step inside. Other students bump into them. Some of them say, "You want to get out of the way." Smarter students make comments like, "Here we go again, the Thursday morning pickle jam."

None of the cadets say anything back. They know I am watching. They know what I expect—never let your emotions get the best of you.

Wait till every cadet is inside the school. Have to make sure no one stands outside and ends up being late for class. Part of my job to make sure no one "disgraces the uniform." That's what Sergeant Maddox calls it when a cadet gets in trouble while in uniform. When a cadet does "disgrace" the uniform, he spends time with Sergeant Slaughter—Sergeant Maddox when he's pissed—instead of me. It's the only time anyone wants to deal with the Pickle Freak instead. Of course, neither one of us hears those names said to our faces by a cadet. But we both know they say them. Doesn't change us one bit.

Look around to make sure everyone is gone. Pick up my bags and head inside, eyes straight ahead and ears wide open, listening for enemies. Of course, I stop at the doorway to remove my cover and tuck it evenly in my belt.

Mrs. Polk, the principal stops me at the door. "Good morning, J.T."

"Ma'am."

"Looking sharp this morning."

"Trying, ma'am." Like Mrs. Polk for two reasons. One: She treats everybody here the same. It's the exception around here, not the norm. Two: She, Mr. Marsh, and Sergeant Maddox are sponsoring me for the Evans Scholarship—only one cadet in Covington County can win it every four years. Not many people on my side. But she's one of them.

Nod at her and start walking. Like the sound of my shoes on the tile floor in the hall. Like it so much that I deliberately smack my heels against the floor to make my shoes go *clap-clap-clap*. The sound is crisp and tight, and it's good. Makes people look and sometimes stare. But I never look at them. Only listen.

"Here comes G.I. Joe."

"Where's the battlefield?

"What a freak."

Words like these whisper and mingle with lockers slamming, music blaring from people's headphones, girls begging their boyfriends not to break up with them, and guys telling lies about how much they can bench-press. Never glance to the side. Never show any sign that I hear them. That's why they keep talking. And that's what I want. Easier to identify enemies that way.

golf

Reach the end of the main hall and square the corner to the right. No lockers on this hall, so it is quieter. I can hear my heels better. *Clap-clap-clap-clap.* Walk fast because I don't want to be late. I have special privileges on Thursday. My teacher knows I double-check that cadets get inside on time, and it's O.K. if I'm a couple minutes late. But I'm never late. Don't need special privileges. Learn how to work within the time I have.

Third door from the end of the hall I square off another turn to the right and walk into Room A 113—history, Mr. Marsh.

One weakness I have is my bad memory. Wasn't always like this. But things change. Adapt. Have to play games in my head to remember some of the simplest things, like names. Mr. Marsh was easy. His last name is Marsh, like a swamp. He's about six-foot-five with long, brown hair and a full beard that hangs about four inches below his chin. I think he looks like a swamp monster. So Swamp Monster equals Mr. Marsh. It sounds like I am being disrespectful.

But Mr. Marsh has my respect. He knows more about wars, battles, victories, and defeats than I could ever know. And he expects nothing but the best from his students. Not a soldier. But a good man.

Square off down the third aisle and walk to the last seat, my seat. Good soldiers keep others where they can see them. My gym bag goes behind the desk. Take out notebook, pen, and textbook. I carry every book and every notebook, all of the time. Just part of my training to be able to carry a lot of weight for a long time. I don't ever miss a chance to make myself better. Just an added bonus to a messed-up situation.

The tardy bell rings. Mr. Marsh shuts the door, stopping late students from being able to enter.

"You know the routine. You can come in when you have a tardy slip from the office. Thank you. Bye-bye." He smiles through the bush that covers his mouth and waves to the small group of students standing outside the door.

Dogs learn better than those kids. It's November, and they still haven't been trained how to get to class on time. Pathetic.

The intercom clicks on and Susan Welsh's voice spurts into the room. "Good morning, North Covington!" Bubbles are almost shooting out of the speaker. Her voice is always so sweet it almost makes my teeth hurt, I swear to God. I guess that's what got her student body president. Everyone knew she was the only person alive with enough sweetness and energy to put up with the mountain of bullshit that comes along with the position.

She spouts off a few announcements that I barely listen to. And then, "Now please stand for the pledge." Here in Georgia, God and country take precedent over almost everything, so the pledge is just as important as textbooks.

Stand, angle slightly to the right toward the flag hanging over the door, and salute. Mr. Marsh steps away from the board and quickly places his right hand over his heart. And the students are doing the same—at least most of them are.

"I pledge allegiance to the flag…," the class says, but the lack of emotion makes it sound like a song meant to hypnotize. "…of the United States of America."

All of us should be standing, but some never do. Mr. Marsh is real big on preaching about individual freedoms and stuff, so he doesn't make people stand for the pledge. It's always the same five kids. They're not trying to make some political or religious statement. They're just too damn lazy to stand up.

Even though the words of the pledge are coming out of my mouth, my brain is on fire.

"For which it *stands*," I say louder than the class. Want the ones sitting down to stand up, to show respect. And my father's voice wants it, too.

"Disrespectful punks."

Couldn't be more right.

"All those soldiers."

Just like him.

"Can't even stand and show a little respect."

Pathetic.

"PATHETIC."

Chris Walker sits in the first desk. He slouches, legs stretched out. He doesn't care what soldiers have done so he can sit in his nice little desk indifferent to everyone but himself. The soldiers that are fighting right now for *him*.

About time he's reminded.

Without hesitating, step down the aisle, slapping my heels. Stop at Chris's desk. Turn away from the flag and stare down at him.

He looks up at me.

My voice is now the only one in the room.

"Indivisible, with liberty and justice for all," I push hard from my gut. Before the intercom clicks back on, I say, "Even you," to Chris. Susan's voice then bounces across the room. "Thanks North, and a have a terrific Thursday."

The class sits. But I don't.

Snap my arm down to my side. Keep staring at Chris. Want him to see how pissed I am, to understand, to know he should've shown respect. He's made my list. Guess he's always been a good candidate.

Chris glares back. "You need something?"

Don't need to answer. He gets the message. Plus, words are nothing. Only action matters.

Behind me a few people half chuckle and snicker. This is not a joke, and I don't care what they think. I know they want me to do something that will let them say, "See, I told you." Not going to do more, not today, not in uniform.

"Uh, J.T.," I hear Mr. Marsh say, "you need to sit down now."

Turn away from Chris to look at Mr. Marsh. "Excuse me, sir." Take a step away from Chris's desk.

Chris says, "Freak."

A girl's voice mumbles, "No kidding," while a few others blow small laughter through their noses.

Sit back in my desk. Don't look around the room. Eyes forward—the opposite of everyone else's. Even though I'm sure half of them look confused, they're not. They know the message I tried to send. They probably even agree. But they'll never say it. That's O.K. Sometimes soldiers have to do the dirty work. Glad to do it when it comes to people like Chris Walker.

Mr. Marsh pulls the class back to reality, away from what they think is impending danger. "O.K., class, if you'll turn in your textbooks to page 158, we'll pick up where we left off yesterday."

Backpacks unzip, feet bang against desks, and desks shift around the room as everybody switches off of me.

I switch, too—from soldier to student. "The best have to adapt to any situation," Sergeant Maddox always says to the cadets. So that's what I do.

Mr. Marsh begins his lecture. Chris and class disappear. Have to focus. Won't let an enemy get the best of me. Won't allow him to keep me from getting my work done. The scholarship goes to the best cadet, which includes grades.

The class flies by. Always does. Most kids can't stand sitting and listening to someone talk for an hour. But history works for me. It's simple—facts, names, dates. Have to work hard to remember, but at least it's not confusing. Don't like being confused. Guess that's why English and math are my worst subjects.

The bell rings and books slam shut. "Everyone have a good day. See if you can make a little history before tomorrow." Mr. Marsh says that every day. He thinks it's funny, but it only makes most students shake their heads.

I'm the last out the door. As soon as I enter the hall I hear, "Hey, Pickle Freak." Chris Walker is behind me. Stop, but don't turn. Make him come to me.

He walks in front of me. "So, you got something you want to say to me?" he says, jerking his head forward.

"Not at this time." No expression, no change in volume.

"What do you mean, 'not at this time'? Seems like a good time to me. If you got something to say, you might want to get your freak mouth moving before somebody sticks a fist in it." Chris looks around to make sure people stop and watch. Like all the times before, he needs an audience.

Keep my face straight and hard. "Chris, unlike you, I respect the rules."

"Oh, so the Pickle Freak is just a good little boy." He laughs, looks side to side at the small crowd starting to assemble, and then jerks his head back to me. "But not too good to get your ass beat." Chris drops his bag off his shoulder. The crowd is silent, waiting to see if Chris will really take a swing.

Don't move. Don't even flinch.

"Gentlemen, do we have a problem here?" Mr. Marsh

stands in his doorway. Chris puffs up his chest. Chris looks at Mr. Marsh, but doesn't say anything.

"No problem, sir," I say, keeping my eyes on Chris. Always keep eyes on the enemy.

Chris drops his arms and picks up his bag. He puts his finger in my face. "Pretty soon that scar isn't going to be the only thing messed up with your face."

Chris walks away, and Mr. Marsh steps back into his room. The muscles in my neck squeeze tight. Let out a deep breath, not because of fear, but for control.

"Good job, soldier."

He's right. Getting better at handling Chris Walker.

hotel

Second period is the same as always, except for me being ten seconds late. Completely unacceptable. But Ms. Rimer doesn't care like I do. She thinks I was checking on cadets. Test in third. Spanish is so easy I can't believe Ms. Guy can even say it's a test—*el banco, la escuela, la tienda, el museo, la farmacia, la biblioteca*. Good to know another language. Just another skill a soldier might need.

Spend fourth period in the dark, which is normally a good place. But we watch another movie on the deadliest snakes in the world. Mr. Finch is a bit of a lunatic about snakes, so we have to watch a lot of videos on snakes. We see so many the class actually gets excited about a worksheet.

Bell rings and Mr. Finch flips on the lights. We herd out of his room while he tries to yell over the class, "Don't forget tomorrow's quiz on constrictors."

I'd like to tell him I'll sleep with a constrictor if he would stop showing us snake videos.

Turn into the hall and march toward the cafeteria.

Sergeant Maddox has lunch duty every day, and he wants

to see us eating together. Says it builds unity, brotherhood. Freddy MacDonald, the platoon smartass, asked him how we could build brotherhood with the girls in ROTC. MacDonald got gigged and spent an afternoon with Sergeant Slaughter. Next day nobody even heard MacDonald clear his throat. And they for sure didn't see him move too quickly because Sergeant ran him till he would have eaten his own legs if it meant he could stop. On top of that, he landed on my squad for me to deal with. So no one else asks questions. We just follow orders.

Sloppy joes and French fries cover disposable trays and create a smell that is unmistakable high school cafeteria. Doesn't matter what they are serving, the place always smells like a combination of cheap cheese, powdered eggs, and chocolate milk. And with the blue plastic chairs and the faded yellow concrete walls, it ain't hard to figure out why schools are referred to as *institutions* of learning.

The tables are bricks. Same shape, size, function, and there might as well be concrete between them. There is no moving, no changing. Call them cliques, "social groups," whatever. Once you're put in place, that's it. Can't take you out or else the social wall might come tumbling down.

My brick is the green one in the back.

About three steps away from the table, Cadet Freeman sees me coming. She stands, and the others follow right behind her. Sit my tray down, drop my gym bag, and pull off my backpack.

"Captain," bounces around the table, and the cadets nod at me.

"Gentlemen, and lady," I say, nodding at Cadet Janet Freeman. She used to be our worst female cadet—overweight, slow, and clumsy. Not so much anymore. When she came back after the summer, Sergeant Maddox said, "Glad to see you grew into yourself, Cadet." Guess that's his way of saying she went through a metamorphosis that's made people wonder if the real Janet Freeman was abducted by aliens. She's hardcore now. Just what a leader needs. Glad to have her.

"Captain, are you eating today?" Freeman asks.

"Absolutely, Cadet. Just wanted to check that everyone was here. Everybody looks squared away." Drop my backpack by the chair. Nod at the table and march toward the line.

The line runs along the wall. Most of the students lean against it with their shoulders or back. Kills me. They're too lazy to even stand up straight. When I step into line, the guy in front of me shuffles forward like I smell bad or something. A few people file in behind me. Look over my right shoulder. They keep a safe distance like there is an invisible fence they don't want to cross. Turn my head forward, keep my eyes straight ahead. But my ears tell me what's going on behind me.

Bodies shove into each other and students try to suppress their laughter. Somebody says, "Watch out." Then another says, "Be careful, he might have a grenade." Some more laughing and shoving. One of them grazes my back. Stay stiff, eyes forward. Whoever it was jumps back and says, "Stop playing."

Pickens is in line a couple of people in front of me. He turns to see what's going on. He says, "Captain, what's happening?" Just shake my head at him. Hear somebody behind me mention Chris Walker, and I know they're talking about this morning in the hall. And right on cue, Chris Walker comes walking down the line with his tray. Of course, he stops close to Pickens.

"Well, if it isn't G.I. Gimpy," Chris laughs.

Keep my eyes on Pickens. This is a good test for him. Got to see if he can be disciplined, ignore the game Chris Walker likes to play with people he thinks are weaker than him.

Pickens looks at me. Shake my head as an order that he shouldn't respond. He nods at me.

"Oh yeah, stumbled in for some lunch, huh?" Chris Walker reaches out and flips Pickens' beret that's tucked in his belt. Pickens doesn't move and neither do I. We're stronger than Chris Walker's little mind games.

Nobody laughs but Chris, so he says, "Just stay out of people's way, soldier," in a mocking deep voice and gives a half-salute before he walks away.

Pickens looks back at me. "Just an asshole, Captain."

Nod in agreement.

india

Pickens and I sit down at the table. Even though I'm sure the other cadets saw and probably heard Chris Walker, they know not to say anything. So they fall right back into whatever they were talking about before we got to the table.

"I am trying to tell you," Janet says, "if you freeze a spoon and then hold it on there, the color will go away."

Across the table, Freddy MacDonald has the top button on his shirt undone. A red spot about an inch wide shines on his neck. Assume it is a hickey. "A spoon? How the hell do you freeze a spoon? It's metal."

"You're not actually freezing it, you moron. Run it under hot water, and then stick in the freezer. It will get super cold in just a few minutes. Hold it on there until it gets warm, and the color will be taken out so you can't see it," Janet says. The others at the table stare at Freddy's neck.

"And just how would you know?" Freddy says.

This could definitely bother Janet—cadets are the only males seen with her. But she fires back without hesitating.

"My cousin who worked at my mom's sign store this summer. I heard one of the guys on the installation crew telling him after Mom reamed him for coming in looking like an octopus got wrapped around his neck. Kinda like you."

This conversation I could do without. Hate it. Girlfriends, boyfriends, high school gossip, and all that shit. Screen it away, thinking about drill formation, practice, and new ways to make this squad better.

Sean O'Malley says, "Man, you need to tell Alexa she should change her last name to Hoover because it looks like you got attacked by a vacuum." Freddy throws a French fry at O'Malley. The table laughs except for me, even Pickens. He just likes feeling part of the group.

"Yeah," Janet says, "why did you let her do that in the first place?"

"It wasn't like I asked her to or anything. We were, you know, just hooking up a little in the garage—"

"In the garage? How romantic," Janet laughs.

"No, we weren't just in the garage. We were in my dad's old Mustang."

"Oh, that makes it better." Janet rolls her eyes.

"Hey, look, when you need some time, you just need some time if you know what I mean." And Freddy throws a fry at Janet. "Anyway, we were just hooking up a little. I didn't even know she had done it. I guess my brain was somewhere in another place or something."

"I know where your brain was, and it definitely wasn't in your head," Cadet O'Malley says. The table bursts out laughing. Freddy's face turns as red as the spot on his neck. O'Malley doesn't laugh at his joke, though. He never laughs at his own jokes.

"O'Malley, just sit there and eat your cardboard and shut up," Freddy says.

"Enough," I say. Too much for one meal.

The table goes quiet, and everyone turns back to their trays.

O'Malley eats MREs (Meals Ready to Eat) on Thursday. He's a senior. He enlisted early, so he spent the summer in basic training. He thinks this makes him better than everybody, even though his rank is not as high as mine. He gets MREs at the Army Surplus and eats them on drill days. Guess he wants to show off.

O'Malley breaks the silence after a few seconds. "It's not cardboard. It's mushroom chicken in cream sauce with rice pilaf and broccoli," he says, shoveling food in his mouth.

"Sounds like the military version of Lean Cuisine, if you ask me," Peter Dixon says. Dixon's stomach presses against the table and the buttons on his shirt strain to hold on. He lost fifteen pounds, so he decided to go down a shirt size. I told him he needed to wear a shirt that fit, but he said if his shirt was too tight it would motivate him to keep losing weight. Couldn't argue with that, so I let him stay with the new shirt.

"If that's the case, then I guess I need to bring you a whole stack of these things," O'Malley blurts back.

Dixon drops his head.

"Enough," I said. Look up from my tray and stare

at each cadet. "We don't need that," I snap at O'Malley. "We're a unit. Act like it."

"Sorry, Captain," O'Malley says to me.

"Don't tell me, Cadet." I nod toward Dixon.

"My bad, Peter."

"Yeah, no problem, O'Malley." Dixon says it, but he doesn't mean it.

Peter Dixon's mom teaches senior English. Amazing she couldn't think ahead to high school when she named her kid Peter with a last name like Dixon. Should have known some bad stuff was coming. Cadets joke on him all the time. Probably the worst is when other kids, and sometimes cadets, call him Double Dick.

Look behind Dixon to see Sergeant Maddox enter the cafeteria and head toward our table. "MacDonald, get that shirt buttoned and tie straightened. Sergeant Maddox is about half a click away." I say it without looking at him.

Freddy's eyes get big, and he fumbles with his top button.

To distract Sergeant Maddox, I stand up and meet him before he gets to the table. I salute. "Good day, Sergeant."

"Tillman, good day to you, Captain." He doesn't salute me because I'm not a real soldier yet. "At ease," he says. Sergeant Maddox looks over my shoulder. "So how are your little sweethearts today?"

"Tip top, sir."

"Well, you know I'm not going to settle for anything less."

"Never, sir."

Sergeant Maddox stands like a brick post. Everything about the man is hard. His legs are sawed-off telephone poles, and his right arm bulges, ripples with muscle and veins that look like rivers. Left arm just dangles, though. Injured in a training exercise. It's useless now. But I think it just makes him tougher.

"Make sure they're ready this afternoon. You know Roper's group wants to knock you off the top."

He's right. Pat Roper's squad has been trying to catch us for weeks. They're the only ones with a chance. Brent Ladner's and Robert Fletcher's squads haven't been able to get it together enough to be real threats. They just don't take it as seriously as me and Roper.

"Yes, sir."

"Don't back off these cadets. You don't want to give Roper the satisfaction." Sergeant Maddox looks at me real serious. "You keep them in line."

"Always, sir."

"And what about the grades? Remember what we talked about."

"Yes, sir," I say without really answering the question. Language arts not going as planned. Don't want a tutor.

"Good then." Sergeant Maddox walks by me toward the table. "See you sixth period, ladies." He strides by the table with his chest poking out and back so straight he almost leans backward. Bet he doesn't even think of this place as a school. It is a training facility, and this isn't a cafeteria, it's a mess hall.

"Yes, sir," the table says in unison.

Turn toward my table of "sweethearts." They were one screwed up group a couple of months ago—parts that just couldn't fit together. O'Malley had everything down from basic so he'd get all pissed at the others. MacDonald spent most of his time staring at Freeman's ass and dropping his rifle. And Dixon and Pickens couldn't even march on rhythm and pace. Pathetic. That's why Sergeant Maddox gave them to me. He said I was the only one who could get a group like this in order. Guess it was a compliment. Compliments are not what I need. Winning, that's all that matters. Everything is just preparation for when the bullets are flying, the IEDs (Improvised Explosive Devices) are real, and I get to find out if I deserve my father's last name.

Squads from eight high schools around the county compete at drill competition every fall. The last two years, the winning squad leaders for the county were offered ROTC scholarships. But the only scholarship I'm worried about is the Evans Scholarship, given by Mrs. Bernadette Evans in honor of her son who attended The Citadel but died in Vietnam. Every four years she picks a winning squad leader from the county because they've proven to be disciplined, respected, motivated, and smart. Can't ask for more than that from a student or a soldier. So the mission is clear: win the scholarship, attend The Citadel, then continue what my father had the courage to do.

Just had to be given this group. But I'll get them there. Not even an option.

Juliet

The bell just rang, but it's not the end of the day, not even close. For every other student in the school, the bell signals shut the book, grab backpack, and head for the door. Not in ROTC, not with Sergeant Maddox in the room. Everyone sits up straight, hands flat on the desk, and eyes straight ahead, waiting for his command.

Students funnel down the halls like a steady roaring river. Sergeant Maddox straightens his desk, making sure his calendar, book, pencils, and stapler are evenly spaced apart. That one good hand making sure the items on the desk look glued in place. No pictures sit on Sergeant Maddox's desk like other teachers. And I've thought a lot about that. No girlfriend or wife pictures. None of his buddies in the service. The cadets want to know why. But I think I've figured it out. He's always telling us to move forward. Pictures tie us to the past. Get the feeling his past is pretty ugly—grenade training accident, forced to leave active service at twenty-eight. Yeah, his desk is just how it should be.

Think about the picture of my father. It's not like other

photos. Instead of holding me down, it pushes me forward. Big difference.

Sergeant Maddox stands next to his desk, staring at us. This is part of our mental training, learning to stay completely still, ignoring the body's urges to twitch, shift, clear the throat. Sounds easy, but it's ridiculous how much your body wants to move when it's ordered to keep perfectly still. Sounds physical, but it's worse on the mind.

He is waiting for someone to move, someone to screw up, so he can make an example. Nobody wants to be the example. Had to fight off sneezes and coughs, ignore urges to scratch my nose, and even hold it together one time when a fly landed on my forehead. Never flinched. Just put brain somewhere else so you don't feel it. Works most of the time. That's why I am a captain—I'm harder.

The sounds in the hallway begin to fade, signaling the hallways are almost empty. Sergeant Maddox's eyes scan the room, but his head doesn't move. He's almost ready to dismiss us. He's just waiting for the silence outside the door to match the silence in the room.

When the hall falls quiet, Sergeant Maddox still doesn't dismiss us. He just stands and stares—testing to see how long we can take it.

The room gets heavy, almost sticky like pine sap. Can tell dread and expectation grab at cadets' fingers and faces, begging them to scratch or twitch so this game can be over.

We all know we're not leaving until somebody screws up. Not worried about me. I like this—sitting without moving.

Makes it easier to feel not real. If I sit still long enough, it's almost like my body disappears. Nice place to be.

"BISCUIT!" Sergeant Maddox yells, killing the quiet. "Stand your butt up out of that desk." Sergeant Maddox calls Dixon Biscuit because he says he's obviously eaten too many. Doesn't hurt his feelings. Most of us have nicknames. It's almost like earning a new patch or pin. Believe me, the ones without nicknames wish they had them.

Sergeant Maddox turns quickly away from his desk and walks three rows to his left. Dixon forces his way out of his desk and stands up.

Had to be one of mine. Looks bad on me. Not the way to earn points.

Sergeant Maddox walks down the isle. "Biscuit, would you like to explain to me why you are moving around that desk like your girlfriend just grabbed your johnson?"

Dixon doesn't answer because he knows Sergeant Slaughter doesn't want to hear his answer, doesn't care what the answer is. But that is what it takes to get people used to holding that line—between being ordinary and worthy. Sergeant isn't going to let anyone walk out of this school unworthy.

"My God, son, how in this world do you think you can be a soldier if you can't even sit still for five seconds? Look around. Do you see anybody else shifting and farting around in their desks?"

Dixon doesn't say anything so Sergeant says, "Sound off, Cadet," to let him know he wants a reply.

"Sir, no, sir," Dixon answers.

"Good Jesus, I didn't think you had room to move in that desk. But I guess you found a way. Hell, I don't know whether to gig you or be proud that you found a way to do something I didn't think was possible. What do you think, Biscuit?"

"Sir?"

"Do you want the gig for screwing up our nice quiet, still formation or not?"

The room's dead quiet. Every cadet knows Dixon better give the right answer. My heart speeds up, knowing that if he doesn't get this right, Sergeant Maddox will come down on me as hard as he will Dixon. My job to train him to get shit right.

"Cadet, I'm waiting for an answer."

"Uh, I, uh."

"Or do you want some special treatment because you're uncomfortable in that desk?"

"Sir, no, sir."

"That's good because you're not going to get any." Sergeant Maddox turns to walk away, but stops. He snaps back toward Dixon. "Biscuit, do you see this?" Sergeant points to his dead arm. "Do you think I make excuses because of this?"

"Sir, no, sir."

"Do you see this slowing me down?"

"Sir, no, sir."

Sergeant Maddox steps closer and speaks softer. "If I can do it, Cadet, then I damn well expect you to. Got me?"

"SIR, YES, SIR," Dixon shouts out—not pissed off,

just proud. That's what Sergeant Maddox will do to you. Make you feel like you are scum of the earth and then turn around and pick you right back up. Doesn't seem like it. But to Dixon, he just got compared to the hardest son-of-a-bitch any of us knows. For him, that is a day-maker.

Regular people don't get it. We get it. Dixon gets it. Pickens gets it. Trying to find a way from point A to point B can be a bitch. So it's best to have an asshole show you the way.

Sergeant Maddox walks back to the front of the room and keeps talking. "Biscuit, your squad has competition in four weeks, correct?" His voice is low, straight, and serious.

"Sir, yes, sir?"

"Are you going to be the one who fails, the one who brings disgrace on this platoon, your squad?"

"Sir, never, sir."

"Well, then I suggest you get yourself together before I have to put my foot so far up your butt it will take a tank to pull it out."

"Sir, count on it, sir."

"Sit down."

I hear Dixon sit.

"Tillman?" Sergeant Maddox says.

Keep looking forward. Stand without moving my eyes. "Sir, yes, sir?"

"Looks like you have your work cut out. Don't disappoint me."

Don't reply because he doesn't need one. He knows what my answer would be. But just hearing him even suggest that I could disappoint him makes my stomach turn, shakes my head up.

"Sit," Sergeant Maddox orders.

I do.

He walks over to the door and opens it with his right hand. None of us in this room even notice the left one not working anymore. Every day he shows us what it means to accept, adapt, and overcome—all with no help except for what he's got inside. No family, no military. Just forty-two kids who screw things up.

"Squad leaders, you have exactly two minutes to get your sweeties on the drill field, in line, and ready for inspection. Dismissed."

Every cadet stands almost in unison. Pickens comes limping up the aisle from the back of the room. When he moves past me he says, "That Dixon," and laughs.

Grab his arm to stop him. He turns and looks at me. Just stare hard back at him. He needs to know this is serious, nothing to laugh at. Let go of his arm and hold up one finger in front of his face. He knows what it means— one gig.

He nods at me the same way cadets do at Sergeant Maddox when they've screwed up. Nothing has to be said. The message is clear.

When Pickens and I walk past Sergeant Maddox, he says, "Puppet, make sure Alpha Squad doesn't rack up any-more gigs today."

Don't give Pickens a chance to answer. "Absolutely, sir. No gigs," I say before heading out for inspection.

kilo

Wait in the hallway for every cadet to leave. Want to give my squad time to line up before I get there. The other squad leaders run out with the rest and stand in front of their cadets while they get ready for inspection. I don't have to. They know what I expect.

Walk stiff and straight out of the school toward the drill field that's really the soccer field every other day but Thursday. See my squad already lined up, standing at attention, while other cadets still fumble and fiddle around with their uniforms. I look at Pickens and try hard not to be pissed at him for what he said. Being pissed won't do him or me any good. Never let emotion get in the way.

Walk faster the closer I get, and the closer I get, the stiffer they stand. Stop only about a foot from O'Malley, who is center of the formation—three on the front line, two in the gaps behind. I stare at him right in the eyes, examine his uniform from top to bottom. Start with O'Malley because he always has it right. After basic and having his ass kicked up one side and down the other, going through drill days is nothing to him.

"Good, Cadet." He hates when I call him cadet instead of soldier. Got news for him. Here, he is a cadet.

"Thank you, Captain." O'Malley knows the routine.

Step to the left in front of MacDonald. The first place I look is his neck to make sure he has that hickey covered. Step back and examine every inch of his uniform. Most of the time I don't have a problem with MacDonald, but he does have his days. Figure with him worrying about his neck so much, he may have missed something. But he's straight.

"Cadet, good job."

"Thank you, Captain."

Turn to make him think I am finished with him. But I stop, face him, and lean my head to his ear. "Cadet, I don't care what you have to do. Tear the skin right off your neck if you have to. But tomorrow, that thing on your neck had better be invisible. Clear?"

"Crystal clear, Captain," he whispers.

I nod at him.

Inspecting Freeman doesn't feel like the others. It is harder to look at her. My eyes have to go over her chest. Something in my brain always expects her to say, "What are you looking at?" Of course, she never says it, but that doesn't keep the sting out of my stomach every time I inspect her.

Walk around behind her. Unlike the others, I have to check her hair. Have to make sure not one strand is touching her neck. Standing behind her I can smell the perfume she knows she is not supposed to wear on drill days. I don't gig her though. I wonder if she wears it to mess with my head. Doesn't work. Just as hard on her as the rest. Never let anything get in the way of leadership.

"Freeman, very nice today. Good job, Cadet."

She doesn't reply. Freeman never says "Thank you" like the others. I like that she doesn't thank me because why should she have to thank me for her doing something that's her job anyway. She's got the right head on her shoulders.

Pickens and Dixon stand in the second row for a reason. They haven't earned the front. But when they do, we'll have just one line, proving to everybody else we don't have a weak link.

I look hard at Pickens. Need him to know he has bad stuff in store. He knows it, and I can see it in his eyes. He wants to apologize, to tell me he won't let me down. I like having my squad trained so well they don't need me to say anything. The fewer words the better.

Don't inspect Pickens. Just glance over him to make sure he hasn't jacked up his uniform since this morning. But Dixon is a different story. When you are as big as he is, the body fights with the uniform, trying to pull it out here and twist it up there. I told Dixon a few weeks ago to cut holes at the top of the insides of his pockets. That way, he can reach in and tug his shirt down tight without making it obvious. Keeps Sergeant Slaughter off of his butt, and mine.

I finish inspecting Dixon. "Cadet, looks like the holes are working out."

"Absolute genius, Captain."

I walk to the right side of the formation and yell, "Sergeant, squad ready for inspection, sir."

Sergeant Maddox nearly runs down to our formation. His steps always heavy and solid.

He only glances over the group. He knows I'm as hard on them as he would be. "Tight. Clean. At ease Alpha Squad."

We are Alpha Squad because we have accumulated more points than any other squad. Points are given in physical training, marching, academic performance, and following the rules of the platoon and the school. But Pat Roper's squad is not far behind us. And all of us know it—especially Dixon. They know I've taken up their slack for weeks, but it is catching up to them.

Sergeant yells, "CADETS." We all snap to the right. He doesn't have to tell us which way to turn.

"Foooorrrwwaarrrd march."

Every cadet steps left foot first, all in unison. Sergeant Maddox calls out, "Left, left, left-right-left."

After ten steps, I glance at my cadets. They march tight and together. Their strides fall evenly with the same crunch, crunch, crunch, crunch in the grass. Even Pickens' limp doesn't look as bad today. They look good. But not everybody can be so fortunate.

"CAAADDEEEEEEETS," Sergeant drags out, letting us know we're about to stop. "HALT."

We only stop marching when somebody missteps, stumbles, relaxes, or fades slightly out of line. Pisses me off when we stop, and the nice rhythm of a good step goes away. Must be a complete waste of a person who can't freaking learn to walk in a straight line. Sergeant pretty much feels the same way.

He walks up in Robert E.'s face. Sergeant calls him Robert E., meaning Robert E. Lee, because he wears shirts with rebel flags on them all the time. He doesn't say anything at first. He just drops his head, shakes it back and forth, and rubs his hand over his eyes. This is worse than yelling. It means he's so disgusted he can't even find the words.

Robert E. doesn't even act like he has anything to say. That's the way to play it. The less you say, the better off you are. Kind of like that in a lot of situations.

Sergeant walks away from Robert E. and weaves in and out of cadets, working his way to the back of the formation. He knows Robert E. has nothing to say. "Cadets," Sergeant Maddox starts, "apparently Robert E. has a major case of cranial rectal inversion. This disease is quite contagious and has the ability to destroy a whole platoon. So, we are going to help Robert E. with his condition and make sure he has not infected anyone else."

Sergeant stops, letting all of us run scenarios through our heads of what his cure will be.

"I'm thinking three miles should do the trick."

The cadets know not to make a sound, not a sigh, not a groan, nothing. That only gets distance added.

"By the way, Robert E.," Sergeant Maddox says, "that'll be five gigs."

"Sir, yes, sir," Robert E. calls.

Sergeant Maddox yells, "CAAAADEEEEETS. FOOORRWAARRD MARCH."

I'm not pissed at Robert E. He's on Roper's squad, which means they just lost five points. Bad for them. Good for us.

lima

"You know, Tillman, some might say this falls outside the boundaries of my position," Sergeant Maddox says as he shoves some of his desks against the wall to make room in the middle of the classroom. "But I'd say it's just teaching you how to operate within the boundaries that have been set." He pulls another desk out of the way with his good arm.

While he clears a space in the middle of the room, I take off my cover, unbutton my shirt, fold it neatly, and place it on top of one of the desks on the edge of the room.

"A soldier's job is to protect others, but first he has to know how to protect himself. Right, cadet?"

"Sir, yes, sir," I say, turning to face him and tucking my white undershirt back in.

On some Thursdays, Sergeant Maddox keeps me after to show me moves that he doesn't show any of the other cadets. He knows I've got the best chance to win the Evans Scholarship, and he wants me to have every edge I can. So that means learning secrets that others haven't earned the right to know. It does mean lying to Mr. Coffeen about when inspection is over, but some lies are necessary. Secrets have to be kept.

"Now, step up, Cadet."

Move to the center of the area Sergeant Maddox has cleared in the middle of the room. Stand at an angle with my right arm facing toward him. Every move he's taught me can be done with one arm or with one leg. "Minimum effort, maximum impact is the key," he says.

Sergeant Maddox steps up in front of me, angles his good arm toward me. "Alright, Tillman, grab my throat."

"Sir?"

"Did I stutter, Cadet? Reach out and grab me by the throat."

Reach out slow like I'm reaching my hand into a bee hive. One thing I never know with Sergeant Maddox is which part of the exercise is going to be what he calls the "teachable moment." So I have to stay alert. Wrap my fingers around his throat.

"Cadet, let go."

Follow the order.

"Now do it again like you mean it. We ain't playing tiddlywinks here."

Repeat the move, faster and firmer this time.

With my hand around his throat, he says, "Now, Cadet, let me tell you something. The throat is just about the scariest place you can grab the enemy. Most just freeze up. But you can't be like most. You got to be better."

"Sir, yes, sir."

"If you get in this position, let me show you how to retaliate. First, squeeze tighter."

Do like he says because this is serious. Feel the muscles in his neck tighten. Then pop, his good hand slams against my forearm, making my hand fly off his throat. Didn't even see it coming.

"See, it's easy, Cadet. One thing about the throat is that it is hard to hold on to. Now grab me again."

Follow the order.

In slow motion he shows me right where to hit the forearm. "And once you've released the hold, you can move in, driving your forearm into the nose." He moves slowly, stopping just millimeters from my face.

He drops his arm and steps back. "Got it, Cadet?"

"Believe so, sir."

"Your turn."

Sergeant Maddox reaches out and grips my throat. Not like Mike used to do, but tight enough to send the blood racing up into my head.

He picks this moment to bust me. "So, you failed another quiz in language arts."

Eyes get big. He timed his attack perfectly. Got me in a position where I can't even respond. Not that I'd have a good one anyway.

"You know the deal. I get to take action now."

Don't nod or anything. Just stare straight ahead, waiting for his order.

"Now remember, palm out, drive with the heel of the hand."

Nod. Suck in air, tighten my arm, and swing my arm across my body, slamming the heel of the hand into his forearm, popping his grip loose. Wish Jason would have known that move.

"Perfect execution, Cadet. Hooah," Sergeant says loud enough to echo off the walls.

Want to smile, but I know not to. Training is serious business. "Hooah, sir," I say back. No emotion, just acknowledgement.

"Now, one more. It's an easy submission." He sets his feet in front of me.

I do the same.

"Reach out like you're trying to grab me."

Stretch my arm out to grab his shirt. Sergeant Maddox grabs over the top of my hand and curls it under my wrist and pulls down. My wrist feels like it will break so I have no choice but to drop to one knee. Sergeant Maddox steps to the side, still holding onto my wrist, but the sharp pain is gone.

"See there, Tillman. Quick and easy. Enemy down. Minimum effort, maximum impact."

He lets go of my wrist. Stand up quick, straight and stiff. Didn't like going down like that, but know it's necessary training. Sometimes it's the only way to learn.

"Your turn, Cadet." Sergeant Maddox plants his feet shoulder width apart. He looks like a wall that outweighs me by thirty pounds. Have serious doubts he'll even buckle his knees. And Sergeant Maddox sees it.

"Cadet, just trust it. You know I wouldn't fool you."

Nod at him.

Sergeant Maddox reaches toward me, much quicker than expected. But I catch the top of his hand anyway, step a little to the side, and turn his wrist under like he did mine. He drops like somebody pulled the floor out from under him. Don't let go of his wrist.

"That's what I'm talking about, Tillman," he says from the floor. "Release."

Follow the order. Snap to attention while he gets to his feet.

Sergeant Maddox rubs his wrist a little. "Cadet, if you can get me to my knees, then you can take down just about anybody."

Nod because I know he's right. Nobody is harder than Sergeant Maddox.

"Just remember, only use what you know if absolutely necessary, when a situation can't be avoided otherwise. Sometimes you only get one shot with an enemy, and you have to make the most of it. Once the enemy knows your strengths, they'll work even harder to find your weaknesses."

"Sir, yes, sir."

"Good work today. Keep working the way you do, and you'll prove a lot of people wrong."

"Absolutely, sir."

"Just protect yourself and keep your eyes on the prize."

"Always, sir."

mike

The hardware store would be better if it was like a library—no talking, just people finding what they need, taking it off the shelf, checking out, and leaving. No such luck. Questions fly as soon as the bell rings on the front door. Where can I find this? What do I do with that? Do you have this size bolt and this length nails? Why does this cost this much when it is five bucks cheaper down the road? Unless the store is empty, they never stop. And neither does Mr. Coffeen.

"J.T., boy, I just don't know where you get all that energy. I guess the good Lord gave you my share." Mr. Coffeen takes off his bright "Yella Wood" cap and wipes his forehead. "I figured you'd spend the afternoon getting that lumber all situated, and here you gone and got that done and started moving all that potting soil into the storage room." He shakes his head. "I just don't know."

Say, "Just doing my job, sir," without stopping or breaking my rhythm. The goal is to get into a smooth pace of work and not come out until it's time to close up. Stopping

61

might lead to thinking—about school, Mom, or how bad arms and back hurt from lugging lumber, buckets of chains, or whatever else is lying around that Mr. Coffeen can't move himself. Probably why he decided to take in a sixteen-year-old foster kid in the first place. That's O.K. Guess we both get what we need out of the deal.

Load the last bag of potting soil onto the hand truck and grab the handle to push it through the garage door at the back of the store. Mr. Coffeen steps aside.

"Oh, look at me. I'm getting in your way. You have to excuse an old man. Sometimes I'm just not thinking."

Pay no attention to his comment and push the hand truck into the storage room.

"J.T., when you get that soil fixed up, if you would, grab the broom and sweep the front. We're getting pretty close to closing up for the day."

"No problem, sir. Get right on it," I say while slinging bags of soil off the hand truck and onto a nice even stack between the peat moss and fertilizer. Stop after each bag to make sure it's stacked with an even squared edge with the bag below it.

"Now J.T., those bags don't have to be stacked just right as long as they don't fall over. Don't drive yourself crazy with them things," Mr. Coffeen says.

"Just want them perfect, sir. Sergeant Maddox says if you're going to do something, do the best you can, no matter what." What I don't say is getting it perfect eliminates trouble, just like Mrs. Hernandez taught us at Honeywell

House. "I know it's hard," she used to say, "but it will keep you safe."

He laughs. "Well, I guess I can't argue with that."

The bell on the front door rings. "Sounds like we got another one. Broom's over in the closet by the bathroom when you're done there."

Shake my head. A year and a half of working here and he still tells me where the broom is.

Finish stacking the potting soil into a perfect cube and push the hand truck back over next to the door. Garage door down and locked. Check the regular door to make sure it's locked too. Mr. Coffeen forgot a couple of months ago. Somebody broke in and stole about $2,000 worth of power tools. He just shrugged and said the insurance would take care of it. But I couldn't let it slide that easily. If you let people take from you, violate you, then they will keep doing it until you are destroyed. Can't let that happen.

He doesn't know this, but after he got robbed, I snuck out of the house every night for a week and came down here. Sat in the dark of the storage room with a crowbar, waiting for the bastard to come back and try again. Never did though. Still want to get my hands on whoever it was. Just drives me crazy when enemies don't get what they deserve. But that's why I train—to be ready to protect, fight for others who can't fight for themselves. The soldier's way.

Grab the broom from the closet and go to sweep the front of the store. The spot between my shoulder blades feels like it is being stuck with an ice pick and shoulders burn. Force myself to move fast. Too close to finishing to let a little pain slow me down. But I don't. I stop. Stare. Our last customer is Chris Walker and his dad.

Mr. Walker is talking to Mr. Coffeen. Chris stands just behind his dad. He's not talking. He's looking at me.

Chris stares at me like it is supposed to mean something. Guess he thinks if he looks at me hard enough then I'll turn away, give in and act like I'm scared. No chance.

Lock my eyes onto his. Start walking down the aisle toward the front counter where the three of them are standing. I stiffen and pick up my shoulders. Step quickly, just on the safe side of a charge.

Square off around the counter and then square one more time to the right and walk straight toward Chris. Don't move my eyes off him.

Mr. Walker and Mr. Coffeen keep talking and pay no attention.

About eight feet away, Chris turns to face me. He tenses like he's bracing himself. He rocks back on his left leg.

Hands squeeze the broom handle. Muscles in my forearms flex. Swing the broom parallel to the floor.

His expression changes. He drops his eyes. He's worried—not scared, but maybe wondering if I'm about to take this broom and turn him into a human lollipop.

About a foot away. His eyes widen and he rocks back a half-step. Chris is scared now.

Battle won.

Swipe right past him, grazing his shoulder. Put the broom back down to the floor and start sweeping.

"So, you need 100 sheets of drywall, 200 two-by-fours, and fifty one-by-sixes?" Mr. Coffeen says, filling out an order form.

Chris lets out a deep breath behind me. I stop sweeping, look over my shoulder, and smile. Hold it just long enough for it to light a fire in Chris he can't do anything about, then turn away, shake my head, and keep sweeping.

"Yeah Louie, I think that will get me done for the time being."

Mr. Walker owns a construction company. He knows he can get supplies cheaper at one of the big chain stores, but he keeps ordering from Mr. Coffeen. Makes him a good man rather than a money-hungry prick throwing up ugly houses.

Mr. Coffeen told me one time after a guy cussed him out over a couple of warped sheets of plywood that you always got to calculate about a ten-percent asshole factor into the regular population. Guess Chris carries his family's end.

"I sure do appreciate your business, Anthony. It's folks like you that keep this old place up and running."

"Aw, heck, don't you mention it at all." Mr. Walker takes his hat off and tosses it on the counter, revealing grey-brown hair. He plops his tall, wide body down on the stool and leans over on elbows that look like they have seen hard miles. "Nah, I can't even think of going out to one of those huge outfits where nobody knows you from Adam's house cat," Mr. Walker says. "A man will get one foot in the grave before he can get some help at one of those places."

They have nearly the same conversation every time Mr.

Walker comes in here. Could just about recite the whole thing for them—if I could get that many words out my mouth at one time.

Chris wants to say something to me. I can feel it. But his dad is the kind to keep a tight rein. He's not about to open his mouth. This is my territory.

"Hey Red," Mr. Walker says. "How's school going for you?"

He calls me Red because of my hair, and every time he does I have to correct him.

"Sir, it's J.T., sir." Make sure I don't sound pissed or annoyed, which I am. Stupid kids are one thing, but stupid adults just freaking baffle me. They've had time to learn, adjust. Should be able to get it right.

"Ahh, I know it, J.T. I just keep hoping one day you'll let me call you Red."

"Don't think that's very likely, Mr. Walker, sir," I say straight but polite. Even though he's a bit of a goofball, Mr. Walker doesn't deserve disrespect. He gives exactly what he gets. Nice to him, he's nice back. And the other way around. Clear, predictable, easy. Besides, he spends a lot of money here when he could just as easily take his business elsewhere. So Mr. Coffeen and me always show him respect.

"I know you're in that ROTC program over at the high school. Heck, when I was in the service we all had nicknames of some sort. Don't y'all have nicknames for each other?"

A spurt of laughter shoots out of Chris's mouth, and then he glances at me.

Mr. Walker looks over his shoulder. "Boy, what's so funny?"

"Oh, nothing, Dad. I was just thinking something funny."

I know what he's thinking.

Mr. Walker looks at Chris for a second and then at me. He turns toward Mr. Coffeen, then Chris, and back to me like he's the only one that didn't get the joke. Chris keeps smiling at me, and his dad just keeps snapping his head around like a dog that doesn't know if he wants to go to his owner or run after the poodle.

"Anyway," Mr. Walker starts, "Y'all use that rappelling tower my guys built for y'all this summer?"

"No, sir, not yet. Sergeant Maddox says he wants to make sure we can take orders first, sir."

"I wish I would have gotten Chris in that program because Lord knows with his grades, the only job he's getting after high school will be at the local Kentucky Fried Chicken. Right? Definitely not like his older brother." He looks over his shoulder again.

"Whatever," Chris says back, and his stupid grin disappears.

My turn to smile.

Chris sees it. "Yeah, well, frying chicken is better than being a freak."

"Whoa, now watch it," Mr. Walker says. Then he points to me. "Ain't nothing wrong with being a soldier. J.T. here gets discipline, training. Country needs them folks, especially now."

Chris doesn't say anything, just shifts his feet and drops his head, bringing a weight down on top of the room.

———————

"Jesus H. Christ. What in the hell are you doing?" Mike, the first foster father, yells at me.

My head snaps up and then down at my soap-covered hands in the sink. "Washing dishes. Like you told me." I look over at Mike and then back down to the frying pan and steel scrubbing pad I'm holding.

"Yeah, I can see that, dipshit. But you are going to ruin the thing." He walks over to me, grabs both my arms, and jerks them out of the sink. He shakes his head, disgusted. "I'll be damned, boy. Don't you have sense enough to come out of the rain?"

I just stare at him, mouth shut like always.

Mike lets go of my arms and points into the sink. "Put it down."

I do.

"Kevin, get away from that TV and get in here," he yells into the living room where his real son sits on the couch.

Kevin comes into the kitchen. "What's up, Dad?"

"Would you please explain to Silent Bob here why you don't wash this"—he snatches the frying pan and scrubbing pad out of the sink—"with this." And he holds them up in front of him.

Kevin laughs and shakes his head like Mike does. "For God's sake, genius, don't you know you can't wash a non-stick pan with steel wool. But guess it fits the rest of you." And then he laughs some more.

I stare at the floor and rock back and forth on my feet, thinking maybe moving will somehow make the situation better.

november

L ooking at Chris right now, I know Jason would feel
sorry for him, but J.T. couldn't care less.

Chris gets one thing right. He doesn't talk anymore.
Guess he's figured out the same thing I figured out with
my first foster father—better to keep your mouth shut
before you say something that will make it harder on you
later. That doesn't mean we're anything alike though.

Mr. Walker turns to Mr. Coffeen, who's been standing
across the counter like he's watching three guys trying to
get a piano into a cardboard box. He doesn't know what's
going on.

Mr. Walker says, "Louie, sometimes kids will just drive
you crazy."

Mr. Coffeen laughs like he always does, trying to
lighten the air. "Yep, boys will be boys."

"Alright then," Mr. Walker says, "we better be getting
on out of here. I still need to take Chris over to the construction site he's going to be working at this weekend. I

figure I ought to teach him the business. Give him something to fall back on, if that's necessary."

"Well, it's a good business to be in," Mr. Coffeen says, I guess to make Mr. Walker and Chris feel better. But Chris looks at the ground, not really looks but lets his head sag. Guess he doesn't know he shouldn't show weakness. Needs to learn a thing or two.

Mr. Walker and Mr. Coffeen shake hands. "Take care of yourself now," Mr. Coffeen says as they head for the door.

"You do the same," Mr. Walker says over the bell ringing above the door.

Start sweeping again.

"Looks like we made it through another day, J.T. Let me get this door locked, count the register, and we can get out of here. Did you lock up the back?"

"Yes, sir. Locked and double-checked."

"Sounds good."

Expect him to ask me about Chris. Mr. Coffeen might be old, but he's not stupid. He can sense things—like when I don't want to talk and when I don't want to be bothered. Don't have to tell him. He just knows. So I know he picked up on the vibe between Chris and me. The tension was so thick, he could have cut it with one of the chainsaws we have for twenty-five percent off.

Push the broom around the back of the store. The bristles swish and scratch back and forth with an even rhythm I've heard before.

"Yes, Jesus loves me,
the Bible tells me so."

Should have known that song would find me today. Too much at one time. Start sweeping faster, banging the broom against the garage door to push the song away. But it's no use.

"Little ones to him belong."

Nearly running with the broom now.

"They are weak, but he is strong."

Mr. Coffeen jingles his keys up by the front door, turning off the song. Never been so glad to hear those keys. He's always jingling those keys in his pocket. A blind man could follow him around this store and not bump into one shelf.

"Be right there, sir," I yell from the back.

Grab my backpack and gym bag from the tiny office next to the bathroom. Sling my backpack over my shoulders, and my shoulders want to scream under the weight. Body is whipped. Good. Sleep should come easy tonight.

Mr. Coffeen locks the door, and we both start walking down the sidewalk toward the house. The hardware store is one of only a few shops left on the old part of Main Street. Just a drugstore with an old soda fountain, Miss Billie's Café, and two shops where only the rich and useless walk through the doors. Kind of sucks because it makes the street quiet, which means Mr. Coffeen will feel the need to fill the air with conversation.

He doesn't say anything, though. Guess his radar is working today, and he can tell I'm not in the mood.

We walk the mile home with nothing but mocking-birds and the squeaky straps on my backpack filling our ears. Muscles between my shoulder blades squeeze my spine and beg me to slump a little. No way. Have to walk straight and stiff. Can't let down until the day is done. And that doesn't happen until my head hits the pillow.

"Keep it up now. No pain. You aren't tired." The voice in my head helps me keep it together.

Take a deep breath and force my back to straighten all the way. Quicken my steps. Mr. Coffeen quickens his too. He likes to keep up with me.

"J.T., I don't know if you've been talking to my doctor, but you sure do love to give my old ticker a workout." He comes up beside me. "I'm telling you, I've never seen a boy so hell bent on going as hard as he can *all* the time."

"Sir, the only way to win," I say back.

"What do you mean, 'win'? We're not in a race are we? Because this old man will for sure lose."

"Win the day, sir."

Mr. Coffeen doesn't say anything back.

"Every day you have a choice," I say, striding hard down the sidewalk. "You can let the day beat you, or you can beat it. I like to win."

He laughs. "Yeah, I guess you're right. But don't forget every competition has a time-out or something. Got to give yourself a break sometime."

Don't agree with him, but I don't say it. Don't like breaks. Makes it too easy for Jason to come back.

J.T. is better.

oscar

Friday, 14 Oct 05, 1142

Fridays mean the weekend can't be avoided. Weeknights, homework and studying make it easier to stay J.T. But on the weekends there's too much quiet, not enough to do. No training with my squad. No homework to occupy my brain. The store closes early on Saturday and all day Sunday. So instead of hearing the bell ringing as customers enter the store, I have to listen to Jason and the past. Don't have to fight that battle for hours, though. Now I just have to focus on the paper in front of me.

Love and hate art for the same reason. No rules or schedules, but little expectation at the same time.

Ms. Teagan does not plan lessons. She does not lecture or demonstrate. Nor does she even pretend to care if we learn anything. She has only one expectation—produce a finished product. Clay, construction paper, or Popsicle sticks. She doesn't care. Just don't bother her when she's working on her own stuff and don't ask any questions about her five-minute disappearing acts in the middle of class.

To be accurate, can't really call this a class. It's the attempt by the Covington County Public School District to promote the fine arts. We are only here for thirty minutes after lunch, and we don't receive grades. But we do what we're told. It's simple, the teacher tells you to do something, you do it or get a one-day suspension. So when Ms. Teagan says you have to work on something every day, better find something to create.

Could be worse. The other choices were drama, creative writing, or choir—after ninth grade, couldn't get dumped there again. Seeing as how words are not my thing, pictures will have to do. So today I draw the same thing I do every day—the school logo for The Citadel.

It's good. Keeps me focused.

The room has tables scattered all over, no pattern or shape, which makes the room uncomfortable. But it doesn't keep students from picking the same table every day. At least that is predictable.

Pickens and I sit at a table by ourselves. Me with a piece of white paper and colored pencils and Pickens with whatever task he's picked for the day. Sometimes he draws the still life that sits in the middle of the table. Other days he messes with modeling clay. Today he's actually painting on a piece of canvas board. One thing about Covington County, the money that flows through some of the families like the Walkers around here keeps the school stock full of supplies.

Reminds me of the only thing that really sucks about this "class." Chris Walker sits just two tables over.

But don't think about him. Just focus on the giant C in the middle of the paper. Keeping my eyes on the prize.

A low whisper hovers over the room that rarely ever increases. If anyone so much as coughs too loud, Ms. Teagan will snatch a referral form off her desk. She and Sergeant Maddox would get along perfectly because they both know how to keep a tight rein on a room.

Almost everybody is working on Halloween masks that Ms. Teagan suggested since it's October. She brought in a pile of chicken wire and buckets for flour and water. And you don't have to push too hard to get students motivated about making a mess in class.

Not me. Never a mess.

Whatever Pickens is painting, he thinks is pretty funny. Laughter spits out of the corner of his mouth, and he looks up at me. Stare him down so he knows he better keep under control. Last thing the squad needs this close to competition is a discipline referral.

Whisper across the table, "Don't even tempt her."

He presses his lips together and holds up his hand. He knows.

Finish the C and pick up the sky-blue pencil. Hear scissors snipping and markers rubbing and squeaking across homemade masks behind me. This is the good part about this class. No questions or answers to find. No forced interaction or quizzes to fail. Just movement from bell to bell.

Best of all, Chris Walker has to keep his mouth shut. At least until Ms. Teagan slips out of the room for a couple of drags on a cigarette we all know she smokes behind the building. The woman always smells like she climbed out of an ash tray.

Don't have to look at my watch to know Ms. Teagan is about to make her daily exit. The whole room can feel it coming because the whisper increases a notch. It's like a dehydrated man coming up on a stream. The closer he gets the faster he runs toward it.

Glance to my left to see Ms. Teagan grab her purse. Every step closer to the door, the whisper in the room climbs closer to full volume.

She stops at the door and says, "Back in a second. Don't kill each other." A few people always laugh like it's a joke. As soon as she slips out the door, it's like somebody turns up the volume on the radio. Don't like radios.

Pickens and I just keep working. He runs the brush across the canvas board, laughing for real now. Let him because he's got a few minutes to get it out of his system.

Just shake my head and concentrate on the logo.

To my left, hear a chair scoot away from the table, and not even three seconds later hear a muffled yell. "Private Pickle Freak reporting for duty, sir!"

The class explodes into laughter.

Jerk my head to the side to see Chris Walker standing at the front of the room. His face is covered with a mask that has a Frankenstein scar down the side and an old red wig cut short on top.

He keeps going. He marches in place and sings, "Dress like a pickle all nice and neat, but I'm still ugly and act like a freak."

The room continues to roar with laughter. They turn to look at me, wanting me to get up, to do something. Maybe go after Chris Walker. Maybe run out of the room. Know better. Not going to let Chris Walker win this time.

Don't even change expression. Just turn back to my paper. Look over to Pickens. He's not laughing anymore. He wants me to do something, too. But we both know this is the best way to handle it.

"What's going on in here?" Ms. Teagan yells from the doorway.

The laughter in the room immediately drops to a muffle of snickers with hands over mouths. Chris Walker snatches the mask off his head.

"Chris Walker, outside." Ms. Teagan waves him over.

He walks toward the doorway with a big smirk on his face. He loves his moments in the spotlight.

Ms. Teagan slams the door. The class continues to giggle. Pickens goes over and throws his drawing in the trash. I go back to finishing my C.

A couple minutes later, Ms. Teagan comes back in the room with the mask in her hand but no Chris Walker. The class goes back to appropriate volume.

She drops her purse on the floor by her chair and throws the mask on her desk. Then she grabs a referral form and starts to fill it out. At least there's a chance that Chris Walker will get what he deserves, but I'm not holding my breath. History suggests otherwise.

The bell rings, but Pickens and I stay put and wait for

everybody else to leave first. From her desk, Ms. Teagan says, "Sorry about that, J.T."

Just nod at her. She doesn't need to be sorry. This is just part of the game Chris Walker has always liked to play. And he'll keep playing until somebody stops him.

———————

"Jason, ready? You're next." Mrs. Benefield, the ninth-grade choir teacher stands behind the piano and motions for me to step up to the front of the class. I don't sing, never have, but I got dumped in this class anyway because that's what happens when you come to a school in April. Every other class is filled.

Stand up and walk toward the piano. Mrs. Benefield looks like she's about to spontaneously combust. I'm sure the rest of the class is, too. None of them have heard my voice. They've only seen my face. And that has been enough to fuel a wave of whispers and points.

Mrs. Benefield smiles at me. "Ready now?"

I nod, and she plops down on the piano bench. She hits a note. I'm supposed to sing a scale just like everybody else in the choir. This is what Mrs. Benefield calls an evaluation to see who will be recommended for the real choir next year.

She hits the note again to signal me to start. I look at the ground because there are way too many eyes in the class, prying, searching for weaknesses. Have the urge to wad myself like a piece of paper. I should've just refused, but foster care has taught me refusal just brings more pain.

So I sing, sort of. "La la la la la la la." I push out the scale, barely staying on key. Just trying to survive. Make it to the end of the first one. Mrs. Benefield jumps up an octave and starts again. Sweat sprouts in my palms and down my back. "La la la la la la la." Eyes staying on the ground.

Make it through the scales without having a major train wreck and nearly run back to my seat.

"Good job, Jason," Mrs. Benefield says. "Chris, you're up."

She's going in alphabetical order, so Chris Walker is next.

Mrs. Benefield sits down as soon as Chris Walker gets out of his seat. He walks by my chair and whispers, "Ready for a show, Freak?"

He walks with his head so low his chin almost touches his chest. Mrs. Benefield plays the first note. Chris Walker's head pops up. Somebody drew a Frankenstein scar with a marker on the side of his face, from his temple to his chin. He doesn't sing. He yells la la las as everybody else erupts into laughter. Everybody but me.

papa

"Ninety seconds, one more lap," I say to Pickens as he rounds the track. When he gets tired, his running is closer to a full-body convulsion than athletic activity. But that tough little sucker doesn't complain one bit. Maybe because he knows it wouldn't do any good.

Made Pickens stand in silence waiting for me to get finished with Dixon. Have to watch it with Dixon because of his asthma. He hates using his inhaler in front of cadets, especially his Captain. So didn't give him both barrels the way Pickens gets.

Some might say I'm too hard on him. But those people don't know anything. They don't understand the benefits of pushing yourself beyond where you think you can go. Can't even comprehend that nice numb feeling at the end of the pain. It's hell getting there, but it's a small price to reach a place not many can get to, where every thought is stripped and the body pulses with energy.

"Come on, Pickens. Don't let up. You got forty-five seconds," I yell across the track. He's at 200 meters. Has to make the time or he's got another lap. Don't want to watch another one.

Pickens comes around the last turn. Hold up the stopwatch. Turn to face him. "Harder. Run harder. You can make it. You got this. Come on. No pain, Pickens. NO PAIN."

He slings his arms forward and back like he's fighting a ghost he can't see. He's leaning so far forward he's about to fall over. But he's almost to the line.

"Fifteen seconds. Push."

Had these days with Pickens before. "Ten, nine, eight, seven," I yell, begging him to dig deep, find that last little bit. "Four, three, two," and when I say, "one," Pickens falls on the ground at my feet.

He's breathing and wheezing and pouring sweat all over the track. He rolls back and forth like he's cramping.

"Pickens, got a cramp?" I ask.

"No, sir," he blurts between deep breaths.

"We'll save the rest until tomorrow." I say it but don't mean it. Just want to see if he's going to take the out.

"Not a chance, sir."

"Only way to win is to climb the wall, right, Cadet?" I tell him.

He coughs a couple of times. "Sir, yes, sir." Normally, he wouldn't call me sir when we're not in uniform, but this is training, so I guess he thinks it's appropriate.

Let him lie on the ground for a few seconds and then tell him, "Water."

Pickens pulls his legs under his body and stands up. "How long?" he asks.

"Two minutes."

He knows everything we do here is timed.

He half walks, half jogs toward the water fountains next to the field house. I reset the stopwatch and walk out on the grass. Watch Pickens hunched over the water fountain sucking in water like it's some kind of contest. He puts his head under the water and leaves it there. If I was Jason, I would let him go home. But J.T. knows that's not going to help him or the squad. Not going to get us closer to winning. Need to take him a little closer to the edge.

Pickens pulls his head out of the water and wipes his hand through his hair. He leans over to rest his hands on both knees.

"Thirty seconds," I call to Pickens.

He hustles back over, still breathing hard but the wheezing is gone. He looks at me, waiting for the next order.

"On your face."

Pickens pops down in the push-up position. "Sixty seconds. Count aloud. Ready, train."

He starts up and down, not going too fast. He knows he's got to make the whole sixty seconds. He's learned something with me—pace, to find that line he can hold for the entire time. He understands that if he goes too hard, too fast, he'll blow out. Good to see he's learning.

"Thirty-one, thirty-two," Pickens strains the words out of his mouth, arms and legs shaking.

"Only ten more seconds, Pickens. This is too easy."

"*Too* easy," he blows out at the top. "Thirty-four, thirty-five." He pauses.

"Don't quit on me, cadet. One more."

He drops down again. Half-way back up, he hits a wall. His elbows shake back and forth, and his body isn't going anywhere.

"Cadet, I said one more. You better give me my one."

Somewhere down in his gut, Pickens pulls out that last little bit that pushes him through the wall. As soon as he straightens his arms, he falls right back to the ground.

"Cadet, do you need ropes to keep you off the ground? Don't make Sergeant Maddox right about you." Even though I respect the Sergeant, I know it is more important to convince my cadets that they can rise above his expectations, no matter how high or low.

Pickens rolls over. "No way, sir."

"O.K. Sit-ups."

He pulls his feet in flat on the ground. I reset the stopwatch. "Sixty seconds. Count aloud. Ready, train."

He starts pumping out sit-ups a lot faster than he does push-ups. Can tell he's been doing them at home. He told me two weeks ago he would catch up to me. Told him good luck with that. But looks like he really meant it.

I'm watching Pickens churn out sit-ups like he is possessed when a woman's voice behind me calls, "Jason Tillman?"

A cold electric chill flashes up through my ears. Jerk around to find who's using that name. Woman, looks to be about twenty-five, black hair, athletic build, bag slung over her shoulder.

"J.T.," I say in a tone that lets her know Jason is no good.

"Sorry. J.T." She sticks out her hand before she reaches me. "Hi, I'm Colleen Francis." She says it like I'm supposed to know who she is.

Shake her hand. "Ms. Francis," I say and nod at her.

She chuckles. "Colleen will be fine." She looks around me at Pickens still doing sit-ups. I look at the stopwatch. "Twenty seconds," I say glancing over my shoulder.

She looks at Pickens like she's confused or something. Don't know why. Not like she's never seen somebody do sit-ups before. She shakes her head, straightens her face, then looks back at me.

"What can I do for you, ma'am?"

"I'm the tutor. Tracy said I could find you here."

"Tracy, ma'am?"

"Sorry, I mean Sergeant Maddox. I'm in graduate school with his sister over at West Georgia. He said you knew—"

I cut her off. "No, I didn't know." Lie. Sergeant Maddox warned me a couple of weeks ago about my grade in Language Arts. He said one more slip, and he'd get me a tutor. "Can't blow your chance," he said. Failed a quiz last week on *The Crucible*. Knew he wasn't bluffing yesterday.

"Time," I say over to Pickens. He stops.

Ms. Francis looks at her watch. "It's about five-till-three."

Ignore her. Not her fault she doesn't know what I meant.

Pickens gets up off the ground. "Fifty-eight. Catching up to you."

If Ms. Francis wasn't here I'd tell him he's a long way from the seventy-two he needs to catch me, but I'll save it for later.

"What are you doing out here?" There's that confused look again.

"Training, ma'am."

"Training for ... ?" She leaves the end open for me to fill. But there's no way to fill it. Kills me people don't realize you can train just to be better, not for anything specific.

She's still waiting for me to finish her sentence. I say, "Sometimes extra training is needed when a cadet gets gigged."

Ms. Francis leans her head toward me. "Gigged?"

"Yes, ma'am. It's like a demerit."

"Oh, O.K. I get it."

"Glad, ma'am." She was sent by Sergeant Maddox so make sure I'm extra polite.

"Well, J.T." She reaches into her bag and pulls out a notepad, flips a couple of pages. "I just wanted to come by, meet you, and set up a time and place for us to start."

Can't believe this is happening in front of one of my cadets. "Sorry ma'am, must have some bad info. I'm doing just fine."

"But Sergeant Maddox," she says like it's hard to get out, "said something about a scholarship and—"

"It's fine." I cut her off again. "Nothing I can't handle." Can't let Sergeant Maddox think I'm some weak punk, not able to get control of the situation. He ordered the help, but he'll respect me more if I do it on my own.

She looks back to her notepad. Writes something down. "Well, here is my number and email address if you change your mind." She tears the sheet out of her notepad. She goes to hand it to me. "You sure?"

"Absolutely, ma'am. Sorry for your trouble." I take the paper from her, fold it quickly, and put it in my pocket. Just want this to be over.

"Oh, no trouble. Tracy has done me more favors than I can count. Just wanted to repay a couple of them." She smiles back at me, expecting me to say something. Got nothing to say.

"O.K., well, I'll let you get back to, uh, training."

"Good evening, ma'am," I say and nod at her.

"Yeah, see you later," Pickens says like he expects to see her in the next couple of days.

Ms. Francis walks away. Once she's far enough that I know Pickens is about to say something, I blurt, "Not a word."

"Yes, sir."

Swing the stopwatch around my hand so the string wraps tight. "Let's go."

Pickens and I walk around to the front of the school where his mom is picking him up. Sure she'll treat him like he's some poor victim like he says she does after these afternoon training sessions. Eventually she's got to see how much stronger her son is—way more than she thinks.

Pickens hurries to stay up with me. "Captain, so what's the deal with the tutoring? You need help?"

"Pickens, do I ever need help?" Keep walking fast.

"Not that I can see. But heck, if it meant spending some time with *her*, I'd fail half my classes." He laughs.

"That's the last thing you need to think about. More important objectives to concentrate on. Got a big competition coming up. Major points on the line."

"Yeah, I guess. Still would be nice, though."

Ignore his comment. "Speaking of points, what about *your* grades?"

"I'm doing good except for Mr. Divine's biology class." Pickens laughs. "I can't concentrate for nothing with Nicole Marbury sitting across the table from me."

I know Nicole Marbury. Everybody knows Nicole. She's an example of what happens when you're fifteen going on twenty-five.

"I'm telling you, J.T., that girl does it on purpose. The other day we were looking at amoebas under the microscopes. So Nicole all slides up next to me and leans in real close, nudging her chest against my arm, and whispers, 'See anything good in there?' Just about fell to my knees when her breath hit my ear. I'll just say this. I was definitely the last one to go back to the table. Lost ten points for taking so long."

"Pickens."

"What? I'm serious."

"You have to be better than that. Not like everybody else."

"Yeah, I know, but—"

"No 'but.' Grades go into our overall score as a squad. Can't lose to Roper's group because of *boobs*. Got me?"

"Yeah," Pickens says, a bit disappointed. "It's going to be tough though."

"Most things are." The moment it comes out of my mouth, my brain is spinning trying to figure out ways to get my own grades up. Can't expect my cadets to perform if I don't set the example.

We turn the corner and walk down the front sidewalk to the main entrance where I can see his mom parked in the minivan that almost looks like the one my mom drove when she didn't take the Corvette.

"Maybe I'll ask Mr. Divine if I can sit somewhere else."

"Now that's thinking, Pickens. Good for you. Good for the squad."

"Yeah, plus I can stop torturing myself fantasizing about going out with her."

Pickens is feeling sorry for himself. And he wants me to join in, too. Don't play that game. "Ask her out."

"What? You've got to be kidding." Pickens lurches along next to me. "Look at this." He looks down at his body.

"Pickens. Real simple. Ask her out. If she says no, then fine. It's what you expect. If she says yes, great. Either way, you get past it."

"Yeah, but it's not that easy, J.T."

"Pickens, do you make excuses when I run you to death out on the track?"

"Never, sir."

"Right. Same thing with Nicole. No excuses."

Pickens starts walking straighter. "Got it, Captain."

We stop walking. I look past Pickens to his mom's parked minivan by the sidewalk. "Even if she shoots you down, it will be good for you. Show you can take a hit. Then people see you differently."

He turns to see his mom waving him over. "Wish it would work with her."

"Pickens, have a good weekend. Got to go in and get my backpack from Sergeant Maddox's room."

"Yeah, you too, J.T." He stumbles off the sidewalk toward the minivan parked in the bus lane. He'll go home and let his mama take care of him. One of these days he'll learn to deal without her.

quebec

Sunday, 16 Oct 05, 0718

"**J**esus loves me, this I know,
   For the Bible tells me so,
   Little ones to him belong,
   They are weak, but he ... is ... "

Little kid voices trail off into nothing as black crawls
to light. Throw back the covers and wipe the sweat off my
forehead. Hear the song all the time. Out of nowhere. Jogging down the road, my feet sometimes pound the tempo.
The rhythm gets caught in the broom when I sweep the
back of the store. Doesn't matter what I'm doing. Blink,
breathe, *bam*—there it is. Tiny voices bouncing along soft
and weightless. Can't stand it.

Sundays suck. Plain and simple.

Folks hate a lot of kids' songs. I'm sure Sesame Street
has caused a few headaches. And the queue to take a swing
at Barney would trace around the Covington County line.
But I'm sure "Jesus Loves Me" doesn't make too many lists.

It makes me want to puke.

Last song I heard my mother sing.

Stand up out of bed. Boards squeaking under my feet sound like hinges on an old car door. Stop. Nausea swims around my stomach and floats up to my throat. Deep breath. Rock back on my heels. Boards squeak again. Drop my weight out from under me and fall back on the bed. That familiar heat pushes sweat onto my forehead. Face gets so hot it feels like it will evaporate the drops crawling toward my eyes. Two more deep breaths. Not working.

Jump off the bed and stomp out of the room. Sling the bathroom door open and fall on my knees. Lay my scar on the cold edge of the tub. Done this too many times. The cold surface cools the side of my face and usually straightens my stomach.

It is not just the tub. Anything cold. Just something that isn't hot—hot like that Sunday afternoon driving home from church in the Corvette. No air conditioning. Reaching a temperature inside that nearly melted the dash. The steering wheel shined like liquid, and the vinyl trim on the seats burned the back of legs. But Mom drove it in the summer anyway.

"Be careful with the seat belt, honey."

Two Sundays before, Jason burned his hand on the metal buckle. Summer in Georgia will get you when you least expect it. Jason was careful. She wasn't. Didn't even put hers on.

Flip my face over to the left side so it will match the right. Turn on the water and pull the lever to switch on the shower. The water mists off the bottom, cooling my face faster. The shower head squeaks, almost hums, and I hear the song again.

"Jesus loves me, this I know,
For the Bible tells me so,"

Not little kids this time. It's Mom. Sang the song every day, all day for a week. Result of teaching the four-year-old Sunday school class. Said if she sang it enough, maybe she could get it out of her head. Guess she couldn't. Now I can't either.

"Little ones to him belong,
They are weak, but he is strong...strong...strong."

J.T. is strong.

Get up off the floor. Turn on the sink. Splash water on my face. Don't like doing this because I have to run my hand across the scar, but I have to get rid of the heat. So hot.

Bolt out of the bathroom and into the living room. Mr. Coffeen's gone to church. Every Sunday. A bowl, spoon, and a box of cereal sit on the kitchen table that he left for me. He never forgets to leave something for me to eat. Can't eat though. Too hot.

Throw open the windows, the front door, the back too so the air can flow through. Got to cool it down in here.

"Little ones to him belong."

Shove the rug in the middle of the room to the side so the floor is bare. Lay face down on the cool wooden slats. Sharp pain shoots through my stomach like somebody is trying to gig me to the floor. Stuck.

Breathe. Breathe J.T. Keep Jason away.

A slight wind comes through the front door, running

for the back. No chill bumps. Nothing but heat coming off my back like asphalt after a summer thunderstorm.

"Yes, Jesus loves me,
Yes, Jesus loves me."

Not just Mom anymore. Jason sings with her.

"Yes, Jesus loves me,
The Bible tells me soooo."

Too close. I know what's next—the white sheet flapping, snapping in the wind.

Got to stop it. Stop it, J.T.

Put my hands flat on the floor. Push up. Body straight, tight. Toes dig into the floor. Train. Just train.

Down, up. Down, up. Down up. "J.T. wins. He always wins. Can't be beat," I say out loud.

They are weak, but he is strong.

That's right. Got to be strong.

Can't let the song win. Shake my head at the top of a push-up. Keep going.

Down, up. Down. Hold it. Let the blood rush to muscles. Up. Down, up. Keep pumping them out until the pain starts to work.

"You are a soldier. Pain is the fun part." The song is gone, and the voice that always gets me from point A to point B rings loud and clear.

"Looking good today, soldier. Looking good."

Stop doing push-ups and pop off the floor. Can't stop. Not enough pain yet.

Room. Chest of drawers. Socks, shorts, T-shirt. Running shoes from the closet. Blood in my chest and arms starts migrating back to where it came from. Jerk the shirt over my head and nearly jump into the shorts.

Fumble with my shoelaces. Sweat rolls down my face. The house fills with cool air, stinging, like somebody lightly rolling jagged glass down my cheeks.

My father's dog tags fall off my chest. Jingle on the road. No one hears but me.

"What's the matter soldier? Can't tie your shoes?" The voice keeps me straight.

Focus. Get shoes tied.

Stomp out of the room. Bang through the front door. Leave everything open. Start running down the street, never the sidewalk. The sidewalk has cracks and ridges that can catch a toe, make me stumble, slow me down.

Not worried about pace, rhythm, or distance. Just need that comfortable place that running hard brings.

The pain always starts in the left leg first. But that pain is almost always there. Used to it, so it doesn't give me what I need. Doesn't push Jason away. Only makes him hold on tighter. He can't hold on for long though. He's not hard enough. Never was.

After five minutes, the pain in the right starts to match the left. Push harder to make it migrate up into my gut and then into my chest. Little humidity makes the air sharp, scraping my throat and stabbing my lungs. This is good. But not perfect. It is only good enough when it reaches my head.

Run through stop signs and intersections without look-ing. Have to keep eyes forward, concentrating on the road, what's ahead. Sweat pours down my back and face, and the cool air makes it feel like crushed ice against my cheeks.

Another half-mile and the pain presses against the top of my head like rocks scraping across my scalp. This is the bad part. The more in shape the body gets, the longer it takes. But it will come.

Pound the pavement for another mile. Then, just like crashing through a wall, the pain explodes into nothing. The body disappears. And Jason is nowhere to be found.

romeo

Mr. Coffeen's truck sits in the driveway when I round the corner. The house is not empty. Safe again.

"Good Lord, J.T. You look like you ran down to the river, jumped in, and ran back," Mr. Coffeen says when I walk in the front door.

"Sir, just around the neighborhood." Go to the refrigerator for the bottle of water I keep there. Turn it up and chug about half.

"Father Rodgers preached a heck of sermon this morning." I like the way he talks about church, never like he wants me to go, just letting me know he enjoyed it.

"That's good, sir," I say between swallows from the bottle. Look around the house. All the windows shut, just like the back door. But Mr. Coffeen doesn't say anything about the house being left open.

Instead, he grabs his keys off the kitchen table and throws them over on the counter. I'm sure I'll have to remind him later where they are. "So, what you got on your agenda today?"

He kills me with this question. Obviously, previous strategy of telling him nothing doesn't work. And when a strategy fails, soldiers have to find a new one. So I answer.

"Sir, 1300 to 1430, homework. 1430 to 1515, review planned maneuvers for drill competition. And 1515 to 1700, wash, dry, and press uniform and write evaluations for my cadets." Preparation, Performance, Success. Everything else just isn't necessary.

Finish the bottle and go to the sink to refill it.

Mr. Coffeen knows there's no way I'll ignore my duties to the platoon or my cadets so he doesn't mention any of that. "Well, that ain't no way to spend a Sunday. I'll be daggum, you do enough school work during the week. Them teachers need to let you have a little fun on the weekends."

Mr. Coffeen baffles me more than anyone I know. People would think this was my first weekend here. Fun is something I don't have a lot of experience with. And he knows this. Think sometimes he just wants to talk, and he'll say anything that pops into his head, whether it makes sense or not.

"Sir, guess they just want to prepare us for after high school." I don't really believe this, but I know it's the kind of statement adults want to hear.

"Yeah, well, I think they could still let kids have their weekends without homework."

"Sir, I think I'll get you the principal's phone number," I say as I put the bottle back in the refrigerator. Mr. Coffeen laughs.

"I can't believe it. J.T., you made a joke." He keeps laughing and slaps his leg. I swear, comedians across the

United States would kill for an audience filled with people like Mr. Coffeen. He just frigging laughs at anything.

Didn't think I was being funny, just smartass. Don't know where it comes from. Jason would never be smartass. But J.T. likes the edge.

"Sir, glad you liked it," I say flat and even.

"J.T., I think you'd surprise yourself if you'd open up that mouth of yours a little more."

His comment makes me stop and face him. He looks at me like he knows he said something he shouldn't have. Don't know if I'm supposed to say anything. Not pissed, just caught off guard. Rarely expect anyone to say what they really think.

Mr. Coffeen stares at me for a few seconds. He's trying to assess how I feel about his comment. But I stone him. He's on his own with this one.

He finally says, "J.T., I didn't mean nothing by that. You go on and talk as much as you want. Don't let some old man try to tell you what to do." He smiles and forces a short chuckle.

"Sir, that's the plan." I nod my head at him to let him know I'm not pissed or anything. Walk out of the kitchen toward my room.

"You got something important you needing to get to right now?" Mr. Coffeen asks behind me.

"No sir, just a shower."

"Well, before you get all prettied up, can you give me a hand out back? I was supposed to have Mrs. Richardson's mailbox done three weeks ago, and I ain't even close to finishing. If I don't get that thing to her this week, she is going to skin my wrinkled butt alive."

"No problem, sir." Don't remember ever refusing Mr. Coffeen. Guess because he doesn't often ask for much.

"Go on in there and throw on some jeans, and I'll meet you out back in the shop."

"Two minutes, sir," I say.

"Two minutes? Take your time. It's going to take me two minutes to get out the back door."

Mr. Coffeen makes jokes all the time about him being old. I think maybe because he doesn't want to be. But as far as old folks go, he's got more fire in him than a crate full of grenades.

Change as fast as I can—still a heavy air in my room— and then head out the back door. The backyard is about half as big as it would be if there weren't two buildings. One is a metal building Mr. Coffeen uses to store stuff he refuses to throw away, and the other is his workshop.

When I come through the door to the workshop, Mr. Coffeen is already wearing his safety goggles and a thick, heavy apron. The room looks like a construction class for a group of Tasmanian devils—sawdust blankets the room, half-finished tables, stools, and a pile of rubber band guns, wooden tricycles, and toy chests line the walls. No organization at all, just piles here and there. He's making the rubber band guns, wooden tricycles, and toy chests to sell at the Covington Fall Festival in a couple weeks.

"J.T., go ahead and put these on." Mr. Coffeen tosses me a pair of safety goggles. Catch them with my right hand.

Put them on and stand there because I have no idea what to do, where to stand. He's only brought me in here once when I first came. But then, I wanted nothing to do with this place, or anything else for that matter.

"Go ahead and grab those square posts over there." He points to the far side of the room where two long, square wooden posts lean against the wall. "Get them over here to the table saw and let me show you how to work this thing."

Both hands don't do certain maneuvers well, so it takes more effort than I'd like to get the posts under each arm. Wedge a post under my left armpit and fight to keep it in place. Pick up the other one securely with the right.

The weight makes the posts teeter under my left arm. Bang into a couple of tables. Back up and knock over the fire extinguisher. Jump forward, left post rocks forward, skids across the concrete floor. Strain to get the post back level with the ground. Almost to the table. Turn. Take out the bird feeder on the table behind me.

My eyes shoot to Mr. Coffeen. He shrugs.

"Here, put one of them on the floor and slide the other up here on the table," he says, not mentioning the jackass waltz I just performed across the room.

Drop the left post on the floor and slide the right one onto the table.

He unclips the tape measure from his belt and hooks it on the end of the post. "Now, you need to cut three pieces. The first is easy. You just need to cut two feet off this eight-foot post. I have to bury two feet, so that will leave four feet above the ground."

Don't say anything, only nod.

He takes a thick square pencil out of his pocket and marks a line on the post. "Now, set the post against the guide like this, flip on the saw right here." He points to a red switch on the side. "Then just pull the trigger and bring it down smooth and easy. Got it?"

———————

"Honey, now take the wrench like this, turn in to the left. Remember, righty tighty, lefty loosey."

"Mom, I'm not in kindergarten," I say. We both lie flat on our backs, under the Corvette on the cool smooth concrete.

"Jason, that might be so, but I'm thirty-six and still have to remind myself." She rocks her head to the side and winks at me.

I smile back, and then look at the bolt she wants me to remove. I strain a little to break it loose.

"Now be careful. You don't want to take it all the way out, or we'll be cleaning oil out of your hair for a week." She laughs.

I turn the bolt slowly, trying to feel where the end is. Have no idea what I'm doing. Just waiting for a river of old oil to come shooting out into my face.

"Right there ought to be good. Now here." She slides a plastic oil bucket over to me. "Put this under the oil pan."

I put the oil bucket in place.

"Now take this." She hands me a dirty rag. "Turn the oil plug the rest of the way with your hand. When you feel the last thread let go, pull your hand away quick so you don't get it all over you. Got it?"

"Got it."

sierra

"J.T., you here?" Mr. Coffeen waves his hand in front of my face.

"Absolutely, sir," I say. Face hot. Breathing weird.

Mr. Coffeen chuckles. "Good Lord, boy, you were a million miles away. Pay attention now cause this thing will get you if you don't."

Look at the saw. Should be simple, but he could be asking me to perform brain surgery and I'd be just as clueless. He thinks it is O.K. though.

"Now let us see what you got." He steps out of the way.

Move next to the saw table and reach over to flip the switch. Grab the handle of the saw, and Mr. Coffeen stops me. "Now, make sure them fingers stay far out of the way or you'll be waving a nub at all the ladies." He laughs.

Nod and look down at the post. Put a heavy left arm on top of the post to keep it against the guide, pull the trigger on the handle. The saw starts spinning with a low electric hum. Stop and face Mr. Coffeen.

He nods. "Now, go ahead. Nice and easy. No sweat."

Apparently his eye sight is getting worse in his old age because beads of sweat are growing like wild fire across my forehead.

Stare at the post. Focus on the pencil line Mr. Coffeen drew. Pull the saw down slowly. It sings all the way through the post. I'm surprised by how much I like the sound. Power and precision zooming into the air. Good stuff. Cools my head.

Ease the saw back up to the starting position. Pull my arm off the post.

Mr. Coffeen slides his goggles up to his forehead. "Looks like we have a natural here, folks. Good job, J.T."

Don't say anything back. I never respond to compliments.

"Now, here's what I need. Take this other post. Cut a two-foot piece and a one-foot piece. On the one-foot piece, I need you to cut a forty-five degree angle on both ends for the brace. Here, let me show you."

Mr. Coffeen shows me how to rotate and set the saw on the correct angle. I repeat what he does to show him I know how.

"Good. Now cut those pieces, and I'm going to get to work on carving the sides of the mailbox." He hands me the tape measure and pencil and walks away.

Before I move, I close my eyes and repeat the steps in my head, making sure I remember. Got to get it right. Not like changing the oil in the Corvette. Said I had it but didn't. Oil all over. Kind of like the blood.

Breathing gets fast. Heat flashes into my chest like I'm opening an oven. Move, J.T. Moving keeps it away. Fast.

Pick up the other post off the floor. Use my body to slide it on the table. Snatch up the tape measure. Hook it on the end of the post. Measure two feet and make a line. Cut the piece just like the other. The saw sings its song again, and I take a deep breath. Set the two-foot piece aside. All the way back here now.

Unsure of cutting the angles on the one-foot piece, but I get it right. Turn off the saw and pull my safety goggles off. "Pieces are cut, sir," I call over to Mr. Coffeen.

"Good deal. Bring them over here," he says without picking up his head.

To keep from continuing my earlier destruction, I carry the pieces over one at a time. He's leaning over a square mailbox, carving a design into the side. Lines swirl all over the place. Don't know how he does it—creates a design from nothing and doesn't screw it up. Makes me nervous. No plan or anything. Too much room for error.

"Sir, how do you know where to carve lines without a pattern?" I ask.

Mr. Coffeen chuckles. "J.T., I can't tell you that. I get a picture in my head, and I just try to put that in the wood."

"What if you mess up?"

"Well, if there's one thing I don't have a shortage of around here it's wood. I'd just start over."

Shake my head. No chance I'd have that much patience with a piece of wood. Or enough nerve to trust I'd get it right. Need rules, guidelines, or something to keep things clear and predictable.

Mr. Coffeen finishes a line and sets his carving tool on the table. "Now let me show you how to nail those things together." He reaches over the workbench and takes a hammer off the wall. Then he opens a drawer and grabs a handful of nails. He shows me how to line up the pieces and tells me how many nails to put in each spot.

"Now, that hammer ain't as bad as the saw, but it will still do a number on some fingers. So watch them thumbs." He turns and goes back to carving.

Situating the pieces and positioning the nail in the right place is a chore, but I manage the first without catastrophe. But on the second nail, I blurt out, "Son-of-a..." and stop it by sticking my thumb in my mouth.

Mr. Coffeen doesn't look up, but says, "Yep, that thing will get your thumb every time."

Shake my hand and go back to nailing. When I finish, I stand the post up. It's just three pieces of wood nailed together, but I like it. Shouldn't have avoided this place for so long.

There's rules, measurements, calculations, precision. Good things I can handle.

Maybe I could build something.

tango

Monday, 17 Oct 05, 0615

Sleep was an instant—a hiccup of dark between lights. Lights out, eyes close, count backward from 100 and never make it to zero. Wake up a moment later. That's the way I like it. Focus yields results.

Made it to another Monday. Tighter routines and schedules. Just the way it needs to be.

Pop out of bed and hit the floor. Deep breath. Mr. Coffeen's aftershave has stormed across the house. He must put it on with a sponge. Distraction. But I just pretend it is tear gas and start busting out push-ups. Arms and chest are burning good when Mr. Coffeen hits the door.

"J.T.? You up?" Mr. Coffeen says through the door.

"Forty-one, forty-two, forty-three." Pause in the up position. Arms ache, especially the left. "Enter."

He opens the door, but I don't look up. Don't move. Don't like being interrupted when I'm PTing, but it's hard to be pissed at him after working in the shop. Keeps me from glaring up at him.

"Good Lord, boy, you keep working out like that and I'll have to widen all the doorways."

Stare at the floor, waiting for him to say what he really came in here to say. He knows it. "Just thought I'd see if you want to go with me to Mrs. Richardson's this evening to put up the mailbox. I could use an extra set of hands."

"Yes, sir. No problem."

"O.K. then. Maybe afterward we'll swing in Ed's Drive-in and grab a burger or something. Lord knows you got to be getting sick of my cooking."

"Sir, no, sir." Arms getting tired. Hope he hurries up.

"That might be so, but let's just say the burger will be payment for the help."

"Your call, sir."

"It's settled then. Well, let me get out of here. I got to get to the store early. Anthony Walker called last night and needs me to meet him down there before he heads out to one of his sites. Have a good one. See you this afternoon."

"Yes, sir."

Mr. Coffeen shuts the door. Glad he said something about Mr. Walker. Makes me think of Chris. And my body instantly recharges. Stare at the floor and watch it disappear. All I see is Chris in his truck pulling up, pushing me, calling me Freak.

Drop down and hold it with my nose only a centimeter above the floor. Let the blood shoot through my chest and pound against my forehead. Chris thinks he's going to get me somehow. He'll try. But he has no idea.

Push up. "Forty-four, forty-five, forty-six," I say loud,

picking up right where I left off. Get to sixty, and my arms begin to shake. Don't stop. My head switches from Chris to Pickens. I think about what he said. He said he was going to catch up to me. I like him, but can't let that happen. Got to maintain that line—that line between me and everybody else. Can't let anybody catch me. I am the Captain. Have to be better, stronger, harder. No other way.

"SIXTY-FIVE, SIXTY-SIX." I scream the numbers because screaming helps. The push-ups get harder and slower. This is the place where people and soldiers are separated. People stop. Soldiers don't.

"Soldier. No pain. No quitting."

Push past the hard ones, and the push-ups get easier. Don't hear the voice in my head. Don't need it. Have my own.

"Go, J.T. Too easy. TOO EASY!"

Push huge breaths out at the top of every rep. Love this.

"Chris Walker. Never get me. Pickens. Never catch me." Start grunting because it's too hard to get words out.

Don't know what number I make it to. Just know I've gone further than my body wanted to. That's the key—finding a way to keep going when everything else says stop.

Collapse on the floor and roll over. That nice blanket of pain covers me. Glance over to the picture leaning against my bedside lamp. He's proud. He has to be. "Don't worry. Won't let you down." Look at the desert ground under his feet, knowing I'll be fighting on ground like some day. And I'll be good, strong, something Mom would be proud of.

It won't even matter if I don't make it back. Either way, things will be like they're supposed to be.

Jump up off the floor. Open the door. The floor creaks. It shouldn't be creaking because I haven't stepped on that board yet. Look up and see Mr. Coffeen. He's looking at me like an alien is crawling out the top of my head. I stop.

"J.T., you alright? My God, I thought you was getting attacked or something."

"Sir, thought you left."

"Can't find my keys."

"TV stand, right side," I say back to him.

"Oh." Mr. Coffeen nods his head. He doesn't move, just keeps looking at me. "What was all that yelling about?"

"Sir, just training." Make a move toward the bathroom. Got to let him know I don't want to talk about it. But he stops me.

"J.T., something eating at you?"

Want to tell him he needs to back off. He needs to keep his questions to himself and get out of my face about it. I want to say, "Only thing eating at me are questions I don't want to answer." Instead, "No. Nothing eating at me. Just training."

Don't wait for him to respond. Step into the bathroom and shut the door, thankful to be in the darkness where everything is clear.

———

"So tell me, how did your mama die anyway?" Mike says, leaned back on the couch with his feet propped up, swigging a can of Pabst Blue Ribbon.

My pencil stops filling in the blank on my language arts worksheet. Heart blasts blood straight into my head. He knows the answer to the question, but he likes to ask it every couple of days anyway. He also knows I won't answer.

Kevin sits in the La-Z-Boy, rocking back and forth, holding a bag of frozen peas on the black eye Mike gave him for stealing one of his beers while he was still at work. Kevin is tougher than me. He just looked back at Mike after getting backhanded and said, "That didn't hurt."

Thought Mike would tear right into him for that. But he actually smiled at him. "You just remember I count them every morning," and popped his first can of the evening.

WWE wrestling blares on the TV. "Yeah, Jason, you've never told us the story," Kevin says after he laughs, because he likes this game almost as much as Mike.

"What? Did she OD? Get stabbed by a crazy boyfriend? Come on, it will do you good to talk about it." Mike chuckles and takes another swig. "We're just trying to help."

Put my pencil in the crack of my notebook and close it. Shove it into my backpack. Don't say anything back. Never do. Mrs. Hernandez said talking back causes trouble.

Zip my backpack, get up off the floor, and walk past the couch.

Mike swings his feet off the coffee table and catches my wrist. "Time for you to talk, little man."

Stare back at him, frozen.

Mike glares back at me, grits his teeth. He twist my wrist, dropping me to my knees. "One of two things is going to happen. Either a story is going to start coming out of that mouth or this wrist is going to snap in half."

Tears fill my eyes, but no words come into my mouth. They can't.

Mike leans his head all the back and chugs his beer. His grip loosens a little.

Jerk my arm away, jump off the floor, and run for the hallway.

"Now where you going?" Mike yells.

Hear the empty can drop to the coffee table. Then Mike's footsteps pounding across the floor like a freight train. Mom said a tornado sounds like a train. Supposed to get in the hall closet when a tornado is coming.

Grab the doorknob, open it, and fall into the dark closet, slamming the door behind me.

Mike pounds the door with his fist so hard the floor vibrates under me.

"Ah, just leave him alone, Dad. Hacksaw Jim Duggan's coming on."

Hear the crowd on the TV cheer. The knob jiggles, but the door never opens. Mike's footsteps head back to the den, his favorite wrestler, and his beer.

Here in the dark, like when I'm asleep, Mike leaves me alone. No questions I don't want to answer. Just quiet. Clear.

Safe.

For now.

uniform

Every leader has to accept he is never really a part of the group. That line has to exist, even if that line is hard to see. But right now, it couldn't be more obvious.

Janet Freeman is trying to teach Dixon how to dance. Not talking about sixth-grade-wearing-a-cardboard-stiff-blazer-at-the-middle-school-Valentine's-dance kind of dancing. This is the kind of stuff that brings in administrators like a SWAT team on a hostage situation—hips popping, swinging, and grinding. Other students like Dixon wouldn't be caught dead learning to dance right out in public, but I guess he's been made fun of so much he just doesn't care anymore.

Stand at the far end of the commons area watching them without my standing over them. Any good leader needs to know what his cadets are like when he's not around. Helps me see every part of their personality. Maybe I'll catch a glimpse of something I can use.

Freeman stands in front of Dixon real close, bumps and grinds him a little. Swear his face turns about two shades short of the red wheelbarrows on sale at the hardware store. He stands there terrified and frozen. Freeman's voice echoes across the commons. "Come on, Peter. You got to get into it. You can't be scared. Just move. Let it go."

Dixon barely sways back and forth like the tiles around him are loaded with mines.

"There you go. Now move your arms. You look like you're in a straight jacket."

He bounces his arms away from his sides and starts snapping to music that must be playing in his head because the commons is silent except for Freeman's voice. It's weird the way the place sounds when it's empty after school.

Freeman prods Dixon. "Good, Peter, now a little bit more." She keeps shaking and popping her hips around. Dixon starts moving bigger. That's when MacDonald pipes up.

"Hey Peter, watch out. You start swinging around too much and you're going to knock Janet clean out of the building."

"Shut up, MacDonald. He's doing fine," Freeman snaps back at him.

Don't know if he's doing fine because I don't dance either. But it does seem like he's having a good time, even if he looks a little like a slug on a hotplate.

Pickens gets up off the floor and walks toward them. He starts to move a little, like he's trying to insinuate he wants a turn, but both Dixon and Freeman ignore him. Probably for the best.

Freeman jumps around, leans over a bit, and puts her butt right against Dixon's leg. "Now you're getting it."

MacDonald has to open his mouth again. "You bet he's getting it—right in his pants."

With that, Dixon shuts down. MacDonald pulled his plug. His legs snap together, his arms fall to his sides, and he jumps back like he got burned.

"MacDonald, I don't know why you can't shut the hell up. Let's see you do better," Freeman shouts.

"Oh, I'd love to, but I have a girlfriend and all."

"Yeah, whatever," Freeman says back.

Pickens jumps right in. "My turn." He points at Mac-Donald. "And don't say a word."

A month ago, Pickens would have never said that. Guess the training has been helping more than his body. Just got to make sure his head doesn't get too big for him to handle.

MacDonald just laughs.

"And that goes for you too, O'Malley," Pickens says. O'Malley looks up from his rifle. He doesn't know what's going on. He's sitting on the floor wiping his drill rifle with an old T-shirt the way he does before every practice. He likes to pretend it's real. But they're just like the ones the band's color guard twirls and flips except ours have fake barrels attached.

Freeman shuts it down, though. She knows MacDonald is not going to keep his mouth shut, and if he goes any further he could ruin the mood for practice. That's the kind of thing I'm talking about—a part of Janet I don't see at drill or during practice. She's going to be a good leader one day. She doesn't judge. Just says what she has to, to get the results she wants.

"That's enough for today. We'll try again later on."

Pickens is disappointed. Can see it, even if I'm twenty yards away.

No mystery why Pickens wants to learn to dance. Guess maybe he's got notions of asking Nicole to the homecoming dance. This is just in case she says yes. Got to hand it to him, he's optimistic. Some of us would rather stay realistic.

Right now, the reality is we have to get ready for a competition. And I have to lead them.

Yell across the commons, "CADETS."

victor

Freeman and Pickens look over toward me, and they all scurry to pick up their drill rifles off the floor. Walk fast across the floor, slapping my heels, even though sneakers don't make any noise.

Freeman is the first one to pick up her rifle. She spins around. The butt of her rifle plants MacDonald right in the balls. He doubles over. Janet barely looks over her shoulder. "Sorry, Freddy."

Can't tell if MacDonald knows, but I do. That wasn't an accident. Don't say anything, though. MacDonald's comments hurt squad unity. Way I see it, Freeman just gave him the gig he deserved.

"Fall in."

All five jump into formation, holding their rifles four inches in front their chests like I've showed them, faces forward. Good cadets. Even MacDonald pushes through the pain. He breathes deep and slow, his face red and sweating.

"Alright, cadets. Two weeks. Competition. Pat Roper's group. Will they beat us?"

"Captain, no sir," they say in unison. Love the sound.

"That's right. Alpha Squad. We don't lose."

"No, sir," they call out.

Stand in front, trying to find some trace of doubt. People's faces always tell the truth. But not even Dixon's shows he second guesses. "Good," I say. "Hit the field."

With their rifles still held four inches from their chests, they jog toward the door. Run ahead of them to get the door. Don't want them to have to slow down. Just like I taught them, the second line, Dixon and Pickens, fall behind the front line to make it single file. They storm through the door and shift back into formation. Trained well, just like Sergeant Maddox knew I would. Never disappoint.

Shut the door and sprint ahead of them to the practice field. Roper's squad's already out practicing. He wants so bad to knock us off. But he can keep on wanting.

Stop at the far end of the field. Face away from my cadets, feet just outside my shoulders, and hands tucked behind my back. Hear their steps stomping behind me in unison with perfect tempo. First time I've heard that. Pickens never quite gets the rhythm right. Different today. The steps get louder until they pass by me and fall in, centered in front of me.

The sun beats into their eyes. They squint and wait for my order. "Cadets, right face." Turn sharp and smooth, snapping their feet together.

"Forward march." Watch their feet to make sure not one cadet is even close to starting out of step. "Left, left, left-right-left." Turn and double-step until I'm in my position to their left. The sun reflects off O'Malley's shiny rifle and catches the corner of my eye. Doesn't bother or distract. Never does.

The squad reaches the corner of the field and turns, maintaining spacing and pace. We'll make three laps around the field before rifle handling, quick turns, and formations.

"Freeman, call it out," I say. Every practice I pick another person. Got to keep it even. Every cadet has to feel important.

"I don't know, but I've been told," she calls and the others repeat. "Not enough training will make you old."

It's corny, but MacDonald already got gigged twice for calling out *inappropriate* cadences. We're too close to competition to let that happen again. Trust Freeman not to step out of bounds.

As we pass Roper's squad, he looks at me and nods. Nod back. Not enemies. Can't be. Just going after the same thing. Our nodding at each other is like when football coaches cross the field and shake hands, just acknowledging the efforts of the other. Don't like or dislike each other. Both just want to be the best.

"CAPTAIN TILLMAN," Sergeant Maddox yells across the field. Look over toward him without missing a step. He points to the ground at his feet. "FRONT AND CENTER."

"Alpha Squad, keep marching."

"Yes sir, Captain," Freeman says for the group.

Break out of formation and double-time it over to Sergeant Maddox. Look at his face. His eyes nearly burn a hole in my forehead.

Stomp in place right in front of him and salute. "Captain Tillman reporting." Snap my hand down to my side. Eyes straight ahead, right at the Sergeant's chin. Never look him in the eye.

"Cadet, let me ask you a question. Are you the best cadet in the program?" His tone is sharp, just on the edge of pissed.

"Sir, wouldn't know, sir. Just try to do my best." Lie.

"Tillman, don't give me that shit." He shakes his head and looks at the ground. He chuckles like a horror movie. "I'll ask you again. Are you the best cadet in the program?"

Raise my chin a little. "Sir, yes, sir. The best."

"That's what I thought." He steps around behind me. "I'll ask you another question. Do you try to display all the qualities of a good soldier?"

"Sir, always, sir."

"Correct again," he says, getting a bit louder. He comes around to the front again and paces back and forth.

"You a leader?

"Yes, sir."

"You always follow orders?"

"Yes, sir."

"You never question what I think is best?"

"Never, sir."

"You respect my authority?" He increases his volume more. So I do, too.

"Absolutely, sir."

"You would never embarrass me?"

"Would never think of it, sir." Know exactly where he's headed. Just waiting for the line.

He stops, turns toward me, and leans in so close I can feel his breath on my face. "Then explain to me why I just got off the phone with Colleen and she tells me you told her you didn't need her help." His whisper is acid and vinegar.

Don't know what to say, so I don't say anything.

Sergeant Maddox doesn't move. "I'm waiting, Cadet."

"Sir, I don't have an explanation, sir." Out of the corner of my eye, I see my squad marching past us. They have to be looking, wondering what's going on. I never get in trouble, never get gigged. Hate them seeing this.

"Well, Tillman, we're going to stand here until I hear you explain why you questioned my decision." He takes a step back and stands there staring at me.

"Sir, I uh, just think I can handle it on my own. Find a way. That's what soldiers do." Only answer I have.

"Tillman, was I unclear about what would happen if you slipped in class again?"

"No, sir."

"Then you must have ignored my request on purpose. Is that it?"

"No, sir. Would never do that." Face straight. Eyes burn because I don't even blink.

"You embarrassed me. I call in a favor. Colleen comes all the way out here to help *you*. And you just sweep it aside, like my judgment doesn't matter. What do you have to say about that? What would you do, Cadet?"

"Sir, don't know what to say."

"You better say something, or I'm going to PT your ass until you puke."

Know what he wants me to say.

"Sir…sir, I uh…"

"SPIT IT OUT, CADET."

"Sir, I was wrong, sir."

"You're damn right you were wrong. Don't you *ever* question me again. You got that?" He steps forward and shoves a piece of paper in my pocket. Don't flinch or budge.

"That's her number. Call her, set up an appointment. You do whatever she asks. No questions. If she asks you to put on a tutu and dance around like a chicken, you do it." He stops and wipes the spit off his mouth. He takes a deep breath. "You have a chance to represent your squad, this platoon, and me. Mr. Marsh and I are working hard to see you really make something of yourself. So you *will* get help with those grades. That is a DI-RECT order."

"Sir, yes, sir."

He stands for a second looking at me. "Now on your face, Cadet."

Drop down in the push-up position.

"Fifty. And at the top of every one I want to hear you say, 'I will never embarrass my commanding officer.'"

Push out the first one. "I will never embarrass my commanding officer." Before the second one, the stomps of my squad pass again. Just as soon somebody shoot me than have them see this.

Start again, going faster on each one. Got to be done

before my squad makes it around for the third time. Sergeant Maddox doesn't say anything until I finish.

"Now on your feet, Cadet."

Jump up and stand at attention. "Tillman, don't disappoint me again."

Those words crack across my legs, almost buckling my knees. He turns and walks away. Sergeant Maddox knows he doesn't have to say anything else.

Stand and wait for my squad to come back around. When they get close, walk over and join right back in step.

"One more lap." Can't let them see me messed up. Got to hold that line. Can't lose my authority, my respect.

We practice the same way we always do. Nobody says a word about Sergeant Maddox. They know better. Maybe it is good they saw it. We have a good practice. Maybe they think if I'm in trouble then they are, too. One thing I do know. That's the last time J.T. ends up on his face in front of his squad.

whisky

Blood simmers under the surface. Every step cranks up the temperature another notch. Don't see the sidewalk. Don't hear cars or birds. Just Sergeant Maddox standing over me. "Don't disappoint me again."

The walk to work couldn't be worse if I was walking on broken glass.

Before today, J.T. had Sergeant Maddox's respect, and now J.T. has to earn it all over again. Know how he works. Getting his respect is like climbing a cliff. Fall and you start over at the bottom. No hope of a slope or tree or rock keeping you from smacking the ground. "Well, dipshit, you screwed up. Lost your grip and down you went."

Don't like the bottom. Not my place. Never there. But here J.T. is, and Jason isn't far away.

My pace slows. Arms get heavy, shoulders roll over like carrying bags of concrete. "Back on the bottom. Can't believe it," I think. "Bound to screw it up, I guess."

My legs stop. Look forward. Shake my head. "Don't

want to work today. Can't do it." I turn around and head back toward the house.

The voice screams like a grenade.

"SOLDIER, WHAT ARE YOU DOING?"

Snap my head up from looking at the ground.

"Feeling sorry for yourself? Feeling weak?"

Stop walking.

"Pick that head up."

I do it.

"You screwed up. So what? Gonna back down? Gonna get beat?"

"Sir, no, sir."

"You're a soldier. There ain't no quitting."

"No, sir."

"Turn your ass around."

Snap in the other direction.

"Now march."

Legs take off.

"No mission is perfect. But a good soldier makes it work."

"Yes, sir."

"No quitting. NO FAILURE."

"Yes, sir."

"Now keep pushing. You got work to do, soldier."

Increase my pace. Jason couldn't be further away.

The hardware store is in sight. Run for the door. Storm through it, making the bell slam against the wall.

"Good Lord boy, you going to take that door right off the hinges." Mr. Coffeen says it light and easy.

Don't say a word, just make a beeline for the bathroom. Can't slow down. Can't disappoint anybody else today. Change my clothes and walk out.

It'd be better if I could go for a run. Pain and sweat would be a gift right now. But I can't run. Stuck right here with Mr. Everything-is-Great-and-Wonderful.

Walk to the front counter for Mr. Coffeen to let me know what he wants me to do. He's ringing up some paint for Ms. Beatrice, so I wait for him to finish. Hate the waiting. Got to get moving. Swear this lady must repaint every room in her house once a month with all the paint she buys. Mr. Coffeen tears off her receipt and tapes it to one of the paint cans. "You want me to get J.T. to help you with those?" he asks.

Don't wait for her to answer. Just start grabbing paint cans off the counter. But she stops me like she always does. Knew it wouldn't be any different this time. Just have to make the attempt.

"Heavens no," Ms. Beatrice says and pushes my hands back down to the counter. "I'm old, but I can handle a couple of cans of paint."

Just look at her like *don't stop me*, hoping she'll see I *need* to help, to keep moving. Mr. Coffeen jumps in.

"Alright then, you have a good evening and you come back and see us." And then he looks at me. Let go of the cans and step away.

Ms. Beatrice fumbles around until she gets a hold of all the cans. She spins around and moves for the door.

Mr. Coffeen waves to her as she bangs out the door,

nearly taking out the window with the can in her right hand. When the door closes, Mr. Coffeen laughs and says, "I'm telling you J.T., there goes the most stubborn woman on God's green earth. I could sell her a flat of bricks and she wouldn't let anybody help her get them to the truck." He turns toward me and ignores the fact that I wanted to help her. "So tell me about your day. How was school?"

"It was school."

"How did your practice go today? You did practice with your troops, didn't you?"

"Yes, I trained with my *cadets*."

"So how did it go?"

"Fine."

"How are they looking, are they—"

"You want to tell me what you need done around here," I cut him off. Don't have time for him asking questions.

And this is the closest to pissed Mr. Coffeen has ever been at me. He puts his hands on his hips, his face tightens, and then looks around the store. "Alrighty then, I guess we do have quite a bit to get done around here."

He looks around the store, making a list in his head. "First, we got to get that tool aisle straightened up. Mrs. Milton came in here with her four-year-old boy, and he yanked nearly every screwdriver and pair of pliers we've got off the shelves."

Nod. "Got it."

"And then, I tell you what, go ahead and move those fall plants we got in Friday out to the garden area. Folks are getting their flower beds ready for cooler weather. Set up one of the tables from the back and put them out there by the garden fountains."

"No problem." A little drum starts beating against my left temple. Start to walk off, but Mr. Coffeen stops me. Wish he'd just let me get started. Got to keep moving.

"After that," he stops, rubs his chin, and looks around the store. The drum travels across my head and bangs the right temple, too.

"I guess we need to get out some more bags of mulch. Once the weather cools off, that stuff goes like turkeys the day before Thanksgiving."

Nod again. Turn and take two steps before the beating gets too loud.

"And I guess once you're done, you can—"

Snap around. "Goddamn it, we close at five-thirty, right?"

My voice bounces from windows to walls and fades away. Any other day I'd feel sorry. Not sorry, though.

Want Mr. Coffeen to be mad. Mad like me. Need him to yell, argue. Better even to slap, push, or shove. Something. Deserve it. Need to get gigged.

Sergeant Maddox didn't give me enough. In this place Mr. Coffeen's the commanding officer. He's got to do something.

Too bad my day is just filled with disappointments.

Mr. Coffeen looks straight at me. He takes a deep breath, softens his voice. "Yes, J.T., I know what time we close." His voice is calm, almost sweet. "The way you came storming through the front door, I just figured you had some energy you needed to get rid of."

Why can't he just give me what I deserve? That's the way it works. Make a mistake. Pay the price. But it's obvious Mr. Coffeen and J.T. don't live by the same rules. "Yes, sir," is all I say and walk to the back.

Open the garage door and push the hand truck over to the stacks of mulch. He said to start with the tools, but the heavy work is the cure. Pliers and screwdrivers will make me want to stab myself—tedious work with not enough movement. Need some kind of pain, even if it's the kind that gets things done.

Throw the bags on the hand truck like they don't weigh anything. Work fast and try not to think. "Just keep moving, J.T.," I say. Sweat sprouts and stings the top of my head. Not like running, but it's something.

When I come back through the store, Mr. Coffeen is helping some man I've never seen with one of the chainsaws. Glad he's occupied.

Stack the mulch almost as fast as I loaded it. Arms and lower back burning now. Walk back into the store and grab a level off a shelf. Use the level to make sure the bags are stacked perfectly even. Focus and execution equals success. Got to get that back in my head.

Set the level on top of the stack of bags and go back for more. Moving good now. The wheels on the hand truck rattle and turn where they want. Slam into one shelf and then another. Don't slow down. Can't. Something might get broken.

Mr. Coffeen calls from the other side of the store. "Good Lord, J.T., you need a license to drive that thing." He likes to make jokes in front of customers. He says it makes it easier to sell.

Slam the hand truck into the stack of mulch so hard it pushes over some bags onto the concrete floor. Pick up one of the bags and hear, "Hey Carter, what do you think would happen if you buried a pickle?"

Look to my left and Chris is standing there smiling like he did when Ms. Teagan called him into the hallway. Ignore him and set the bag down on the hand truck. Don't need this now.

Chris walks forward. Still ignore him. Grab another bag and stack it on the hand truck.

"How you doing there, Pickle Freak?" He pauses and waits for me to answer.

Don't say anything, but do turn and face him.

He's closer, staring at me. Our heads level at the same height, but Chris Walker's body lacks the results of hours and weeks of training I've put myself through. He lacks the motivation.

Measure the distance at about six feet.

"You need something?" I ask. This thing is either going to end or move forward. Right now, don't care which.

"I just came by to pick up some nails for the new nail guns my dad bought."

"Nails inside. Talk to Mr. Coffeen."

"Yeah, I know. But I wanted to make sure you got the message the other day."

"And what message is that?" Know good and well what he means but want to hear him say it.

Chris Walker takes a big step toward me like that's going to intimidate me. He points. "Best stay out of my face." He smirks. "I can make things pretty tough. More than you can handle. Somebody could get hurt. Wouldn't want that, would we?" He stops. His smirk disappears. "You hear me, dumbass?"

"Seem to be handling things just fine. Not the one who got suspended for a day. So who is the dumbass?"

Chris Walker takes another big step toward me. Don't even flinch. Tighten the muscles in my chest, abs, and shoulders.

He pushes me in the chest with both hands. "Oh, so you're calling me a dumbass?"

Stumble a half-step back. Got him right on the edge, where I want him. A little more and he'll give me what I need, what I deserve, because Sergeant Maddox didn't do enough.

"Nah, figure your father calls you that enough."

Chris Walker's eyes turn into flames. He clenches his teeth. Balls his fist.

Don't move a muscle.

Chris Walker's fist crashes into the side of my face. Head snaps to the side. Light flashes. The sharp, copper taste of blood spurts over my tongue. And the pain makes my brain want to explode out of my head.

Two reasons I let him punch me. One: It's the gig I deserve. Two: Makes Chris Walker think he has me.

"You getting the message now, soldier boy?" he yells.

Spit blood on the ground, turn and look at Chris. His hands are by his sides because he thinks I'm going to back off now, let him win this battle. Can't ever let the enemy win again.

"Was that supposed to hurt?"

Chris Walker cuts his eyes, rears back, and takes another swing.

My right hand reaches across my body and latches onto the top of his fist. Squeeze. Step slightly to the left. Rotate the hand under the wrist, just like Sergeant Maddox showed me. Chris Walker crashes to one knee. Sergeant Maddox would be proud.

Remember Mom saying in kindergarten, "Don't let anyone push you around." But Jason did let them. He never fought. And that cost him—with other kids, with a foster father. J.T.'s not paying that price.

My father's voice barks, *"That's it soldier. Perfect execution."*

Chris Walker tries to get up to his feet. Fold the hand under more, almost bringing his elbow to the ground. A sound almost like a whimper squeaks out. Jason used to make that sound when Mike kicked him for forgetting to push the chair back under the table or putting the milk on the wrong shelf. Didn't help him much either.

Hear footsteps. Look up to see Mr. Coffeen walking out the back door. He looks like he just came up on a car wreck. Seen it before.

"What in the Sam Hill is going on here?" Mr. Coffeen looks at Chris, then back at me. "J.T.?"

Let go of Chris Walker's wrist. Spit blood on the ground. "You have a customer," is all I say. Walk past Mr. Coffeen, heading for the bathroom.

x-ray

Push the bathroom door open with my foot and flip on the light. Turn on the cold water. Lean over and suck water into my mouth. Swish. Spit.

Brownish red liquid splatters in the sink. Glance up at the mirror. Jason looks back. Blood trickles out of the left corner of his mouth and runs over the scar.

Look down at the sink. Drops fall in rhythm, tapping an even tempo on the white surface and splattering my insides against the sides of the sink. Mrs. Hernandez hates the sink messed up.

Red contrasts against white. The snapping in my ear.

Too much to stop.

Slap off the light and drop to my knees. Heat rises.

———

I know the sound. Lying on the asphalt, trapped, the only thing I notice or can make sense of. Sounds like a flag snapping in the wind. Maybe an American flag like the one my dad used to wear on his uniform.

Folks on the way home from church bustle outside the wreckage. But I don't listen to them. Close my eyes and listen to the flag. Whip whip snap. Whip whip snap.

"Get the saw. Now. Come on," a man yells outside the car.

More feet run and shuffle on the asphalt outside the car. Can't see anything except the sky through the driver-side window. Just feel the skin-melting heat on the street. Maybe it has already started because the side of my face is wet and warm.

Hear a motor cough a couple of times. "Come on, damn it," a man's voice says. "Start." The motor coughs one more time and then screams outside the car.

Can't hear the flag anymore.

Grinding drowns everything. Look up to see sparks flying into the hole in the windshield. When it finally stops, someone pulls the metal away to let in the burning hot sun.

"Don't move, son. Don't move."

I don't. Just listen.

A man kneels next to me. His blazing yellow fireman's jacket swings in the wind, the metal clasps bang against the car. They're almost in rhythm with the flag that I can now hear again, snapping in the wind.

On his knees, he begs for me to lift my shoulder. I obey. He eases his arms underneath my melting body and slides me out of the car. Lies me flat on the asphalt. The hard surface feels like hot coals.

Another man, white shirt and black pants, crawls his hands over my legs and stomach. Someone I can't see places a cloth on my face. It covers my eyes. Swipe it away.

"Don't move now," the man in the white shirt says.

Don't listen to him. Lean my head to the side so I can find it. That American flag snapping sharply in the wind. But there is no flag. Only a white sheet with blood soaking through.

yankee

Knock knock.

Shake my head in the dark and swallow blood.

"J.T.?" Mr. Coffeen stands outside the bathroom. "J.T.? You alright in there?"

Don't answer. Just try to catch my breath.

"J.T. I'm going to open the door now. O.K.?"

Mr. Coffeen cracks the door a little and then opens it the rest of the way. The shop is dark. All the lights have been turned off.

Look up at him.

"How bad are you hurt?" he asks.

"Not hurt." Grab the bathroom counter and pull myself off the floor.

Mr. Coffeen lets out a deep breath, rubs his forehead. Studies my face. "You sure?"

"Yes, sir. Not hurt. Just got gigged."

zulu

Ice cubes clink and forks and knives scrape across plates. Tension.

Wondering how long it is going to take him. One minute? Two? It will kill him to last that long. Cut. *Scrape*. Bite. Chew. Swallow. Drink. *Clink*. Focus on tempo, rhythm. Cut. *Scrape*. Bite. Chew. Swallow. Drink. *Clink*.

"So, you want to tell me about the store?" His voice low and slow, cutting his food.

Made it three minutes. Better than expected.

"No, sir."

He sets his knife and fork down, takes a deep breath. "Well, I think I'm going to need you to tell me anyway, J.T."

Keep eating. Stay in the routine. Hamburger steak and mashed potatoes. Chew slowly, something else Mrs. Hernandez taught us at Honeywell House.

He waits, patient as always.

"Nothing to tell, sir."

He wipes his hands on his napkin and sets it back on

the table. "Now J.T., that's a lie." He's not accusing. Just stating a fact.

Can't tell him he's wrong. Hold silent.

Mr. Coffeen leans back in his chair. "You think I've never been in a fight?"

Shrug.

He tilts his head all the way back with his face looking up at the ceiling. "See that?" He points to his chin. A one-inch line I've never noticed marks the skin. He brings his face back down level with mine. "That one was because of a girl. Guy she dated before me. One heck of an uppercut." He shakes his head, remembering.

"Oh, but that wasn't the bad one. No, sir. That was just a scratch."

Mr. Coffeen puts two fingers in his mouth. Pops out three teeth and sets them on the table. Not good in front of a plate of food.

"There you go," he says like I'm supposed to be impressed. Far from it.

"Got nothing to blame but my own mouth for that. Just couldn't shut it up. I's eighteen, had a new Chevy that I treated better than a mother's first born. A bunch of us was parked out by Lake Martin. This guy opens his door and bang. Put a dent right in the side. Oh, he tried to apologize, but I wouldn't let it go at that. Kept running my mouth and pushing on that old boy. So him and two of his buddies finally shut me up." He shakes his head again. "Whew, I had a hot head."

He picks up his teeth off the table and snaps them back in place. "Hard to imagine."

He's right.

"J.T., there's always a story. And the only thing all them stories got in common is ain't none of them good."

He looks at me like this is going to get me to talk. No chance. Pick up my fork and knife.

"So, what is the story with Chris Walker?"

Keep looking at my plate. Shrug. Another bite. Chew. Swallow. Drink. *Clink*. Tempo off.

Mr. Coffeen realizes he's not getting anything out of me. "Well, whatever it is, there's only one question you got to answer. Same question that my daddy asked me when I came home holding three teeth in the palm of my hand. He was a good man who never raised a hand to me or nobody. He stood right there in the living room and asked me, 'Was it worth it?'"

He stops for a second, looks above my head into the past, then says, "And I's too stupid then to answer that question correctly. Took me a lot more years to get that one right."

Keep eating.

"Still nothing to tell me?" He's not mad. Thinks he's helping.

Shake my head. Got to keep Jason away. He doesn't handle these situations well. "No, sir."

"There's one more thing." He sets his elbows on the table and leans over his plate. "J.T., I can't have that kind of stuff going on at my place of business. You understand that, right?"

Nod.

"This town is too small to be upsetting folks, especially folks like the Walkers."

"Sir, maybe you should fire me."

He doesn't respond right away. Considering it maybe.

Mr. Coffeen thinks I'm talking to him. "Can't do that, J.T."

Breathe deep. Squeeze my eyes shut, waiting to see if Jason has anything to say.

"J.T., look at me."

Open my eyes and look up to see Mr. Coffeen looking straight at me, not like Sergeant Maddox with sharp lines on his forehead pointing down to bullet eyes. Mr. Coffeen's lines curve. Guess I'd call it concern.

"You know that's not going to happen. I need you too much around there. But you might want to think about letting me help you straighten out whatever is going on with you and Chris Walker. I could tell the other day there was some awful tension between the two of you."

Jason pushes at my mouth, trying to make me spill it all. Jason would pick this time to come after me, when I'm tired. Drop my fork and rub my hand over my face. Need to get up, out.

My hand stops on the scar. Fingers feel the raised skin. Too much at one time. Push away from the table. Grab the plate and glass.

Move fast. Don't wash the dishes. Just put them in the bottom of the sink and run water over them. Turn to leave the kitchen and Mr. Coffeen.

"J.T., just hang on a minute, son," he says.

Stop. Look at him hard. "Not your son."

"J.T., sorry. But fighting ain't going to get you nowhere. Done been down that road."

His voice sounds sharper than what normally comes out of him, like he's warning me. Only one thing to say. "Sir, don't worry about it."

"J.T., I do worry about it. And whether you want to believe it or not, I worry about *you*."

Turn sharp to the right and march out of the kitchen.

"J.T., just a second now."

Snap around to face him. "Sir, don't worry. Won't happen again. Won't disappoint you."

Before he gets in another word, I retreat fast. Soldiers anticipate. Act.

Hear Mr. Coffeen behind me. "J.T.?"

Yes, J.T. Not Jason.

Mr. Coffeen says again, "J.T.?"

Step into my room and shut the door. Almost safe.

Drop quickly down to the floor, chest on the ground, palms flat on the floor. Push up. Stare at the picture. Start banging out push-ups. Eyes stay on the picture. And the voice makes me feel better.

"Good soldier. That's the way. Assess a bad situation. Retreat if necessary."

Arms and chest churn like pistons through pain and

weakness. Focus on the picture. "Keep your eyes on the prize." That's what Sergeant Maddox says. Only prize is winning. Getting to The Citadel, then the real thing, victory. Never break. Keep firing. Winning. Every battle.

alpha-alpha

Thirty minutes of training brings me back into balance. Jason is nowhere near. Can focus on the next task at hand.

Stare at the phone and the piece of paper Sergeant Maddox gave me, pissed off and racking my brain to find some way around this situation. But I've been given an order, and that's all that matters.

Pick up the paper, study the numbers. There might as well be a secret code that spells, "Weakness." My fault, though. Sergeant Maddox was right. Had my chance. Now I pay.

Read the numbers over five times, memorize them. Don't have to, but my brain needs practice whenever it can get it. Pick up the phone. Dial quickly. Get this over as fast as possible.

Three rings, four.

"Hello," a girl answers on the other end.

"Yes, ma'am, may I speak to Ms. Francis, please?"

"This is she." Her voice is light and bouncy, almost like Susan Welsh's during the morning announcements.

"Ms. Francis, this is J.T. Tillman, one of Sergeant Maddox's cadets."

"Oh, hey. How are you?"

"Fine, ma'am."

She laughs. "J.T., you don't have to call me ma'am."

"Ma'am, I'd just rather if it's all the same to you."

"O.K. then. Not going to cause me any harm, I guess."

A few seconds of silence hangs on the line before she says, "So, did you change your mind?"

Could tell her no. Had it changed for me. Got my orders. Just following through. No need. "Yes, ma'am."

"Great."

Silence again.

"Well," she chirps in, "when do you want to get started?"

"Guess Wednesday."

"Wednesday will be fine. What time?"

"1700?"

"Seventeen hundred? Oh, that's five o'clock, right?"

"Yes, ma'am."

"That will work." Hear her scratching the info down on paper. "How about we meet at Billie's Café, Main Street?"

"Certainly, ma'am."

"I love that little place. I have to go there every time I'm in town. It's like a disease I have." She laughs.

I remain silent. This is business, training, not pleasure.

Her laugh trails off. "Alrighty, well, see you then."

"Thank you, ma'am."

"Oh, no problem, J.T. Bye-bye."

"Good-bye."

Set the phone down and wad the piece of paper. Could stay pissed off, but that's not what soldiers do. Some missions require sacrifice. This is just another one on the list.

alpha-bravo

Wednesday, 19 Oct 05, 1658

If it wasn't for the crowd at lunch, Billie's Café would've had to close up shop a long time ago. Mr. Coffeen says there's no reason for her to open at night. "Guess she figures like I do. If we stop working, we're liable to fall over dead." But from the looks of it, Ms. Billie has a better chance of dying from boredom. Not even a handful of people. May be bad for profits, but good for me. No chance of seeing someone from the platoon.

Can't lose any clout.

There's no bell on the front door, so I stand in the doorway until Ms. Billie comes bolting out from the back at about a hundred miles an hour. Probably a habit she got into when this place was packed 24/7, before the cluster of chains out by I-75.

"Just sit anywhere, sweetheart. I'll be with you in a second." She grabs a coffee pot and fills a cup for the one man sitting at the counter.

I drop my backpack on the floor and slide into a booth

by the front window so I can see Ms. Francis coming. Always better to keep things in front of you so you can see them coming, good or bad.

Mr. Coffeen let me off a few minutes early. No reason. The place is just across the street. But he got the sense that this is important.

"Now go on, J.T. I'll get this place closed up. Don't want to keep her waiting."

Hated explaining the whole situation to him. I think he enjoyed it as much as I hated it. He acted like this was some kind of date or something, even though I told him it was for school.

"Smart women are the best kind," he said. "Figured that one out too late, let me tell you. Now get on out of here."

Would've taken too much energy to argue with him.

Ms. Billie comes over to the booth and pulls out a small notepad from her apron. "What'll it be this evening, handsome?"

Handsome? Not funny. "I'm waiting on someone."

"Alrighty then. You just wave at me when you're ready." She flips the notepad closed, winks at me, and tucks it back in her apron. She starts to walk away, but stops. "Oh, and tonight's special is chicken and dumplings."

"Thank you, ma'am, but I don't know if we're eating."

She looks at me like I just asked her the square root of 388,944. "Well, O.K., whatever then."

She's disappointed.

Look out the window and see Mr. Coffeen locking up

the store. Doesn't feel right watching from over here. Like something's missing, wrong. Guess it's the routine.

As soon as I turn my head away from the window, Ms. Francis comes through the door. She gives a quick scan of the room, then spots me at the booth. "There you are." She smiles, walks over, and slings her bag into the booth. She plops down. Immediately whips her hair up into a ponytail. Kills me the precision some girls have with that.

No need for me to wave at Ms. Billie because she's five feet from the table by the time Ms. Francis barely hits the bench.

"So, we eating tonight?" she blurts out all excited as Ms. Francis settles in the booth.

Ms. Francis looks at me.

"I'll just have water," I say.

"And what about you, honey? Special is chicken and dumplings," Ms. Billie says like a car salesman.

"Yeah, O.K. Sounds good. And coffee."

Ms. Billie jots it down on her notepad. "You won't regret it."

I watch her leave, and her walk reminds me of Ms. Hernandez the way she just about burned up the ground whether she was in a hurry or not. That picture hangs in my eyes for a few seconds before I push it away. Not here, now.

Ms. Francis pulls off her jacket and sets it on top of her bag.

"So J.T., where do you want to start?"

Right to business.

Shrug. Don't know how to explain.

"Well, can you tell me why you're having a problem?"

"Not exactly sure, ma'am."

"Is it a lack of preparation? I mean, are you reading, studying? Do you understand the material?" She pulls her ponytail out, just to sling it right back up as if something was wrong with it in the first place.

Hear the door open behind me. Look over my shoulder to see Pickens and his mom. She's quartered away so I can't see her face. Never have seen it. She always seems to be hidden by the glare of the windshield or the shadow of a tree. Pickens' head scans the room quickly. He sees me, but he doesn't even acknowledge me. Good cadet. He knows why I'm here and that I hate this whole situation.

The two of them walk to a booth and sit down, his mother's back to me, like she did it on purpose.

Ms. Billie ignores that they've walked in and sat down. Instead, she zings up and sets my water and Ms. Francis' coffee on the table. "Be just a minute on the chicken and dumplings," she says and scurries away.

Watch Ms. Billie walk to the back without saying anything to Pickens and his mom and figure out real quick why this place is empty.

Ms. Francis brings me back. "Well?"

Turn toward her. "Not sure." That low simmering heat crawls over the top of my head. Not even five minutes into this thing. Sweating already. Hate questions.

"J.T.," her face gets serious, "you have to try to tell me

what you're having trouble with so I know how to help you. Understand? That's the only way this works."

Instead of replying, reach in my bag and pull out my English notebook. Open it and pull out the quiz on *The Crucible* that landed me in this situation. Stare at the 60% glaring up in red. Hesitate, but know I got to hand it over. It'll explain better than me.

Ms. Francis looks it over. She nods as she scans down the page. "Well, I guess the good news is the only ones you missed were the ones you left blank." She chuckles then stops, looks away from me and back at the page. "But I think I see the problem."

She gets up out of the booth and comes over to my side of the table. "Scoot over and let me show you."

Glance over to Pickens to see if he's watching. He shakes his head like I just beat him in a race.

Want to tell her I'd like it a lot better if she'd stay on her side of the table, but figure everything I say and do is going to get relayed right back to Sergeant Maddox. Her orders might as well be his, so I scoot against the window.

She slides in next to me. My nose catches her smell. Don't know if it's perfume, lotion, or just soap and water. It's simply female—a mixture of cream, flowers, fruits, and sugar.

Forgot that smell. Every girl in school maintains a safe radius so it's been a long time since that soft sweetness invaded my space. It's too nice. Makes me think of Mom.

Ms. Francis places my quiz on the table. "Now take a look."

"I've seen it, ma'am."

"Yes, J.T., I know you've seen it. But look at the questions you didn't answer." She points her finger toward the page. "What do they have in common?"

Pick up the paper and look at the unanswered questions. Read each one.

Clueless.

"Ma'am, I don't know."

"Well, look again, then." Orders sound so much nicer coming from her mouth.

Read them all again. And then one more time. I can only come up with one answer. "They all start with, 'How do you know?'"

"Exactly. Good." She pats my shoulder.

Flinch.

Ms. Francis gets nervous. "Sorry."

"No need."

She looks at me like she doesn't believe me. Then she says, "J.T., do you have your book with you?" Moving things forward.

"Of course, ma'am." Scoot toward her. She gets out of the booth. Reach over and pick up my bag and sit it on the bench. When I pull the zipper open, Ms. Billie comes up to the table.

"Here you go, honey. Chicken and dumplings that will 'bout near make you weep." She sets the plate down on the other side of the table. Good.

Pull out my book while Ms. Francis sits back in her place and picks up her fork.

"Turn to Act I." She stabs a piece of chicken and puts it in her mouth. "Lord, I love this stuff," she says and shakes her head.

Flip open the book and turn pages until I find Act I. When I get there, look across the table. "O.K.?"

She chews a couple of times and swallows. "Read the first question you didn't answer."

Pick up my 60. Read the first question. "How do you know Parris is greedy?"

"Now see if you can find the answer." She goes back to eating. And I start scanning and flipping pages."

Ms. Francis is nearly finished with her plate before I give up. Look up at her. "Ma'am, don't see it. Can't find it anywhere."

"J.T., you can't find it because none of the characters say it."

What I'd like to say is, *Why in the hell am I looking for something that nobody says?* But her smell floats across the table. Cools the heat beating in my head. Take a deep breath. "Then how am I supposed to know?"

"How do you know Sergeant Maddox is a good commander?"

"Ma'am?"

"Do you think Sergeant Maddox is a good commanding officer?"

Straighten up in my seat. "Absolutely, ma'am."

"How do you know? Did somebody tell you?"

"No, ma'am. It's just obvious."

"Why?" She smiles like this is a game she's winning.

"Because, because he trains us hard, pushes us to be better, doesn't take any crap."

"Right. All of those are actions. His actions speak for themselves. Nobody has to say it. Got it?"

"Maybe."

"Look again. Find what Parris *does* that would tell you he's greedy." She shovels the last bite of chicken and dumplings in her mouth.

Ms. Billie zooms over with the coffee pot in her hand. "Here you go, sweetie, let me warm that up for you." She fills Ms. Francis' cup and takes her plate. "So what'd you think?"

"Makes the food at the university cafeteria seem like dog food."

Ms. Billie laughs, breaking my concentration. "Anything else I can get you two?"

"We're fine," Ms. Francis says.

I'll be fine if I can get one second of quiet.

"Well, you just let me know."

This time I answer. "We will," I bark without looking up from the book.

She scurries away, and I look up to see if she stops to wait on Pickens and his mom. But they're gone. Guess they gave up on Ms. Billie.

Ms. Francis' coffee cup settles on the saucer the way Mom's used to in the morning. The dishes knocking together used to remind me of wind chimes for some reason. Don't need the memory.

Every couple of minutes her smell twitches my nose, stirs my brain. Impossible to focus.

Force my eyes and head to concentrate on the words in front of me. Reading only Parris' parts. Got to be fast and efficient. Get through one page, then two and three.

Found it. Look up from the book.

"Ma'am, think I got it."

She takes another sip of coffee. The saucer chimes. "Well, let me hear it."

"Ma'am, he complains about his salary."

"BINGO," she yells. Then she reaches across the table and grabs my hand with both of hers. Soft palms and skinny fingers warmed from the coffee cup tug and shake my hand. "Perfect."

———

"Now, come on, honey. Just two more." Mom holds my spelling book in one hand and her coffee in the other. This is our routine every Friday morning. She calls out the word, and I spell it. Only way I can learn them. Fourth grade shouldn't be this tough.

"Ready?" she asks.

I nod. Push my plate of half-eaten scrambled eggs away from me like I need the room to concentrate.

"O.K. Here's the next one. Extraordinary."

My brain spins, finds the letters, piecing them together. "E-X-T-R." Pause to gather the next letters. "A-O-R-D . . . I-N-A-R-Y."

Mom sips her coffee and sets the cup down in the saucer. She swallows and reaches across the table for me to give her a high five.

I slap her hand.

"Alright, here we go. This is for all or nothing." She tries to act so serious, like this is the National Spelling Bee or something.

I play along. Make my face serious, too.

Mom flips the book closed and stares across the table. "Catastrophe."

This one is easy. I mispronounced it in class and made some people laugh so it was the first one I learned. "C-A-T…A-S-T…R-O…P-H-E."

"BINGO," Mom yells, and raises both arms in the air like we're on a game show.

I smile.

She drops her arms and grabs my hand with hers. She shakes it. "Perfect, honey."

alpha-charlie

Ms. Francis shakes my hand, a bit harder. "J.T.?"

Blink a couple of times and pull my hand away. "Ma'am?"

"You with me?" She smiles across the table, trying to hide that she is freaked a little. But she is doing better than most do.

"Yes, ma'am."

She nods. "Good. Ready to try the next one?"

Nod back at her, even though the only thing I'm ready for is leaving. I read the next unanswered question. Doesn't take me long to find the answer. Feel weak for missing it in the first place.

When I get it right, at least Ms. Francis keeps her hands to herself.

Within ten minutes, we finish the other questions, and she makes me summarize the first act.

"Well, looks like you have a pretty good handle on things."

Only way to have it.

"Remember, most of the time with this stuff, the answer isn't going to be right in front of you. You have to look at the evidence and draw a conclusion."

"Yes, ma'am."

Ms. Billie comes by and drops the check. "Hope to see y'all again."

I snatch up the check before Ms. Francis can get her hand on it.

"J.T., you only had water."

"Ma'am, can't let you pay."

She doesn't argue.

I pull my wallet out of my back pocket and place the bills on top of the check on the table.

"Well," Ms. Francis says as she grabs her jacket, "I'll call Sergeant Maddox and let him know how it went."

"Thank you, ma'am."

"So, you want to meet again next week? Same time and place?"

"That will be fine, ma'am."

She stands up out of the booth, puts on her jacket, and grabs her bag. "You did well, J.T. You'll be back on track in no time."

She better be right. Got to get that grade up.

alpha-delta

Thursday, 20 Oct 05, 0714

Crowd. Blue lights. Bomb squad. Together in front of a high school. Not a good thing.

Walk up to the back of the crowd. No one sees, speaks. Just bodies pressing against the yellow police tape holding them back from whatever has brought two sheriff's cars and a truck with "Covington County Bomb Squad" painted in black letters on the door.

Stand behind everyone else and look over their heads. Fifty yards away, next to the main entrance, two men in bomb suits examine something. Looks to be about four-feet tall, odd shape, mostly dark green and gray, a square hanging on it. They walk around it, scanning it with some kind of detection device.

This many students are never this quiet. They wait, probably hope that something will happen.

The two bomb men make two more trips around the object, then turn off the detector, and pull off the heads of their suits. Ten seconds later, two deputies walking German shepherds come out the front entrance with Mrs. Polk and Mr. Schmitt, the school security officer. They walk slowly. They don't seem worried.

Look at my watch—0722. The day already off track.

A deputy with a dog yells something to the bomb suit guys. They nod. The deputy, Mrs. Polk, and Mr. Schmitt have a short conversation. Then Mrs. Polk and Mr. Schmitt walk toward the crowd. Students and teachers start to mumble.

Mrs. Polk approaches the yellow tape keeping the students back and raises her hand to quiet everyone. "Students and staff, your attention please."

The crowd gets still.

"There will be no school today."

Students clap and cheer. They're thrilled. I'm not.

Mrs. Polk raises her hand again. "Now please listen. We have a situation. Everything seems to be fine, but we need to investigate further."

More mumbling.

Mrs. Polk continues, a bit louder. "The buses will be pulling up here on the street to pick up bus riders. Those of you who walk or drive need to leave immediately. The school will release a statement on the evening news to notify everyone about tomorrow."

Just like a movie, a van with WLOX News 13 painted on the side pulls up behind the crowd right on cue.

"Now, we need all walkers and car riders to please disperse immediately."

Nobody even acts like they're going anywhere.

The deputy who's in charge of holding the line steps forward. "Come on kids, let's go." The radio clipped to his belt comes alive, and a slightly crackled voice spurts, "Deputy Johnson, everything seems to be clear." He snaps his hand to the volume knob and turns it down. But he's too late.

Somebody ducks under the yellow tape. Then another, and another. Within seconds, the crowd busts through the tape like a dam breaking.

"Whoa, whoa, whoa, now stay back. Stay back," one of the deputies yells. But it's useless.

Students flow toward the school like an avalanche, leaving the faculty behind. Two deputies can't stop a few hundred students. Let them all go in front of me. Don't need to get caught up in that. Uniform has to stay crisp, even though there will be no inspection today, no points awarded, no routine.

They all jostle, shove, and nearly climb over each other to get a look. Just hang back, easing closer to watch, evaluate the situation. And then slowly, bit by bit, some of them start to turn, to look.

Most people look at me with a quick glance up and down or cut to the side, hardly ever right at me, especially on Thursdays when I'm tip to toe in green. They don't want to get caught staring at the scar. They wouldn't say it, but I know it.

Today is different.

Something is up. Because everybody looks.

One person can give off a funny vibe. But two hundred.

They don't give off a vibe. They give off a shock wave that pricks like pins. It makes me move.

Try to ignore them, keeping my head forward. March toward the school, straight and stiff like my shirt and pants. About twenty yards away, more heads turn. They don't dart away like they're supposed to. Catches me off guard. Keep my eyes fixed straight ahead where my cadets are standing with their backs turned. They're looking at the object.

The crowd tracks every step. Ignore them. Have to. It is what I've learned to do. A few feet away I say, "Cadets." They snap to attention and turn in unison. Love when they do that.

Something's wrong with their faces. They are scared.

Pickens tries to speak up first, but Freeman cuts him off. "Captain, uh, good morning."

I nod back. "Morning, Freeman. What's going on?"

As I say it, my cadets press their shoulders together, obviously trying to hide what is behind them.

"Oh, it's nothing you need to see," Pickens says.

Glance over their heads and see a piece of camo. Looks like fatigues. Look back at them.

"Step aside, cadets."

They don't move. All the eyes that watched me walk up now bear down on me.

"Cadets, step aside." More serious this time, not playing.

Dixon pipes up, "Captain, sir, how does my uniform look today?"

Pickens follows up, "Yeah, how do we look?"

"CADETS, STEP ASIDE!"

In the middle of my voice echoing off the walls, the crowd gasps. Cut my eyes at my cadets, and they know they have about two seconds to step aside or they will pay for it.

They move away to reveal Chris Walker's counter attack. It took him three days. Knew something would happen. But never expected this.

Sitting on top of a blob of concrete poured onto the grass is the torso of an old mannequin. The mannequin is dressed in a long-sleeve fatigue shirt I'm sure was bought at the same place O'Malley gets his MREs. The mask that Chris Walker made in art class covers the mannequin's head. And a sign hangs around its neck. The sign reads, "BOOM, YOU'RE ALL DEAD."

Stare at the figure. No one says anything. They're waiting for me. But I'm not going to give them the satisfaction. They want me to be the freak. They want me to do something that will let them say, "I told you so." If I say or do the wrong thing, their insults, rumors, and hate will be justified. Chris Walker will win. J.T. won't.

Keep staring. Ripples sent from my heart expand all the way through my fingertips like one of those vibrating massage chairs that are supposed to make you feel good. But these almost make me sick to my stomach.

The tardy bell rings, even though nobody is going to class today. Nobody moves.

Look up, turn to my cadets. Even though they try, their faces give them away. See it right behind their foreheads. They wonder if I'm about to freak out. At least they're trying to be loyal, hold their belief in their leader.

163

"You look sharp this morning. Too bad no inspection today."

"Thanks, Captain," Freeman says.

"Let's get moving, cadets," I say and turn my head back toward the street.

Deputies scurry around the crowd like cowboys herding cattle, except with nightsticks that everyone knows they won't use. They force the crowd back toward the street.

"LET'S GO, PEOPLE! MOVE!" one yells.

As I walk, the crowd parts like I'm carrying a flaming ten-pound bag of dog shit. Hear my cadets marching behind me. Good. Chris Walker can humiliate me, but it might make my squad stronger.

Look over my shoulder to see everybody but Pickens marching straight and hard, just like real soldiers.

alpha-echo

Friday, 21 Oct 05, 0715

The front of the school looks like it is supposed to this morning, but good sense tells me it won't be the same. A lot of stories can be created in twenty-four hours. A lot of things can change. But J.T. won't. Just adapt, focus, and move forward. Just like yesterday.

Mr. Coffeen was happy to have me at the hardware store all day. So he didn't ask too many questions like expected. He didn't even barrage me when the news showed video of the mannequin. But I was ready, like I am today. Always.

Time my steps perfectly so students finish entering the school just as I reach the entrance. Love when a plan works out. As soon as I step through the door, heads turn and students gasp and recoil. My eyes stay straight ahead. Won't let them affect me. Then I hear, "Tillman."

Sergeant Maddox stands in the doorway of the main office with Mrs. Polk, Mr. Schmitt, and Mr. White, the school counselor. Perfect.

"Front and center, Cadet," Sergeant Maddox says.

When I step in front of Sergeant Maddox, Mr. Schmitt takes a half-step back. He's so scared of everything. Dixon would even make this guy sweat. "Sir," I say to Sergeant Maddox and pop my heels together even though I'm not in uniform, keeping chin high.

Sergeant Maddox doesn't say anything. Mrs. Polk, the principal does instead. "J.T., we need to speak with you a second, please."

Show her nothing but respect.

"Yes, ma'am." They step aside to let me walk past.

The students in the office nearly climb the freaking walls when I come into the room. One bangs against the counter so hard I think for a second he's going to dive over it. Can't even say I mind people being this scared of me. Reminds me I'm the kind that does the job they could never do. War. Battles. Blood. They couldn't hack it. But they know I can. That makes them scared. Makes me glad.

Walk into Mrs. Polk's office. Stand in front of the chair by her desk while the others walk in behind me. They sit. I wait for my order.

Sergeant Maddox knows what I need to hear. "Have a seat, Cadet."

Sit quick, stiff, tight. Hands go to my lap. Brace myself for the interrogation.

Where will it come from? Will Sergeant Maddox start? Will Mr. Schmitt make some sorry speech? Will Mrs. Polk preach policies? Or will Mr. White, the counselor, make some lame ass attempt to "talk" to me? Whatever it is, they can bring it. Got nothing to say.

"J.T., would it be alright if I ask you a couple of questions?" Mr. White asks.

Looks like they're going with the counselor. Angle to the left to face Mr. White. We've talked before, the first week I got here at the end of freshman year. He had all the dirt on what had happed to me—the wreck, the messed-up foster family. He thought he was going to be able to pat me on the shoulder, say a couple of nice things, and I was just going to spill my guts. He got one hell of a disappointment. Like he's about to get now.

Sergeant Maddox is in the room, so I keep it short, respectful, leave the smart comments out. "Sir, go ahead."

"Tell me, how are you feeling this morning?"

Oh, for Christ's sake. Can't believe this guy. I know what he wants, but I stone him. "Sir, never better."

Mr. White nods his head. "Are you angry or anxious in any way?"

"Sir, no, sir."

"I mean, has anyone in the school upset you?"

"No, sir."

He nods and rubs his hands together, looks at me for a second. "How do you feel about other students here at North Covington?"

Swear he got these questions from some guide they must give all high school counselors. The only thing that would be more obvious would be if he had a pamphlet in his hand.

He loves this crap. He's living in a dream world where he thinks he can save some kids with a few words. Know the type. Talked to enough "counselors" when I was at Honeywell House. Got the whole routine down.

"Sir, I don't understand the question."

"Do you like them, not like them? Do you feel like you have friends here? Do you like coming to school here?"

"Sir, I feel fine about the students here," is all I say. If I give them even one little morsel of the truth, I'll get a one-way ticket straight out of here. That means no more cadets, no more Sergeant Maddox, no Citadel. Everything J.T.'s focused on, worked for, will disappear. Have to start over. Can't go backward. Always move forward.

Mr. White leans forward and places his hand on my arm. I flinch and the temperature in the room jumps about ten degrees. He pulls his hand away but stays leaning forward.

"Maybe I should ask how you feel about Chris Walker?"

"Sir?" Now this catches me off guard. Don't like it.

"What about," he looks down at a notepad sitting in his lap, "Chris Walker?"

"What about him, sir?"

"About a week or so ago, Mr. Marsh says he saw the two of you having a small altercation in the hallway. He says he didn't think much about it then, but now he just wants us to check it out."

No response.

"So, what about Chris? What were you arguing about in the hall?"

"Nothing, sir. We weren't arguing. Mr. Marsh is mistaken."

"Cadet," Sergeant Maddox says. I look over at him.

He's giving me that look that says I better tell it straight. That's just like him. He doesn't put up with bullshit. And he can smell it a mile away.

Turn back to Mr. White. "Sir, I just made a comment about him not standing for the pledge in the morning. He didn't like what I said. He said something to me in the hall. I apologized. That was it."

Wait for Sergeant Maddox to say something because I'm sure he can sniff that one. He knows I'd never apologize to somebody like Chris, especially not for something like that. Figure he doesn't say anything because he knows he would've said something, too. In fact, bet he's glad I did.

"So, that was it? Nothing else?" Mr. White asks.

"Yes, sir."

"J.T.?" Mrs. Polk's turn now.

Angle back toward her. "Yes, ma'am?"

"We got some information that Chris Walker made the mask that was on the mannequin yesterday morning. Can you confirm that?"

"No, ma'am, I can't."

"So, the referral Ms. Teagan turned in for Chris disrupting class didn't have anything to do with the mask?"

Obviously, Mrs. Polk knows the story, but her information didn't come from Ms. Teagan. That I would bet on. She's not going to chance getting busted for her smoke breaks. So I feel comfortable in denying a story I know came from another student.

"Not that I know of, ma'am."

Mrs. Polk nods her head. "J.T., we really need to find

out who pulled this, this prank. It's very serious. We lost a whole day of instruction."

"Understand, ma'am. Help you if I could."

This is a perfect opportunity for me to bust Chris Walker. Could guarantee he'd get expelled, not that he'd care. But can't let others fight my battles. Have to win on my own. Face the enemy instead of running from him. If they do get Chris Walker, it won't be because I punk out.

"J.T., I think I know the answer to this question, but you know I have to ask anyway. Did you have anything to do with the statue outside the school yesterday?" Mrs. Polk asks.

"Absolutely not, ma'am. Would never."

She nods. "Well, somebody obviously wanted to make it resemble you, maybe lead us to believe you had done something, would do something destructive."

Kills me the words she uses. What she means is somebody wanted to make it look like I was about to blow this school into the next hemisphere. It'd be a lot better if people just used the words they mean. Keep things clear and straightforward. But that's not Mrs. Polk's style.

"Guess so, ma'am. But would never think of it."

Mrs. Polk examines me closely, not sure if she wants to believe me or not. But I've never given her a reason to doubt. Never been in trouble. Just do my duty and that's it.

She looks at me a bit longer and then puts on her reading glasses and shuffles some papers. She takes off her glasses and looks at me again.

"J.T., here is the problem. We need help figuring out

who would do this. We can't have this kind of thing go unpunished. This is very serious."

"Yes, ma'am."

"So, can you think of anyone, anybody that might want to get you in trouble? Because right now, it looks like either you or Chris Walker." Mrs. Polk's face sags, and her eyes drop from mine.

"Ma'am, don't have a clue. Really."

She nods her head, disappointed. She looks at Sergeant Maddox and then back at me.

"J.T., I have no proof that you did this." She stops and takes a deep breath. "We'll just have to wait and figure this out."

"Until then?" Look at Sergeant Maddox. "I can still compete with my cadets?"

"Yes," Mrs. Polk says. "But please, J.T., try to think of something that could help us."

"Do my best, ma'am."

She starts shuffling papers again. "Now, I've already talked to your foster father this morning. Unfortunately, he couldn't leave the store to come in. He knows we're talking to you, and I'm going to talk with him more this evening."

Just nod back at her.

"Fine then." Mrs. Polk picks up a pen. "J.T., can we have permission to look in your locker? We just need to take a look, just to be on the safe side." She is not happy about this.

"Sure, ma'am."

"Could you give us the locker number and the combination?"

That's just like Mrs. Polk. Here I am, some kid who might be ready to blow a gasket and go on a rampage all over the school, and she's still polite as ever. Don't know if she needs permission, and she sure doesn't need to ask me for the combination. She could get that with the punch of a few buttons. But being that way is just not in her. Whatever she has, she needs to spread it around.

"333," I say. "But it's empty. Carry all my books with me." Point to my bag on the floor.

"Well, can we search your bag?" Mrs. Polk asks.

"Absolutely, ma'am."

She looks over at Mr. Schmitt. He strains to get out of the chair and walks over to my bag. He nearly blows a blood vessel picking it up and sitting it on the desk. He pulls out all my books and binders until the bag is empty and a pile of clean books and tabbed binders nearly hides Mrs. Polk.

She flips through my binders. Guess she's looking for some kind of crazy drawings or some plan to blow up the school. They have to look. When she finishes, she looks over at me. "Very organized, J.T."

"Ma'am, I try."

"Now I see why Mr. Marsh and Sergeant Maddox think so highly of you."

Just nod back. Nice to know somebody's on my side, even if I'm willing to fight on my own.

Mr. Schmitt puts all my stuff back into the bag and

then nearly falls over sitting it on the floor by my feet. "There you go. I guess you young bucks can carry all that weight. But I got enough weight to carry." He pats his big stomach.

Room much lighter now.

"J.T., we're still going to have to look in your locker."

"That's fine, ma'am."

Pick up a pen from the holder on her desk. "Here's the combination." Scribble the numbers on a Post-it note.

Set the pen back in the holder and straighten up. "Am I dismissed?"

"Not quite. We'll need you to come with us to your locker."

Everyone stands almost in unison, like they've been trained. Mr. Schmitt motions for me to walk out first. The rest file out behind me.

Chris Walker sits in one of the chairs on the other side of the counter. He smirks at me like he's won this game. He hasn't. He's just temporarily leading.

When we pass, Mrs. Polk says, "Mr. Walker, we'll be right back."

Chris Walker doesn't even have the common courtesy to reply. No respect.

We all walk to my locker. I stand to the side while Mr. Schmitt turns the dial on the lock. He screws it up the first time and has to try again. He looks nervous. Guess he's not as sure as Mrs. Polk seems to be.

He finally pops the lock and opens the door. Empty, just like I said.

"Well, J.T., that's all we needed to see. Thanks for your cooperation."

"Anytime, ma'am."

"Cadet, you're dismissed," Sergeant Maddox says.

Walk fast toward Mr. Marsh's class. Don't want to miss any more of class than I have to. Halls empty, but the air isn't. It almost buzzes with the stories already flying out of mouths, pens, and phones. Stories? Truth? Doesn't matter. Nobody cares.

alpha-foxtrot

Radars go off like crazy when I walk into Mr. Marsh's room. Twenty-two brains and forty-four eyes switch on, find me, and try to figure out what they should do, what to believe. Of course, some have already decided.

Like Michael Chilton, third row, second seat. And Misty Hariel, fifth row, third seat. Both press buttons on their cell phones like they're about to burst into flame. Guess they have the responsibility of giving the play by play for first period. They're the only two not looking at me.

Step toward my desk at the back of the second row. Eyes track me, even Mr. Marsh's. He's still standing by the door waiting for me sit down. A few words between me and Chris Walker days ago in the hall, and he watches me like I'm loaded with grenades. And the rest of the class watches me like I'm a rattlesnake in the corner of the room. They should know they don't have to. I don't have the same problem with them as with Chris. So for now, they're safe.

Get to my desk and drop my bag off my shoulders. Turn to sit down. Lesley Murray stops writing and covers her paper with both arms. That's fine. Like I don't know what she's writing about.

Sit down, face the front. As soon as I do, Mr. Marsh says, "Class, up here."

Most of the heads in the room snap to the front, but a few still linger behind. So Mr. Marsh says, "Class, please."

The rest of the heads turn, and so does mine.

———————

Mrs. Hernandez guides me out of the office at Rabun Creek Middle School where she just finished signing a bunch of forms for me—forms my mother would have signed. But now Mrs. Hernandez does that stuff, at least until she finds me a foster family.

Mrs. Hernandez's heels click on the tile floor and her perfume wraps around me like a cloud. "Now Jasonito, I know you're nervous, but it's going to be fine, just fine."

"Yeah," is all I say back.

The halls are empty because school has already started, and that makes it easy for us to navigate the hallways. Not that Mrs. Hernandez would have any trouble. She does this all the time, she says. Wish I could feel as comfortable as she does.

She stops about halfway down Hall D and places a hand on my shoulder. "Room 32 is just down there. I'll let you go the rest of the way, O.K.?"

I nod.

She steps away, and I turn toward the classroom. Don't move though.

"Jasonito, go ahead. Really, it will be O.K. You have to do this."

She's right. I do. But that doesn't mean I can't take my time about it.

"Oh, and here." Mrs. Hernandez gives me a Post-it note with "Bus 24" written on it. "The bus will drop you off at Honeywell House."

I take the note and put it in my pocket.

"See you this afternoon. Have a good day." Her white teeth beam between her bright red lips. She waves and walks away.

"Yeah," I say back to her.

Walk to the classroom and knock on the door.

Ms. Ladner opens the door with a big smile and says, "You must be Jason."

Don't say anything back to her. Just hand her my schedule.

She looks at it for a second. "Yep, you're in the right place. Come on in."

Walk through the door, looking at the floor.

"Class, this is Jason. I want everybody to welcome him."

Look up at the class. Everybody stares. Mouths hang open. My face.

My forehead still has cuts on it, and stitches run from my left temple to my chin like a railroad track. Doctors said a few more days with the stitches. Mrs. Hernandez wouldn't let me wait.

"Jason, you can take the seat there." Ms. Ladner points to a desk at the back of the room.

Every eye sticks to me, clinging, stinging, cutting. Try to ignore them. Sit down and look back at Ms. Ladner.

"O.K. class," she says, but nobody looks away.

"Class," she says again. Still nothing.

Then a little stronger, "Class, please." And that gets them off.

alpha-golf

Been stared at ever since, but rarely by a whole class. Until today. Only difference is I don't care anymore. One day, if I come back from the war, they will have to thank me.

Don't even get my book open before the bell rings. Slide my book and notebook back into my bag while the class empties like a busted bag of potting soil at the hardware store. Guess they have stories to tell.

Stand out of my desk, sling my bag over my shoulders.

Mr. Marsh stands by his desk instead of in the doorway like normal. March down the aisle and turn toward the door. He stops me.

"J.T.?"

Stop, snap around. "Yes?"

He grabs and strokes his beard. "I guess Mrs. Polk talked to you."

"She did."

Mr. Marsh nods.

"And so did Mr. White, Mr. Schmitt, and Sergeant Maddox," I say.

He nods some more. "What did they have to say?" he asks and moves his hand from his beard to his pocket.

"Stuff about what you told them." I stop, thinking about all the other questions they threw at me. Mr. Marsh doesn't need to know that stuff though.

"Just trying to keep you out of trouble."

Stare back at him.

Mr. Marsh asks, "You understand, right?"

"No."

Mr. Marsh looks at his desk and lets out a big sigh. "J.T., you have the grades, for the most part. Sergeant Maddox tells me you perform better than any other cadet. You're doing all the right things. That's why I nominated you for the scholarship. Can't see you mess that up because of somebody like Chris Walker." He doesn't ever bother to ask me if I had anything to do with that thing out front. He's smarter than that.

"Got nothing to do with Chris Walker."

Mr. Marsh gives me the same look he gives kids when they ask him a question about something he just covered. "J.T., you forget I taught Chris' older brother and most of his cousins, too. Let's just say they all left their mark on the school, so to speak." He tilts his head and strokes his beard again. "Like I've said, history is the best predictor of the future and explanation of the present."

Mr. Marsh smirks, but it bounces right off me. He's not reaching me today.

If he really wanted to help me, he would have just left it alone and let me handle things instead of churning up ideas in Mrs. Polk's head. Need her recommendation as much as Mr. Marsh's.

"So steer clear of Mr. Walker. You got me?"

"Guess so." Just say it for Mr. Marsh. Don't get it. And don't want to. Problem is, people like Chris, that foster father, that driver who crossed the center line but still walked away, get away with it unless somebody stops them. They make the world worse. A soldier's job is to make it better. Protect. Serve.

"That's what I want to hear," he says and steps from around his desk. "So, are you in trouble?" He steps closer, and I turn and head for the door.

Before hitting the hallway, I say, "Not yet."

alpha-hotel

Even though fall has arrived in North Georgia, the body still bakes under all the polyester. They're not happy about having to change after school, but we need to practice in our uniforms. Only one more week until drill competition. Got to see if my squad can get through all the maneuvers in full dress.

"Cadets," I call out, and before I can say "fall in," they jump into position. Rifles at their sides, shoulders straight, and chins up. Step up in front of them and take a look at each cadet. Want to see if they're thinking about this morning. It was easy for them to hide it during inspection because Sergeant Maddox gives them more to worry about than me.

Scan their faces.

Like they rehearsed it, each cadet looks me straight in the eye and nods. Freeman almost smiles.

They're ready.

Take two steps back and call out, "Right, face."

Every rifle snatches off the ground and pops into position, their hands slap against the wooden stocks. Good sound. They spin to the right and knock their heels together like their bodies are attached with invisible string. First time ever.

First day me and Roper and the three others became squad leaders, Sergeant Maddox gave each of us an index card with one sentence written on it. He said, "Cadets, read it, learn it, strive for it."

We all looked at the card and read, "Leadership is the art of getting someone else to do something you want done because he wants to do it. General Dwight D. Eisenhower."

For the first time, my cadets look like they want to do this.

I call, "Forward, march."

Watch their feet as they step off to make sure not one foot is the least bit out of step. Pay special attention to Pickens. With his limp, it's almost a guarantee he'll be off. But today you'd never know it.

"Left, left, left-right-left."

Their steps fall in rhythm and their spacing is perfect. Look up at their arms. Every cadet holds the rifle exactly four inches away from their chests, tight, no bouncing or shaking.

Usually, I'd just take them around the drill field a couple of times before throwing something harder at them. But today they are different. So I am too.

Roper's squad marches around the field. They look pretty good. Not this good though.

Roper looks over at me and smiles. Stone him.

"Alpha Squad, let's show Bravo what they have to beat," I say to my cadets.

In unison, they call out, "Yes, sir."

Straight ahead is the fence that separates the field from the student parking lot. Keep my cadets heading straight for it.

"Left, left, left-right-left." Their steps stay in rhythm.

Twenty yards, still smooth. Fifteen, looking good. Keep marching them straight at the fence.

At ten yards, look over to see if they're going to break, misstep or stutter. Not a chance.

Five yards, but wait to give the command. Just before O'Malley marches right into the fence, I call out, "About face."

Everybody spins on the same foot and heads in the opposite direction, like the fence was never there. Almost impresses me.

Give another command. "Left, face."

They turn.

Let them take three steps, and then, "Right, face."

Three more steps. "About, face."

Ten steps this time. Don't want them to anticipate. "Right, face."

My cadets snap to the right like they're running on railroad tracks. Perfect. Satisfaction.

Don't know what's up with them. Just hope it's not a fluke.

The rhythm of the marching sounds good. Too good not to enjoy it some.

Give the command. "When I say Alpha, you say huh. ALPHA."

They yell back, "HUH!"

"ALPHA."

"HUH!"

If the drill field stretched to the next county, I'd march them all the way there. Nice to see the work, the leadership pay off. Every decision is an opportunity for success or failure. And a good leader figures out which decision will lead in which direction. Seem to be getting it right with Alpha Squad.

Reach the other end of the field and call, "Cadets, halt."

They slam to a stop. Their chests rise up and down. Nobody moves.

"Right, face."

My squad turns to face me, rifles still in position. I know their arms are burning. Just want them to push a little harder.

Let them stand there while I walk around behind them. "Attention."

The butts of the rifles shoot to the ground, and arms jerk to their sides.

"At ease, cadets."

They all step out with their left foot and place their left hand behind their backs.

Step back around to the front to see how bad they are hurting. Dixon tries to hold his face straight, but the agony can't be hidden. He breathes like an asthma attack.

"Freeman."

"Yes, Captain."

"Explain."

She pauses a few seconds. "Sir, explain what, sir?"

"Why Alpha Squad looks so good today."

Freeman lifts her chin a bit and says, "Just want to be the best, Captain."

Nod back at her.

"MacDonald."

"Captain."

"Your explanation."

"Can't explain it, Captain. Guess we got tired of looking like shit."

Nobody even smirks.

"Pickens, what do you say?" Step over in front of him because he'd never lie to my face.

"Sir?"

"What's your answer? Alpha Squad has never looked this good. Makes a captain wonder."

"Sir, uh, we just thought." He stops.

"Thought what, Cadet?"

"Sir," Pickens straightens up. "Sir, we just thought we owed it to you."

That small empty spot at the back of my gut urges me to say, "Thank you." But that would be too soft. Might throw practice off. Can't lose focus. Just nod and give another command. "Right shoulder, huh."

Rifles fly off the ground in unison, hands slap stocks, and every cadet gets their rifle into position.

"Freeman."

"Captain."

"Take Alpha Squad through rifle maneuvers. Got ten minutes."

"Yes, Captain."

Snap around and walk toward the school. Ordinarily I wouldn't leave them during practice. But Freeman can handle it. Some are just better at giving orders than others. After seeing her with Pickens and Dixon the other day, I think she's one of them.

Behind me, I hear her give the first command followed by hands slapping rifles. It's one thing for them to be good while I'm watching, it is another thing when I can't see them. Good cadets. Good captain.

part II
preemptive strike

alpha-india

Any good soldier knows the key to a successful exercise, maneuver, or mission is timing. So Chris Walker will have to wait and wonder. Just like I've been doing all evening, waiting for Mr. Coffeen to pipe up and say something about whatever he and Mrs. Polk talked about.

He disappeared after dinner, leaving me in the kitchen to clean up. He didn't ask me to, but I do a better job than he does. Finish the last plate and glass and put them on the drying rack. Take a towel and wipe the drops of water that fell on the counter and floor. Still haven't figured out a way to keep that from happening. Grab the towel by the corners. Guide it between the oven door and handle, folding it over evenly.

———

"Mom, what do you want me to do with this?" I wave the wet towel at her.

She wipes the kitchen table and picks up the twelve birthday candles from my cake. "Just hang it there on the oven."

I cram the towel between the handle and the oven and start to walk away.

"Jason, not like that. It will never dry. Straighten that thing out."

Snap the towel off the handle and re-hang it. "Like it really matters anyway," I say and shake my head.

"You're only getting away with that comment because it is your birthday." Mom wags her finger at me and smiles, trying to make me feel better. But how can I feel better when the three people I invited over for my birthday dinner all said they couldn't come. Sucks to find out your best friend is your mother.

Mom drops the used candles in the trash, then opens the door to the laundry room and tosses in the towel she wiped the table with. She spins around on her heel almost like a dancer. "Now, time for presents."

No doubt I'm the only kid in the United States who has to wait until after wishes, candles, and cake to even see my presents. Most kids get to blow out the candles, tear open the paper, then stuff their faces. Not me. Not ever. Then again, most don't open their gifts in front of a whopping crowd of one.

Mom leaves the room, nearly skipping. She is definitely more excited than I am. Hear her fumbling around in her closet for a second before she comes whooshing through the room, twirling around with two boxes wrapped in blue and red.

She plops the boxes on the clean table and then drops herself into a chair. "This one first." Mom slides the box across the table in front of the chair I'm supposed to sit in.

Slide into the chair and unwrap the gift—football video game. Surprised. She thinks I'm obsessed with playing it out-

side, and now she's letting me bring it in the house. But that's Mom.

"Thanks, Mom." Smile.

"And now this." She shoves another blue and red box in front of me.

Tear the paper off the top. Immediately see the logo. The shoes she said we couldn't afford.

Snatch off the rest of the paper. Yank the shoes out of the box, eyes ready to fall out of my face. "You did it."

"Yeah, well," is all she says.

Slide away from the table. Kick off both my old shoes. Lean over and put the new ones on. When I sit back up, another box sits in front of me on the table—a small one. The box is not wrapped. Look at the box, then at Mom.

"Figured you're old enough to take care of these now." She nods her head forward, telling me to open it.

Slide off the top of the box. Lying on a small bed of cotton sits my dad's dog tags. Pick up the chain between two fingers like I'm scared to break them. Mom shined them so bright the kitchen light bounces back into my eyes.

Slide the chain over my head and around my neck. Look across the table at Mom. She's crying. Don't ask why.

"Jason, your dad was a good soldier and a great man. He'd love to see you wear those." She wipes the side of her face. "Happy birthday, honey."

alpha-juliet

Feel my father's dog tags swinging under my shirt as I wipe the drops of water off the floor. Doesn't really matter if I do or not, but I like paying attention to the details that others would let slide.

Mr. Coffeen walks in, sees me on the floor. "Jesus H., J.T., you alright?"

"Sir, just finishing cleaning."

Mr. Coffeen looks at the dry floor then back at me. "J.T., you better get off that floor. People would think you're Cinderella and I'm an evil stepmother with you crawling around like that."

"Absolutely, sir." Stand up.

"So, you finished in here?" He knows to ask. Just because the room looks clean to him doesn't mean it meets my standards.

"Yes, sir."

"Good deal. In that case, come on out back. I could use your help."

Bolt for the door. Bang it open. Leap over the steps. Need out of that kitchen.

"J.T., slow down, the place ain't on fire."

Reach the workshop and wait.

Mr. Coffeen walks across the backyard. "Five, twenty-three, thirty-three," he says.

"Sir?"

"The lock. Combination is five, twenty-three, thirty-three," He says strolling up to the door.

"Yes, sir." Turn around and start turning the dial on the lock.

"Now, make sure you give it three full turns to clear the dial."

Hit all the numbers and pop the lock off the hinge. Go to hand it to Mr. Coffeen.

"Nah, you put that in your pocket. You can lock up later."

Mr. Coffeen walks in and flips on the light. He grabs two aprons hanging on a nail and hands one to me. "Grab a couple pair of safety glasses out of that drawer over there." He points to his workbench.

Do like he says.

He waits at the table saw. Not the one I used before. This one is different, bigger.

Hand him the safety glasses and put on my apron. Slide the glasses on, too. Figure any second he's going to say something about talking to Mrs. Polk. He won't be able to hold it in long.

"Alright now. Here's what we got." He reaches over and grabs two pieces of wood leaning against the wall. "Two pieces this size, three pieces this size."

Mr. Coffeen walks over and slings the two pieces on a an empty table. He unclips his tape measure off his apron and tosses it to me. He motions to the wood. "Go ahead."

Hook the end of the tape measure on the end of the small piece. Measure width—twenty-two inches. Length—thirty inches.

"You need this?" Mr. Coffeen holds out a pencil.

"No, sir. Got it."

"Got a smart boy here, do we? Guess you're tutoring session is paying off." He laughs.

Ignore his comment. It's about the third joke he's made about Wednesday night.

"The other one." He points to the larger piece.

Width—twenty-two inches again. Length—forty-two.

"Alright now, J.T. Here's the hard part." Mr. Coffeen walks back over to the wall where a large piece of wood leans. He grabs the sides, walking backwards until he has it in front of the table. "Help me get this up here."

Take one side of the board, and we lift it up onto the table. "Now, you're going to need this." He hands me the pencil. "Figure out how we can get all five pieces from this piece here."

Look at the board on the table.

"Now, this thing here is four feet by eight feet. Get after it."

He steps back and folds his arms.

Stare at the board for a few seconds, running numbers through my head. Never been good at stuff like this in math class. But then I only get the problem wrong. Screw this up and an expensive piece of wood becomes useless.

Pick up a half-torn sheet of paper off the floor and shake off the sawdust. One thing Mr. Coffeen doesn't have a shortage of around here is trash. Draw a rectangle on the paper and start figuring out the measurements. Mr. Coffeen just sits back, breathing slow and easy, waiting like he's got the rest of his life for me to get it right.

A few minutes later, put the pencil down. "Got it."

"Let me take a look there." He takes the paper and holds it out away from his face so his eyes can focus on it. "Yes, sir, I believe that will do it." He sets the paper down and motions toward the board. "Well, hope you ain't waiting on Christmas. Get to measuring."

Pick up the pencil and tape measure. Walk around the table, hooking the tape measure in place and making pencil marks in places I drew on the paper. When I'm done, Mr. Coffeen walks over with a metal box-looking thing with a dusty blue string hanging from it.

"J.T., let me tell you something. I've been working with wood since my daddy could fart and blow me over, and I still love this part."

He hands me the end of the string. "Now, walk around there with that and hold it tight against the mark you made on the other side."

Do like he says.

Mr. Coffeen holds the string down on the same mark

on the opposite side. He pulls the string tight, then grabs with his fingers, pulls it up and *pop*. The string makes a blue chalk line across the board.

Mr. Coffeen laughs. "Could live to be a thousand, and I still wouldn't be tired of that sound."

Both of us move around the board marking lines in all the right places. Mr. Coffeen chuckles on every snap of the line.

He lets me cut all the pieces. Better than last time because the cuts take more time, the saw's song is louder and longer. As I cut, Mr. Coffeen stacks the pieces on the table next to the saw. After the last piece, it finally hits me to ask what we're supposed to be making.

"Sir, what is this going to be?"

"I's wondering when you was going to get to that. Toy chest for Mrs. Richardson's grandson. Little boy ain't but two. I swear to you, she's going to have that boy spoiled rotten right down to the core."

"Sir, she definitely won't be doing him any favors if she does."

"Nope, not at all."

Mr. Coffeen knows what I mean. Spoiled makes you soft, and that means the world will put a whole lot more dents in you.

He walks over to his workbench, picks up a bottle of glue, and takes a small nail gun off the wall. "Now, here's where we need two sets of hands."

He takes one of the long pieces and sets it flat down on

the table. On the short end he runs glue all the way down. "Now hold that piece in place. Don't let it move now."

Mr. Coffeen picks up a small piece and presses it against the long one. Put my weight down on the long piece to keep it from moving.

He stares where the boards stick together. With his head still down, he says, "Talked to Mrs. Polk this afternoon."

Don't say anything. Just keep pressing hard against the board. Knew this would come sooner or later.

He lets go of the board and picks up the nail gun. "Come here and let me show you."

Take my weight off the board and step over next to Mr. Coffeen.

"Now you got to make sure you got it right up against the wood. Keep them fingers out of the way. If you think that hammer did a number on your thumb, this thing here will definitely ruin your day." He holds up his thumb to show me a small scar. "Wasn't paying attention. Nail hit a knot in the wood, shot sideways, and near about went all the way through." He shakes his head and chuckles. "Father Francis would have had me in confession for a month if he would have heard the words out of my mouth."

Mr. Coffeen places the nail gun against the corner of the board and pulls the trigger. *Pop*. He pulls the gun away to show a small nail flushed into the wood. "Lots better than swinging a hammer." He steps back and holds out the nail gun for me to take. "Rest is yours."

Take the gun from him and face the boards. Hesitate.

"Now go on. You ain't going to mess it up."

Press the nail gun against the opposite corner and pull the trigger. *Pop*. Feels good.

"See there. Nothing to it. Now put three more down the side there, about four inches apart."

Move slow. Can't mess up.

"Yeah, Mrs. Polk don't know what to do about all that craziness down at the school this morning," Mr. Coffeen says behind me.

Ignore him and just shoot the nails into place.

"Let's get this other side up." He grabs the glue. "Here, trade with me."

Hand him the nail gun, and he gives me the glue.

This time I glue while Mr. Coffeen holds the long piece in place.

"I think Mrs. Polk felt better after I talked to her, though. Told her she didn't have to worry about my J.T. One thing for sure, I told her, she can trust you to do right."

He pulls his weight off the board and hands the nail gun to me.

"Yep, wish folks could have said that about me when I was your age. But I had to do a lot of messing up to finally learn my lesson. Cost me quite a bit, I can tell you."

Still no words from me. Just want to keep moving, get past this.

Shoot nails into the end piece like the other one. Go to hand it back to Mr. Coffeen, but he points to the table. I set it there.

Mr. Coffeen waits for me to turn back toward him. He looks straight at me. Makes sure I look at him. "J.T., let me tell you something. Folks can be as cruel as the devil. And when they are, you just remember it ain't got nothing to do with you. Something's just wrong with them. Got me?"

Nod back at him. Don't have a choice.

"Good then." He grabs the two other long pieces and leans them into place, where they need to be glued. He pulls off his safety goggles and unties his apron. "You go ahead and glue and nail those other pieces into place. Tomorrow we'll get the lid made, and we'll finish this up."

Look at him like he's kidding.

He turns away from me, ignoring my look. Walks over to the workbench, tosses the safety goggles on top instead of putting them back in the drawer, and heads for the door.

Still stare at him, waiting for him stop and say, "Nah, I'm just messing with you, J.T."

He doesn't. Instead, he hangs the apron on the nail by the door, looks around the room, and says, "This is a good shop for making things. You feel free any time."

Mr. Coffeen walks out the door.

Stare at the boards. Hope I don't screw things up.

alpha-kilo

Hate the way a knock at the front door sounds when you don't expect it. Something just not right about it. Has to be bad—salesman, missionaries handing out pamphlets, maybe the cops even.

Eight o'clock and Mr. Coffeen has already gone to his room for the night. He likes to sit in the chair next to his bed and read his woodworking magazines or work on a crossword he will never finish. But it doesn't matter.

My situation is not the same. Books, notes, and handouts that have to be learned are stacked on the coffee table. Heaps of information that almost seems impossible to get it all. Like when a glass breaks on the floor. No matter how much you sweep and clean, there always seems to be a shard left behind that will one day stick in your bare foot. But have to finish it all because everything matters. Or The Citadel won't be anything but a dream.

The house is quiet, which makes the knock at the door sound worse.

Set my history book on the coffee table and get off

the couch. Through the curtains on the front window see headlights in the driveway. The floor creaks and another knock hits the door. Mr. Coffeen says nothing from his bedroom. Maybe he's already asleep.

Open the front door. Pickens stands on the steps.

"Pickens?"

"Hey, Captain."

"Pickens, how'd you know where I live?"

"Ah, easy. The cadet directory."

Nod. Suspicious. "Pickens, why didn't you just call me on the phone if you have the directory?"

"Captain, no way. If she heard me talking on the phone she'd ask me a hundred questions about who I was talking to and what we were talking about. Just trying to be smart."

"Can't argue with that." Stare at his mother's figure through the headlights. She always seems to be in a position where I can't see her face. Not sure I want to. Know what kind of look she'd give me.

Step down to the first step and shut the door. "What can I do for you?"

"Well," he looks back at his mom's minivan for a second and turns back to me. "I need your ROTC manual. At least that's what I told my mom so she'd get off the couch and drive me over here. Told her we have a procedures test Monday and I forgot my manual at school."

"But that's your cover."

"Yes, sir." Pickens picks his chin up, proud.

"What is it you really need?" No telling with Pickens.

"Chris Walker."

This throws me off. "Chris Walker?"

"Yeah, we all know he put that thing outside the school." Pickens' face changes. Eyes sharpen, jaw sets.

Keep my face straight, voice flat. "How's that?"

"Captain, everybody knows," Pickens pops, then lowers his voice. "You know how that place is, rumors spread faster than people can keep up with."

Nod. "Correct. But still doesn't explain why you're here."

"Sir, want to help you make a plan. You know, to get him back."

Could try to make Pickens believe I don't plan to retaliate, but that would be a lie. Can't lie to my cadets. Doesn't make for good leadership. Plus, the only people he has to tell are on my squad, and they're not going to bust me.

"My battle, Pickens. Not yours."

"Sir, that's where you're wrong."

Cut my eyes at Pickens. He knows better than to question me.

"Sorry, sir, but—"

"But what, Cadet?" Voice hard now.

Pickens rocks on his feet. Shoves his hands in his pockets. "I used to be Chris' favorite target, sir. A few days ago in the cafeteria, that was nothing. He used to do all kinds of stuff. Walk behind me in the hall, imitating the way I walk, falling all over the place on purpose. He'd come up behind me in the bathroom and push me into the urinal. That was his favorite."

Pickens stops and glances over his shoulder at the minivan then back at me. "Then today."

"I can handle today, Cadet."

"No, I'm not talking about what he did to you. To me."

"What?" Chris Walker can come after me if he wants, but my cadets are another story.

"Well, Captain, I did like you said. Decided to ask Nicole to homecoming."

"And?"

"I stopped her outside the classroom. Chris was standing against the opposite wall talking to Patrice Banks. You know who I'm talking about?"

"Yeah."

"I mean, I started to just forget it, but I had to say something. I stopped her and all. So, I just blurted it out. Guess I said it too loud. Nicole just stood there like I told her I had cancer or something. Before she could say anything, Chris walked over, put his arm around my shoulder, and said, 'Well, Nicole, if you go with the cripple here, at least you'll get the good parking spot.'"

Pickens drops his head. "Then he laughed. And so did she."

He looks back up at me. Study Pickens' face. Know that look. Like when somebody rules over you, traps you, and makes life hell. Doesn't go away. Until you do something to stop them. Not about revenge, just protecting yourself and maybe others from further damage.

"Not letting him get away with that kind of shit anymore. I'm stronger now."

Nod at Pickens. Think. See his face.

"You sure?"

"Absolutely, sir. Soldiers got to do what they have to do, right?"

Before I can respond, Pickens' mother hits the horn a couple of times. He turns and waves his hand at her. "Just a second," he yells.

Then he turns back to me.

"No, Cadet. Soldiers follow orders, defend and protect."

"Yeah, but sometimes when an enemy proves to be dangerous, soldiers have to take action, especially when they've been attacked."

Can't argue. Pickens has learned something. "Let me think about it, Cadet."

Pickens' mom hits the horn again. Wish she wouldn't do that. Can't stand horns.

"So, can I get the ROTC manual? I'll give it back in the morning."

Open the front door and walk over to my backpack by the sofa. Pull out the ROTC manual. Look at the title—*Leadership and Development: ROTC Guidelines and Procedures.* Too bad they don't have one of these for dealing with people like Chris Walker. Then again, one's not needed. Real soldiers use their own wits to get out of a bad situation.

Walk back to the front door and hand Pickens the manual. Grip it tight so he can't pull it away. "Keep a tight lip, Cadet."

"No problem, sir."

Let go of the manual and watch Pickens limp to his mom's minivan. Shut the door. As soon as I latch the bolt, Mr. Coffeen walks in from the kitchen. "Somebody at the door?"

"Pickens, one of my cadets, needed the ROTC manual." Sit back down on the couch and pick up my history book.

Mr. Coffeen walks over and tosses his magazine on the coffee table. "So that didn't have anything to do with yesterday?"

"Sir?" The question surprises me.

"Oh, I know how boys work. Somebody gets you, so you get them back."

Don't look up from my book. "No, sir. Not me. Definitely not Pickens." Have to lie so he doesn't interfere. He's not a soldier. Wouldn't understand.

"Alright, alright. Just want to make sure."

I flip a page in my book.

"Studying hard, I see."

"Yes, sir."

Mr. Coffeen chuckles. "J.T., you just don't ever slow down, not even a notch."

"Only way to stay on top of things, sir."

"Well, make sure you don't blow a gasket." He pats the back of my shoulder.

Don't flinch, though. "No way, sir. Not part of the plan."

alpha-lima

"Fifteen, sixteen, seventeen." My count in sync with my father's dog tags jingling on the floor. But it doesn't cover up everything I've heard today.

Mr. Marsh said, "Can't see you mess that up because of somebody like Chris Walker."

"Twenty-one, twenty-two, twenty-three."

Mrs. Polk told me, "This is serious, J.T."

"Twenty-seven, twenty-eight, twenty-nine."

Pickens complained. "He laughed, and so did she."

Blood pumping good. But too much in my head to find that line, to cross it where shit evens out, then disappears. The day just keeps folding over on itself, refusing to break and leave my head alone.

Jingle. "Thirty-two." *Jingle.* "Thirty-three."

"You need to tell Mr. Coffeen. He'll help," Jason says.

Not now. Not him, too.

Let my chest slam the floor on each push-up to knock Jason away. "Thirty-eight, thirty-nine, forty."

Roll over to do some pike-ups because crunches just won't hurt bad enough. Get to twenty-five when my abs burn enough to make me dizzy.

Then finally.

My father's voice.

"Soldier, you are a machine." Best sound there is.

"Yes, sir."

"That's what it takes. No stopping. Keep pushing."

Dog tags swing off my chest, hitting the floor behind me. Body on fire. Churning up down, up down. Wrapped in spikes. The best pain. Paradise.

The number keeps climbing higher until my stomach locks up, refusing to give me anymore. Not even close to being done, though.

Go the closet for pull-ups. He keeps talking.

"Hard as steel, soldier. Got to be hard as steel. Enemies are waiting."

Close my eyes. Think of his picture. Need to see him, what J.T. is working for—the fatigues, the rank, the respect, that smile.

Hit fifteen before my back and shoulders even notice. Low heat creeps from the bottom of my spine up into my neck. Keep my eyes closed.

"Come on, soldier. Show me what you got."

"Yes, sir."

Sweating so hard, hands slip off the bar. Jump right back into position. Can't stop yet. Hold my chin above the bar. Breathe, breathe, down.

Hit ten more, or what feels like ten. Don't care about

the count, just the hurt that makes everything numb. Can't feel anything anymore. Only the hardest soldiers find this place.

"Getting close, soldier. Almost ready."

"Sir, ready?"

Drop to the floor.

"Battle, soldier."

Lay back for crunches. Stomach not burning anymore. Got to keep moving. Don't want to lose his voice.

"Today was a public strike. Can't let that go unanswered. Just like 9/11."

Hear him loud and clear.

"Next time will be worse. Strike hard. Prevent escalation."

After fifty crunches, hop off the floor and go back to the closet. Hang from the bar. Pull up and lift my chin. Stomach twitches and jumps. The picture is behind me, but his voice stays.

"You've got a strategy for victory, soldier. But you need to eliminate obstacles."

Fight through pull-ups until my chin can't make it to the bar. Drop and hang until my fingers won't grip anymore. Fall to my knees. Sweat races down my face, chest, back. Exhausted.

Maybe sleep will come easy now.

Take deep breaths. Roll back and lie on the cool wooden floor. Almost expect to see steam rise. Instead, the image of that mannequin floats from the back of my brain and covers my eyes.

No doubt every house in Covington County buzzes with talk about the "bomb scare" at the high school. The stories are mounting one on top of the other. Theories getting sifted through like rotten fruit, people finding and taking the ones they like. People will have made up their minds. That's O.K., because J.T. has made up his.

Sit up and jump to my feet. Breathing slow now. Go to the shower. Grab the towel hanging on the back of the door and go to the bathroom. Shut the door. The lights in the house are off, so no light seeps under the door. Can't even see my hand in front of my face.

Lots of people hate the dark—young, old, don't matter. Just another reason why I like it. Most people can't function in the dark. They need eyes. But eyes can fool you. Touch and instincts are way more reliable.

Turn on the water and step in. Wash fast. Under two minutes. Muscles want me to stay longer. Can't tonight. Don't need Mr. Coffeen waking up and asking me why I'm up so late. Getting harder to lie to him.

Dry off and open the door. Make sure to step over the board that usually gives me away. Close my door and step to my chest of drawers. Boxers only. Body still barely hot from training. Muscles starting to relax, though, give up, and get ready to go down for the night.

Hang the towel back on the hook on the door. Step over to the bed. Peel back the corner of the blanket and sheet, making a forty-five degree angle across the bed. Slide in. Click off the lamp and pull the blanket and sheet over my chest.

Slow, deep breaths. Start my backward count from 100. "Ninety-nine, ninety-eight, ninety-seven, ninety-six…"

Just as my head reaches that cliff right before it falls over into sleep, hear something that sounds like an object dropping to the floor in the living room. Open my eyes in time to hear it again. But it's not on the floor. Walls vibrate.

Again, a muffled boom sounds in the house. Then another, and another, getting faster. Then *SMACK* against my window.

Snatch and kick off the covers. Bolt off the bed. Look at the window. Street light lets me see slime running down. Egg.

SMACK.

Another one hits the window. Jump back and drop to the floor. Eggs start hitting the side of the house like rain. Laughter echoes in the yard.

Don't hesitate. Roll over to my chest of drawers. Reach in and grab a pair of shorts. Jerk them on while staying on the floor. Get up and run into the hall. Plow into Mr. Coffeen coming from his room, slamming against his chest.

"What in the hell?" he says as he catches himself against the wall.

Don't slow up a notch. Got to catch them. The enemies are attacking.

Go blowing out the front door. An egg hits me square in the chest so hard it feels like a rock. Run straight through it.

"Oh, shit!" somebody says. "Go, go, go!"

Two guys holding what looks like a huge sling shot

jump into the back of a truck already filled with guys hold-ing eggs. The engine cranks. The tires squeal and smoke.

Run straight for it. Turn down the street behind the truck. Try to see who it is in the back. Know who the driver is. The yellow paint gives it away. Can't see the others. Eggs, laughter, and hoots and hollers pummel me.

Keep running, but the truck pulls farther and farther away. As it screeches around the corner, somebody in the back yells, "Better luck next time, Freak."

alpha-mike

Mr. Coffeen sits on the steps when I get back to the house. He stands up as I walk down the driveway. I speak first.

"Sorry, sir," I say with egg dripping off my arms and fingers.

"Oh, don't worry 'bout me. I played halfback when I was your age, and a hit like that just brought back memories."

"Not that, sir. The house."

Mr. Coffeen glances at the house. "Well, no harm done. Don't look like anything's busted or broken. Heck, I got a pressure washer down at the store that will take care of that." He points at me. "Looks like you got the worst of it." He doesn't chuckle, just looks at me like he's not surprised.

Don't say anything. Stand there with my hands on my waist, trying to catch my breath and ignore the burning in my bare feet.

Mr. Coffeen waves his hand toward the house. "Come on, let's get in the house and get you cleaned up."

He walks up the steps in front of me. Shuts the door behind me.

Mr. Coffeen goes to the kitchen instead of his bedroom. "How 'bout some milk and cookies? Know you don't eat that kind of stuff, but this once ain't going to kill you."

Don't reply. Just walk to the kitchen and stand by the table.

Mr. Coffeen takes a clean dish towel from the drawer and throws it to me. Then he grabs two glasses and a box of vanilla wafers out of the cabinet. He gets the milk from the refrigerator.

Start wiping the egg off my arms. Look down to see a red spot the size of a baseball in the middle of my chest. Must have been one of the eggs from the slingshot.

Toss the towel on the table. Sit down.

Mr. Coffeen pours the milk and shoves a glass in front of me. He takes a couple of cookies out of the box. Tosses one across the table to me. Catch it and pop in my mouth. Haven't had anything sweet in a long time. It almost hurts my teeth.

He chews and swallows the cookie. Takes a drink of milk.

"So I guess that had something to do with Chris Walker."

Swallow the cookie. "Don't know, sir."

He takes another cookie and tosses one on the table in front of me. "Makes you mad as a hornet, doesn't it?"

Last thing I want to do is get Mr. Coffeen going with a

bunch of questions. Just shrug at him. Pick up the cookie off the table. Roll it over my fingers.

"So what are you going to do?"

"Nothing, sir." Pop the cookie in my mouth.

Mr. Coffeen watches me for a second, stares without even a flinch. He nods a couple of times. "J.T., I surely hope you don't think this old man believes that."

Stop chewing because Mr. Coffeen is not supposed to sound like that, his voice sharp. Look at him to verify he means it.

Swallow the cookie and chug the rest of the milk. Can't get into this. Too tired. Too pissed off at those guys that think they can come here and do that to his house.

Strategic retreat.

Get up from the table. Wash the glass and place it in the drying rack with the dishes from supper. "Good night, sir. Need to get some rest."

Mr. Coffeen gets up from the table and stands in the doorway to the living room. "J.T., can't let you walk away on this one."

Take a half-step toward him, hoping he'll just get out of the way, let me go to my room where it's safe—used to be. But he doesn't budge. Look away from him.

"I'm serious. J.T., I'm a patient man, but this is getting to be too much. Bad things happen."

He's right about that.

"Much worse than a few eggs."

"Sir, would you just let me—" Make another move to get by him. Heart races.

"You can go to bed once we get some things clear." He holds his arm in my way.

Could just push through him. He can't stop me. And he'd never lay a hand on me. But can't make myself do it.

"Now sit down for a minute."

Don't want to sit down. Need to retreat. He wants answers that I can't give. My battle. Stand solid. Heart pounds. Heat rises off the top of my head. Jason tries to convince me to listen.

"J.T., sit down. He's trying to help."

"No. My battle," I say out loud to Jason. Press my chest lightly against Mr. Coffeen's arm, but he holds it stiff.

"Sir, please."

"Nope," Mr. Coffeen shakes his head. "We've both avoided this too long as it is."

"Come on, J.T., just for a second."

Don't want Jason to win.

"Now, go ahead," Mr. Coffeen says and motions toward the table with the arm that isn't blocking me.

"Yeah, go ahead."

Only one way to go at this—like a soldier. Run my fingertips across the top of my head, raking Jason back. Lift my face. Straighten my shoulders. About face. Go to the table and sit.

"That's better," Mr. Coffeen says and sits back in his place.

Sit straight and stiff. Ready.

"This thing with Chris Walker has got to stop, J.T." He says it soft. "Don't like where I see this thing is headed."

"And where is that, sir?"

"I don't know, but it ain't going to be pretty."

No, it won't be.

"J.T., you been here long enough for me to know how you go at things—always with a full head of steam."

"Absolutely, sir."

"Well, I didn't take you in to see that head of steam get you mixed up in this kind of trouble."

Good soldiers seize opportunities.

Turn the questions on him, off me. "Sir, with all due respect, why did you then?" Keep voice even.

Mr. Coffeen looks at me for a second. "Guess you have the right to ask. Course, figured we would have got this out of the way a long time ago." He gives a nervous chuckle. "Now, I ain't so prepared."

"Still, sir, it would be good to know."

He rubs his hands together, looks at the table, then up at me. "Well, let's just say sometimes in life we get second chances. And when we do, we can't make a mess of it, especially at my age."

The answer confuses me and cuts into the cloud hanging in the room.

Shoulders relax. "Sir—"

Mr. Coffeen jumps in. "Look now, let's not get off track. This is about you and Chris Walker." He's always sharp.

"Yes, sir." Lift my shoulders again and pick up my chin.

His face searches for what to say next. He opens his mouth several times without saying anything.

I sit like a stone, waiting.

Finally, he says, "You know when I'm out there in the shop carving on a piece of wood for somebody?"

"Yes, sir."

"Well, with every piece I carve, I have the same decision to make—when is enough enough? Sometimes I ain't quite happy with what I got, and I keep on carving here and there trying to make it work. By the time I'm done, all I do is end up turning it into a piece of trash. Should have just stopped while I was ahead. Might not have been perfect, but at least it could have been something I could live with. You get me?"

"Believe so, sir."

"So, I'm telling you," he leans across the table, "you need to get this thing with Chris Walker fixed. Now, before you carve too many lines, and you end up having to start over. Or worse, cutting yourself beyond repair."

Mr. Coffeen almost sounds like he's giving me an order.

"Plus, I lived long enough to know things work their way out if you leave them alone."

Head doesn't move. Don't decline or accept.

"Sir, are we done?"

He looks at me, trying to see if his words got to me. "Guess so."

Push the chair back from the table. Get up and finally head to my room.

Mr. Coffeen forgot one thing. Sometimes things don't work out—unless somebody makes them.

alpha-november

Sometimes to win, you got to beat yourself. No trophies, no applause. Just the pure blood-pumping satisfaction of not letting your head get the best of you.

"You thought this was going be like a day at the county fair. Now, look at you." Sergeant Maddox blows air through his nose like he does to remind us he was right and the cadets were wrong.

He paces between the line of cadets and the thirty-foot wooden tower we're supposed to conquer. But it's not really the wood we have to conquer. That much I know.

Since the beginning of school, cadets have been talking shit about how they couldn't wait to get on top of this thing. But now, after Sergeant Maddox made each cadet go up and take a look over the ledge, words are scarce.

"Cadets, this is the Victory Tower. And the only thing you have to do to win is beat your own fear." He stops, turns toward us, and scans each face. "Oh, now some of you are thinking, *I ain't scared, Sergeant. This is nothing*. But that's before you got your butt hanging out in the breeze with nothing between your brain and the ground but a piece of ten-dollar plastic and the hope that maybe you can hang on to that rope."

Can hear a few cadets' breathing get a little heavier. And Sergeant Maddox hears it, too.

"Any task can be accomplished, even when it seems impossible," he barks.

Already know what he says is true. I'm a captain, survived Mike, going to win the drill competition, the Evans Scholarship, then battles, and a war. Nothing impossible when you're a machine, like me. Just turn it on and do what has to be done. So I know Sergeant Maddox's words are not meant for me. They're for the faces turning white.

"All you need today is guts and rope." Sergeant Maddox almost laughs again. "Alpha and Bravo," he calls, "you're up first."

My cadets, along with Roper's squad, step up toward the tower that took half the summer to build. At the bottom of the tower lies a pile of black harnesses and hard plastic helmets we're all supposed to wear. Behind the piles, a sign that reads "Walker Construction" reflects the sun just coming up over the vo-tech building.

Chris Walker's dad donated the money and labor to have this built. Mr. Walker doesn't miss an opportunity to put his name on something. That's why you can't go anywhere in Covington County and be more than a mile away from a sign, a building, or even a freaking tree with the Walker stamp on it.

"O.K. gentlemen," a thin, muscular guy Sergeant Maddox introduced earlier as Rick says, without noticing Freeman. "Grab a harness and helmet and line up single file, shoulder to shoulder." His voice is light, like this is just for fun. Maybe for him. But not for us. This is training. Find out who can really turn the screws when the time comes.

Before any of us move, we look to Sergeant Maddox. We know who gives the orders around here.

"Cadets, you heard the man," he blurts at us. "Get moving."

Each cadet takes a harness and helmet, steps back, and gets in line. The other cadets sit on the ground behind us. Only half the platoon here today. The other half will have to wait two weeks for their chance at victory.

"O.K., guys," Rick says. "Just put your helmet on the ground at your feet."

The cheap plastic hats, which everybody knows will do nothing to save their brains, bounce on the dry dirt and leaves.

"Now, hold the harness like this."

He grabs his harness on both sides in front of his waist. We do the same. "Now step through, pull snug, clip, and tighten." Rick goes through the motions slowly so we can see.

We mimic his movements, but no one does it as easily as Rick.

Freeman is the first finished so she helps Dixon, who is having more trouble than anyone else. Just like Freeman to be the one to step up and help out, without a word. She'll be a hell of a leader one day.

My hands and feet fight with the harness. Legs just don't want to cooperate with the holes. Force the harness into place. The straps dig into my crotch. Uncomfortable, but not nearly as bad as Dixon looks. He stares up at the wooden tower, sweat pouring down his sideburns. He definitely would trade his share of the fun today, but he'll never say it. Not to Sergeant Maddox or me.

Rick laughs. "Well, alright then. That wasn't quite a nightmare." He walks down the line, tugging and checking every harness. He yanks so hard on mine, I stumble forward. But not a single snicker comes from the cadets. They only see the wall.

"Rick, one second," Sergeant Maddox says.

He walks over in front of our line. "Cadets, listen up. This is about overcoming fear, building confidence and trust. Rick here has climbed everything from water towers to El Capitan. If he says it, you do it. Period. No buts, no can'ts, and especially, no whining. Remember who you are."

No way I could forget.

Rick waits to see if Sergeant Maddox has anything else to say. Then he claps his hands together. "O.K., now let's get after it."

"Alpha, get up top," Sergeant Maddox points up to the platform.

My squad hops to it. Everybody but Pickens. He stands off to the left of the tower, separated from the other cadets, face hard. His mother wouldn't sign the permission slip. Didn't want him to get hurt. But he's hurting anyway.

"Not you, Tillman." Sergeant Maddox stops me. "Got another task for you." He walks over to me. Watch my cadets go to the ladder without me.

"What's the job of the squad leader?" he asks.

Snap my heels together, pick up my chin. "Sir, motivate, lead by example, sir."

"And?"

"Sir? And?"

"Yeah, Cadet. And. The job of every soldier, but especially the squad leader."

Brain spins looking for the answer that I obviously should know. Look over at Pickens with his arms folded, leaning a bit on his bad leg. "Captain, you know this," he says.

"Sir, protect?"

"Are you asking or telling?"

"Sir, protect, sir."

"Exactly."

Sergeant Maddox looks over to Rick. "Rick, hook him up."

Rick looks back at him for a second. "You sure, Sergeant?"

Weird hearing somebody question Sergeant Maddox and not have his ass handed to him. But obviously Rick has proven himself in ways Sergeant respects. So he's earned the right to say what he wants. That's just the way it goes. Everything has to be earned. Nothing's free. Even the right to talk.

"Absolutely. If there's one cadet out here you can trust to do what has to be done, it's Tillman here."

"Good enough." Rick knows what the rest of us know. He can trust Sergeant's judgment.

Rick walks over and grabs the rope hanging from the rail at the top of the tower while my cadets climb their way up the ladder. He hooks a metal piece onto the front of my harness. "J.T., right?"

"Yes, sir." Hold my chin up. Getting an endorsement from Sergeant Maddox erases the disappointment of not being up top with my squad.

"Alright, J.T.," Rick talks while he loops the rope through the piece he hooked to the harness, without looking at me. "This is the brake."

Drop my chin to look down.

"Now you see how I got the rope hanging about five feet off the ground?" He points where the rope curves away from the tower and runs to my harness. "That's so if one of the cadets loses his grip, he won't end up bouncing off the ground like a basketball. Your job is to maintain that height until they reach the bottom. Then feed a little bit of rope through the brake," he says and shows me how to feed the rope through. "Just enough for them to get their feet down. When they unclip, pull the rope back to five feet." He pulls the rope back up to the starting height. "Got it?"

"Absolutely, sir."

"Alright then. Now if somebody does have a meltdown and comes screaming toward the dirt, lock the rope on the brake like this."

Watch his hands carefully.

"And dig those feet in. You'll both get one heck of a jolt, but no broken bones. Or worse."

"Got it, sir."

"Well, then, let's have some fun then." Rick smiles big like Pickens did the first time he made fifty push-ups. "Sergeant," he calls, "stick close to J.T. here, just in case he needs a hand." He walks over to the ladder and shoots up the thirty feet like he was born in a tree house.

Sergeant Maddox walks over close, three feet to my left, watching.

Up top, Rick clips O'Malley to the rope and walks him over to the edge. Knew he'd be first because he's already done this several times in basic. Rick then clips himself to the second rope and slides over the edge of the platform and plants his feet on the board nailed there. He motions for O'Malley to do the same.

Both get into position, legs squatting, ready to push off. Rick nods and they push off the tower in unison. Rick doesn't even bother looking at the tower. He's fixed on O'Malley. No need, though. O'Malley bounds down the tower about eight feet at a time, feet bouncing off the tower like it's a trampoline. He stops perfectly at the curve in the rope.

Look down at the brake on my harness. Feed the rope through exactly like Rick showed me. And O'Malley pushes one more time off the tower, planting both feet on the ground.

"O'Malley just had to be a show off, didn't he?" Pickens says, behind me now.

Should jump on his ass for making such a comment about a fellow cadet, right next to Sergeant Maddox. But know he doesn't mean it. He's just pissed he has to stay on the ground. Sergeant Maddox must know it too, because he doesn't even glance at Pickens. Sure it's because he's got twenty juvenile skulls to worry about instead.

O'Malley unclips from the rope. Rick, who hit the ground in two bounds off the tower, high-fives O'Malley. "Good job, Cadet."

O'Malley says, "Thanks." He still hasn't learned. Don't need to say thank you when you just do what you're supposed to.

Pull the rope back to five feet.

Rick shoots back up the tower. Guess he's coming down with every cadet.

Dixon's next. He sits down, rolls over, and scoots back to the edge of the platform with not even half his legs hanging off, gripping the rope like he's choking a rattlesnake. He stops, and Rick has to grab his pants and pull Dixon's feet down to the board.

Rick says something and shows Dixon how to squat against the tower. Dixon just shakes his head. Rick keeps talking and Dixon continues shaking.

Sergeant Maddox yells, "For the love of God and country, Dixon. Get yourself down that tower. PRONTO!"

Rick keeps talking to Dixon, patting his shoulder, obviously from a different school of motivation than Sergeant. Dixon finally nods back. Then Rick yells down to me. "J.T., pull in about five more feet."

Do like he says, raising the curve in the rope to ten feet.

Instead of bounding down like he did with O'Malley, Rick takes only two steps down. Dixon follows, only he pulls his feet away like they're velcroed to the wood.

Step by step, Dixon actually makes it ten feet down the tower. He takes another step, but lets out too much rope. His ass falls below his feet.

"Pull yourself up and get a better footing." Rick says it loud, but like it's no big deal.

Dixon pulls against the rope with everything he has, but Dixon's muscles haven't caught up with his weight yet. He fights and sways, fights and sways. His body betrays every bit of will he has.

In the middle of his straining, his left foot slides off the tower, spinning him a quarter turn and bumping his shoulder against the tower.

Dixon starts flailing his legs likes he's drowning, trying to get his feet back around to the tower.

The meltdown has begun. Definitely know a disaster when it's about to happen. Go ahead and lock the rope on the brake. Rock back on my heels.

Rick lets go of his rope with one hand and gets a handful of Dixon's shirt to settle him. But Dixon won't have any of it. Without even thinking, he lets go with his left hand and pushes against Rick. One hand won't hold him.

Plant my feet and lean back.

Dixon's body hits the curve in the rope, and it feels like somebody is trying to snatch my spine through my stomach. Dixon's weight and force is too much.

My feet slide across the dirt and dead leaves. Sergeant Maddox doesn't make a move. He wants me to handle this. A test.

"Release the brake," Rick yells. But he's not my commanding officer. Have orders. Protect.

Dig in to slow down, to keep Dixon off the ground. The leaves make it impossible. But nothing is impossible. The leaves just pile up in front of my feet as they slide across the ground. Speed increases. Dixon falls. Helpless.

His body hits the ground, and the force slings me over him. Don't even let go of the rope.

Face plant right into the Walker Construction sign.

Fall to the ground. And the lights go out.

———

"Jason?" Mrs. Hernandez calls out the back of Honeywell House. "Jason? You boys know where Jason ran to?" Hear her call back into the house. Can't see her though. At the bottom of the pile of leaves. We always have to rake. Part of Mrs. Hernandez's plan to teach us how to work, do chores. She said it would be easier when we got families. But not for me. That's why I ran back here instead of getting on the bus with Kevin. He stepped on, and I ran away. Just want to stay right here at the bottom of this pile where it is dark, quiet, safe. No Mike. He'll leave me alone.

"Marcello, you check the shed, we'll check the house," Mrs. Hernandez says at the back door.

"Yes, ma'am," hear Marcello say. His feet hit the ground and hear Mrs. Hernandez shut the door.

Squeeze my knees harder into my chest.

His feet run so close to the pile of leaves that some of the leaves move. The door to the shed slides open. Marcello knocks over some of the tools, probably the rakes he just threw in the door.

"Hey Jason, you in here, man? You need to come on." He's shoving stuff around the shed and cursing the way he does all the time. "Damn it, man. I don't want to be out here looking for your no-talking ass. Got TV to be watching"

He slides the door shut, but don't hear his feet move.

Breathing gets heavier. Pieces of leaves get sucked into my throat and stick to my lips. Makes me half-cough.

His hand slaps across my arm, knocking the leaves away. The cool dark is gone. Sunlight blasts my eyes.

"Man, what the hell you doing?"

Roll over on my back. Eyes dodge the sun to see him standing over me.

"Mrs. Hernandez looking all over for you. Time for you to go."

Just lie there, not moving, not saying anything.

"Mrs. Hernandez," Marcello yells at the house. "Come get this crazy fool." He walks away.

Mrs. Hernandez comes out the back door. She says, "Thank you, Marcello," as they pass each other.

She kneels down next me.

I wipe away the leaves from my face and spit them out of my mouth.

"Jasonito," she says, like when she wants me to do something. "We need to go. You have to go back to the Travis'. I

know. It's hard getting used to a new place." She reaches out her hand to help me up.

Don't take it. Won't give her the arm that Mike will twist and nearly break again. Might not make it to the closet next time.

She pulls her hand away. "Jasonito, don't worry. It will be O.K." She nods at me like everything is fine. But it isn't.

Still don't move. Just lie in the leaves, wanting to sink into the ground.

Mrs. Hernandez gives me her look that says she can't put up with this.

"Jason, this is the situation we have. Some things just have to be done." She doesn't wait for me to reach for her hand. She takes mine and pulls me up out of the leaves. She lets go of my hand and looks me in the eyes. "What's wrong, Jasonito?"

Too many things. Don't say anything.

Mrs. Hernandez looks at me, then runs her hand down my arms, looks at my neck, my hands, like she's looking for something. She won't find anything. Mike knows how not to leave marks, at least on me.

"You're not hurt, are you?"

Shake my head because I'm not. Not yet.

"You just be brave, and everything will work out."

Jason wasn't, and it didn't.

alpha-oscar

In the dark, you can't see what's coming. But that's not necessarily a bad thing. The eyes can fool you. Smell, touch, hearing, tasting. Much more reliable. They tell the truth. Like when Mike's hand would reach into the closet to pull Jason out. If it smelled like aftershave instead of beer, dirt, and grease, it meant it was morning. And Jason didn't have to pretend to be asleep—or dead.

J.T. never pretends.

A calloused hand grabs my arm in the dark. Shakes me. "Come on man, wake up. Wake up!"

Eyes pop open and my right hand clamps down on the arm shaking me at the same time. Snatch it off me.

"Whoa, whoa, hang on." Rick's face comes into focus. And so do the faces of the other cadets standing behind him. "Just a second, now."

Sit straight up. Can't let my cadets see me down, weak. A wave of dizziness pulses through my head. Ignore it. "Fine, sir."

"Well, just hang on." Rick puts his hands out to keep

me from getting up. "How many fingers am I holding up?" He holds three fingers in front of me.

Just stare at him like he needs to forget this. Not here, now.

"Come on. Just want to make sure you didn't mesh up your squash."

"Three."

"See there, looking good so far. Now what's your name?"

Look around Rick to see my cadets looking at me, silent, scared. Pickens looks the worst.

"Cadet, what's your name?" Sergeant Maddox says, standing over me.

"J—"

"Captain, you alright?" Pickens cuts me off.

"Fine."

"Then what's your name, Cadet?" Sergeant has to ask again.

Take a deep breath. Look at Sergeant Maddox. "Sir, Captain, sir."

He smiles. "Go ahead, Rick."

"Just a couple more."

"Go ahead, sir."

"Five times three?"

"Fifteen."

"What county do you live in?"

"Covington?"

"Who's the hottest girl in school?"

"Good try." Sharper than he thinks.

Rick smiles at me. "He seems to be alright. Just a heck of a goose egg." He stands up and reaches his hand out to help me up. Nobody moves except for Pickens. He comes over and takes the other arm. When I get to my feet, Pickens says, "You should have said Nicole Marbury."

Ignore him.

Don't see Dixon.

"How's Dixon?"

"Nothing but a serious bruise to his pride, and his ass," Sergeant Maddox says. Some of the cadets stifle laughter. Sergeant Maddox snaps a finger at them, shutting them up.

"Could have been worse. You slowed him down pretty good."

Nod back at him.

"See there, cadets," Sergeant Maddox yells, "that's what you got to be willing to do." Every cadets' face fixes on Sergeant. "Are you willing to sacrifice your body to try to protect somebody else? That's why Tillman's a captain. The rest of you better step it up."

The other cadets look at me like there's no way they want to be like me. Don't even give them a second glance. Need to check on Dixon.

Me and Pickens walk over to Dixon. He's sitting on one of the trees that was cut down to make room for the tower. We sit down beside him.

"Sorry, Captain." He pulls his T-shirt down over his stomach like he's hiding something. Doesn't look at me or Pickens. "No victory today," he mumbles.

Any other of my cadets I'd probably crawl their ass for losing it like that. But can't handle Dixon like that. It'd make it worse. And can't have him going backwards. Forward is the only way.

"No, but our day's coming."

alpha-papa

Monday, 24 Oct 05, 0616

This is the last Monday that will ever be like this. First drill competition Saturday. After that, know where the squad stands in the region, how J.T. measures up to the other cadets going for the scholarship. And Chris Walker. Maybe he'll go too far. And I'll have a chance to stop him.

Stare at the ceiling trying to convince my body to get out of bed, hit the floor like I do every morning. But Monday.

Monday.

———

"Jason? Jason, honey, can you wake up for me?" A soft female voice breaks through the anticipation that my skull will split open any second. A hand lightly pats my chest. And for a few seconds I let this comfort stay, protect me from the reality waiting for me on the other side.

Force my eyes open. Eyelids stick together. They weigh so much. Crack them halfway. Let them fall back down.

"Now come on, honey, need you to get those eyes open for me. You can do it."

Strain again to get them open. Focus. A young red-haired nurse stands by my bed, and I remember where I really am. Real. White.

"That's it. There you go." She presses a button on the side of the bed. The bed raises me up into an almost sitting position. The sharp smell of urine mixed with the unmistakable chemical smell of a hospital fills the room. Body feels like it's been drug through a keyhole. But it hasn't. Just been in a car wreck.

Look at the nurse, smiling back at me, her hair pulled up in a ponytail.

Before I can stare at her too long, she says, "Do you need to go to the bathroom?"

Shake my head.

"You really need to try to go." She looks at me a second, her arms folded. "Got to make sure all systems are working the way they should." She holds out her hand.

Take it because I'm too tired and heavy to argue.

She holds up the covers to let me swing my legs out of bed. The hospital gown slides up, and I see my thighs, a huge bruise across both. The car.

The nurse steadies me as my shaky legs support my body.

"Take it easy now, sweetie. Be slow and easy." She smiles again. No way she knows because if she did, she wouldn't be able to smile.

Shuffle my feet across the floor. Look beyond the empty bed next to mine to find the bathroom door.

The nurse helps me over to the bathroom. "Can you stand by yourself, or do you need my help?"

Nod at her.

"Yes, you can stand or yes, you need my help?"

"Got it," I force through my clogged throat.

"O.K. I'll be right here if you need me." She lets go of my hand.

Place my hand on the counter and shuffle over in front of the toilet. Lift the gown. Nothing happens. Can't start. Keep waiting until my body decides it wants to go. Seems like forever.

"You doing O.K. in there?"

Don't reply. Just try to finish.

Flush the toilet and grab the counter to shuffle back to the door. Then I see. A white bandage covers the whole left side of my face. Tiny spots of blood trace the edges of the bandage from my temple to my chin. Stare at the mirror. Hear the tires screech and the glass shatter. See the white sheet, the blood.

Press my lips together, but the hurt spurts out anyway. Eyes sting and throat tightens. Another whimper comes, and I let it out. Tears fill my eyes. Want to hear my mom singing. See her face. Not the sheet.

The door swings open. "No, no, no, honey. You can't cry like that. You might tear those stitches out."

I didn't do it on purpose.

She puts a hand on my shoulder and rubs my back with the other. "Come on, now."

Look in the mirror. I'm sorry, Mom. Shouldn't have touched the radio.

A few tears spill over. The salt stings my dry face. Clench

*my teeth together and force the tears away, somewhere down
in my stomach.*

"There you go. Let's get you back to bed."

She helps me climb in bed and pulls the covers up to my
waist. "In a few minutes we'll have breakfast in here for you.
And when you're done, a couple of policemen are going to come
in." She stops and looks at me, her eyebrows raised like she wants
me to tell her that it's O.K. "They won't be here long. Just want
to ask you a couple of questions."

"No. Can't."

"Sweetie, I know. It's hard."

Not hard. Impossible.

"Not talking."

"It will be short, I promise."

Shake my head.

She ignores me. "I'll sit here with you if it will help."

No escape. Stuck.

"Let me get your breakfast. Then we'll take it slow, O.K.?"

*Not O.K. Know what they're going to ask. How did it
happen? What did I see? What did I do? Have to tell them it
was my fault.*

alpha-quebec

Snatch the covers off and roll out straight to the floor. Can't let that kind of shit get me this week. Not this week. Too many important missions.

Push up off the floor and hold it. Stare at my father's picture. There it is. Right there. One day it will be me in the desert. Strong. Proud. Respected. What Mom loved.

By the time I finish training, everything is clear again. Muscles tight, hard like armor.

Shower and dress like I'm in a race that has to be won. Want to the get the day started, moving forward, get it finished.

Mr. Coffeen is pulling the cushions off the couch when I come in. Know what he's looking for. And for once, don't remember seeing where he put his keys. Maybe the shot to my head caused more damage than I think.

"Good Lord, did you have a fight with a baseball bat?" Mr. Coffeen said when he saw my forehead.

Told him it was nothing, but he looked at me like he didn't believe me. "Has nothing to do with Chris Walker,"

I said, knowing that was he was thinking. That was good enough for him, so he let it go at that.

"Ha, there they are." Mr. Coffeen reaches into the crack below the back cushion and pulls out his keys. For once he found them before I did.

Mr. Coffeen looks up from the cushionless couch. "I'm telling you, J.T., I work my brain more looking for these things than doing my taxes."

Don't reply. Go to the kitchen to eat a bowl of cereal that's already out on the table.

"I don't know what you got planned this evening, J.T., but I figured you could go over with me to take the toy chest to Mrs. Richardson. You let me go by myself, and I'm liable to take all the credit." He laughs.

Pour the milk in the bowl. "That would be fine, sir."

"Oh, no. Mrs. Richardson needs to thank the worker, not the supervisor."

Sit down at the table. "Your design on the lid. I just nailed a few boards together."

Mr. Coffeen walks into the kitchen. "Is that what you think, J.T.?"

Just shrug and shove a spoonful of cereal in my mouth.

He slides a chair away from the table and sits down. "J.T., do me a favor. Hold out your hands."

Look at him like maybe he really has lost his mind.

"Come on now. Ain't going to chop them off."

Place the spoon in the bowl and hold out my hands. The back of my hands rest on the table.

"Now look at them," Mr. Coffeen says.

Do like he says. Feels a lot safer than expected.

"Those hands, your hands, created something from nothing. That little boy is going to have something he can use for years because of those hands right there. You need to be proud of yourself. Like I am."

Look at my hands and don't know what to think, feel.

Mr. Coffeen reaches over and takes my hand. "You did a good job, J.T." He grips my hand. Grip back. He shakes it short and firm. Feels good, I guess.

Mr. Coffeen lets go and gets up from the table. "I know you're hell bent on being the best soldier you can be. And I know you want to fight overseas—if we're still fighting by then. But try to remember those hands of yours can be used for something else besides pulling a trigger."

He waits for me to respond, but I ain't convinced. Nod anyway so he'll leave.

"Now, let me get out of here before I start running late. See you this afternoon."

"Sir," I say, stopping him, "going to be late every day but Wednesday. Got practice with my cadets. First competition Saturday."

"That's right. I remember you telling me that. You go right ahead. Got a big scholarship to win, right?"

"Sir?" Never told Mr. Coffeen about the scholarship. And he never goes in my room so he's never seen the brochure Mr. Marsh gave me from The Citadel. He can't do anything to help me get there so didn't see any reason to tell him. Some missions need to be kept quiet.

"Yeah, Mrs. Polk over at the school told me all about it

the other day. The Citadel." He shakes his head. "Boy, that is big time stuff right there."

"Yes, sir."

"Well, don't you worry about it. Can't imagine anybody working harder than you."

Nod.

"Well, you have a good one today. Me and the store will still be there when you show up this afternoon."

He jingles his keys and walks out the front door.

Pick up the spoon and start eating again. Stare at my hand lifting the spoon up and down. Guess they did do something.

alpha-romeo

Instincts. That feeling down in the gut that pulls and tugs, telling you which way to turn, when to act, what to decide. All good leaders have them, trust them. The more they turn out to be right, the easier it is to listen to them. Never doubted my instincts about Freeman. And here she is, proving me right again.

My cadets meet at the sidewalk by the street in front of the school instead of where they usually stand in the morning. They all wear jeans and black T-shirts. They obviously coordinated this without me. But that's fine. I know I'm separate.

"Morning, cadets," I say, examining each one of them.

"Good morning, Captain," Pickens says first.

Stare at them waiting for someone to explain why they are all wearing the same thing on a Monday.

"Cadets," Freeman says, and they all straighten up like they're ready for inspection. "About face." They all turn in unison to face away from me. The backs of the shirts say in yellow letters, *Alpha Squad: One Unit, One Mission. VIC-TORY!*

"Cadets," Freeman says again. "About face." They snap back around. Freeman's face beams. "So what do you think, Captain?"

"Very sharp."

"It was Freeman's idea. Her mom did them for us," Dixon says. His face tells me he has recovered from his failure Saturday. Good to see.

Look at Freeman.

"Yeah, well, my mom had some extra time, so it was no big deal." She tries to play it off, but she's proud of herself. Should be.

Before I can say anything to Freeman, MacDonald spouts off. "Yeah, Bravo Squad is going to be pissed. They'll probably copy us."

"Just make sure that T-shirts are all they can copy," I say.

"I hear that," O'Malley says.

Look them all over again. When I get to Dixon, he smiles. "Captain, down from a double-X to just an extra large."

Glance over at MacDonald, but he doesn't even act like he wants to make a joke. "Good work, Cadet."

Dixon smiles even bigger. He takes his victories where he can get them.

"O'Malley, what do you think of these?" Out of the group, figure O'Malley would be the only one to have a problem. Still thinks he's above this school stuff.

"Just wish it was my idea, Captain." Know he's telling the truth. He's always liked being a step above the others. Guess Freeman got him on this one.

Look over their heads to the school. "Let's get moving."

Take a step. Freeman stops me.

"Captain, wait." She reaches down into a bag lying on the sidewalk at her feet and pulls out three shirts neatly folded, one black, one red, and one camo. "These are yours."

Take the shirts from her. Don't even hesitate. "Hold these." Hand the camo and red T-shirts to Freeman. Drop my backpack off my shoulders. Yank my shirt over my head and toss it on top of my backpack. Pull on the black T-shirt. Tuck it in. Look at my cadets. "One unit, one mission, right?"

"Yes, sir," they say back.

Take the other shirts from Freeman. Unzip my backpack and shove them in. Sling the bag up on my shoulders. "Let's move, cadets."

We all turn and march toward the school. "Sir, what's up with the bruise?" MacDonald asks.

"Cadet, what bruise?"

"The one right in the middle of your chest."

Didn't even think about that before I took off my shirt. Got to think ahead better than that. "It's nothing."

Pickens knows, but he doesn't say anything.

Halfway across the front lawn the bell rings. People see us, point, some even stare. Don't avoid their stares, though. Look right back, daring them.

We join the bottleneck at the front entrance. The usual

talk vibrates through the crowd—except for one voice. Chris Walker's.

"Guess the Pickle Freak has a cult now." He laughs that fake, too-loud laugh, and so do a few other guys. Probably some of the same guys who paid me a visit the other night. Want to turn around, see who they are so I can add them to the list. My cadets keep their heads straight ahead, so I do the same.

When we hit the commons area, I say, "See you this afternoon, cadets." No reason to tell them to be ready. They're primed.

"Good day, Captain," O'Malley says.

"Yeah, later, Captain," MacDonald follows.

They all go separate directions.

Before she gets too far, I call out, "Freeman." She stops and turns. Give her a thumbs-up. "Excellent work, Cadet."

She smiles without reply. Just nods and continues to class.

Mr. Marsh stands outside his door when I make the turn to his room. He leans against the wall and strokes his beard, nodding good morning to students as they walk by. He never does this. Doesn't want to be away from the door when the bell rings.

"So J.T., got a big week ahead," he says, stopping me in the hall. Mr. Marsh knows our schedule for the season as well as I do. Heck, he knows all my dates—tests, inspections, even down to the project deadlines in everyone of my classes. Don't know how. He never asks, just knows everything. Mr.

Marsh didn't lie when he said he'd be supporting me 100 percent.

"Yes, sir. Big week."

"How is your squad looking?"

"Tip-top, sir."

"Well, I got a little piece of information this morning from Sergeant Maddox." He stops and strokes his beard a couple of times. "Not that you need any extra motivation, but the word is, Mrs. Evans..." He stops to see the name register on my face. "Yes, the one awarding the scholarship. She might make an appearance at the drill competition this weekend."

"Didn't think she ever saw the candidates. Not her style."

"From what Sergeant Maddox told me, she does this once a year. Sometimes it's at the first competition, sometimes the last."

"Sir, doesn't matter. Won't change my performance."

Somebody brushes behind me. Know it's Chris Walker. Just like him to pull this right in front of Mr. Marsh.

Mr. Marsh nods at Chris as he walks past me into the room. He glances over his shoulder to look at me, too. Nod at him. Need Mr. Marsh to think I've let things go.

Turn my head back to Mr. Marsh. "So how is that going?" he asks.

"Should ask *you* that, *sir.*"

"You first."

Look him straight in the eyes. "Nothing to report, sir."

"That right?" Mr. Marsh gives me his don't-lie-right-to-my-face look. "So Chris and some of his buddies didn't egg your house Friday night?"

This blindsides me. Mr. Marsh notices.

"J.T., don't look surprised. Teachers have ears, too. The whole back row yesterday at church just about roared talking about it. Those guys couldn't keep that to themselves."

"And who would that be?"

Mr. Marsh laughs a little. "Nice try, J.T. But you know I can't tell you that. Not that I *would* even if I could."

"What about Chris Walker?"

"What about him?"

"Any info about the situation last week?"

"All I'll say is they questioned him just like you. Of course, I'm sure it helped that his father is Anthony Walker." Mr. Marsh stops again and shakes his head. "It isn't fair, J.T. People and names around here."

"Know it, sir."

The bell rings. Mr. Marsh reaches back and grabs the door handle, then turns back to me. "I know it's hard, J.T., but you got to just let all this stuff go. You're better than them." He steps inside, and I walk in behind him.

The announcements start before I make it to my seat. Don't sit, just drop my bag and wait for the pledge.

When the pledge starts, the same people that always do stand and place their hands over their hearts.

Chris Walker doesn't. No honor, respect. Some just have to learn the hard way.

alpha-sierra

Guess it was too much to expect that the ROTC room wouldn't feel like every other room in the school. Figured maybe after a few days, they'd let last Thursday evaporate like all the other rumors seem to do. Or the talk about those who won and failed on the Victory Tower would erase their memory. But they're holding on tight.

Doesn't matter I'm a captain. The rank just means they have to follow my lead, show respect. Doesn't mean they can't fear me. Then again, fear isn't that bad.

Cadet Jordan bumps into me when I enter the room. My body plus the weight of my backpack spins him half-way around. He jerks back around fast, finds me in front of him, and his eyes nearly come out of his head.

"Captain, oh, sorry about that. Wasn't watching. I mean, I just, you know, I was just going to my desk…" His eyes get bigger the more he talks. "Look, if you want to tell Sergeant Maddox to gig me—"

Hold up my hand to stop him. "Cadet, forget it.

Crowded in here." Jordan takes a breath to say something else. Cut him off. "Just sit down, Cadet."

He closes his mouth, slides by me. A few cadets sitting close stare like they're waiting for somebody to jump off a building.

"Cadets." Nod at them. They drop their eyes and look at their desks.

Go to my desk in the front. Bell rings as I slide into the desk. Sergeant Maddox walks out of his office.

"Alright, sweethearts," he booms over our heads. "Time to see just what your brains have absorbed." He walks behind his desk and picks up this wooden stick about a foot long, painted Army green. Every time we have a test he walks around the room, twirling it in his fingers. If he sees you've answered a question wrong, he taps the desk. Doesn't say which answer is wrong. Drives cadets crazy. Not me. Never been tapped.

Sergeant Maddox gives the first order. "Cadets, prepare."

Every cadet gets out loose-leaf paper and a black pen, black only. We all set the paper square in the middle of the desk with the pen parallel with the top edge of the paper. Palms go flat on the desk.

Sergeant Maddox walks from behind his desk, gets ready to call out the first question. All of his tests are oral. Says ninety-nine percent of orders are spoken, not written, so we better learn to listen or one day we'll get somebody killed.

"Question number one: What is a soldier's most use-ful, but also most dangerous weapon? Explain why."

Sergeant Maddox apparently wants to start with an easy one. Build a little confidence. It's almost too easy. He's said it a hundred times. But I get why he's asking it now, after the Victory Tower. Everybody should know this answer—a soldier's mind.

Nobody moves. We wait.

"Now answer."

Every cadet snatches up the pen and starts writing. No time to think. Just write, complete sentences. Get the answer down before he goes to the next question.

Finish my answer and set the pen back where it belongs. Palms go back to the desk. Shoulders straight. Face ahead. Cadets continue to scribble. Don't have to look around. Know I'm the first to finish.

Hear Sergeant Maddox tap a desk. Can't believe somebody screwed that one up. But the cadet should consider himself lucky. At least he knows which one he got wrong. Hope it isn't one of mine. Not this week.

Sergeant Maddox keeps asking questions all the way up to the bell. Every question comes from his head, and he never stops until the bell. And nobody leaves until they give an answer for the last question. Cadets think he's too hard. But those are punks who don't want to find out how far they can go.

First to turn in the test at Sergeant Maddox's desk. "Well, Tillman?" he asks.

"Too easy, Sergeant."

He smirks back at me. "Yeah, maybe. But can't send the rest of these ladies home crying to mama."

"Understand, sir." Turn to go back to my desk to wait for my cadets to finish, but Sergeant Maddox stops me.

"Tillman. Need a word." He looks over to the other side of the room. "My office."

"Yes, sir."

Pick up my bag. Glance over at Pickens finishing his test. He takes a chance and mouths, "Too easy." If Sergeant Maddox saw him do that, he'd get gigged and then a zero on the test. He might be getting better, stronger, but if he doesn't get his head completely out of his ass, it is going to kill the squad.

Cut my eyes at him to make him look back at his test, then march over to Sergeant Maddox's office to wait.

The office is exactly what you'd expect from him. No pictures, no color, no plants. Just a chair for him, two chairs facing the desk, two shelves filled with military manuals and magazines, and a telephone on the desk. It's good—simple, functional, no distractions.

But it is a problem now. Nothing to keep me from wondering. Nobody comes here unless they're getting gigged or worse. Many jacked-up cadets have sat in this office. Definitely not one of them.

Head runs back over the past few days, wondering what he might know, thinks he knows, or heard. Might be pissed about the thing last Thursday. Know he can't stand actions that would bring unwanted attention to the program. But he would have already gigged me for that, even though I had nothing to do with it, couldn't control it. Maybe he doesn't care. Wouldn't blame him. Got to protect the program, all the cadets. He worries about all of us, like I do about mine.

A couple minutes later, Sergeant Maddox walks in carrying the pile of tests. He shuts the door with his elbow, walks over, and puts the tests on top of his desk. Sits down.

Straighten up in the seat.

"So, Tillman, how'd the tutoring go?"

I'm sure he already knows how it went. Look at the phone, knowing he had a long conversation with Ms. Francis about it. But I answer like I'm supposed to. "Very well, sir. Got another quiz tomorrow. Guess we'll find out for sure then."

"Yeah, Colleen's as hard as they come."

Ms. Francis hard? "Sir?"

He smirks. "Wouldn't know it, would you? Three high school state championships in the 5K. Didn't get a fourth because she ran on a busted knee. Tore it all to pieces. And still finished third." Sergeant Maddox shakes his head. "Thank God she was as tough on her brain as she was on her body."

Sit completely baffled.

"So you listen, do whatever she says. No questions."

"Yes, sir."

Sergeant Maddox nods. Studies me for a second. "Good. Now for more serious matters."

Pick my chin up and straighten my shoulders a bit more. Here it comes.

"Your squad ready for this Saturday?"

"Absolutely, sir."

"Good to hear, good to hear." He looks at me straight, hard, jaw flexing slightly. "So last Thursday doesn't have you distracted?"

"Not a chance, sir."

Sergeant Maddox rocks a bit in his chair. Looks down at the desk, then back up to me. "What about your cadets?"

"Focused and motivated as ever, sir."

"Yeah, saw the shirts. Should have gotten my approval first, but can't complain about cadets motivating themselves."

"Freeman's idea, sir. Didn't know until this morning."

"Freeman, huh?" Sergeant Maddox rests his chin on his thumb. Taps the side of his face. "Going to be a good one."

"Yes, sir."

"Tillman, just know that if you're going to wear something like that, be ready to back it up. Piss off some people and they'll come after you for sure."

"Plan on it, sir."

Sergeant Maddox looks at me for a few seconds, studies me, then cracks a smile. Looks weird on his face. "Just keep your edge."

Keep my back straight, stiff.

He presses his finger against his lips, smile disappears, then he drops his hand.

"Tillman, let me tell you about plans." He stands up out of the chair. "Think I planned this?" He points at his dead arm, not pissed, like he's showing me something he just discovered.

"Sir, no, sir. Just meant we'll do our best."

"That's what I'm talking about, Cadet. Sometimes you got to be prepared for forces outside the squad." He sits back down. "This right here," he points at his arm again, "is proof that the thing that takes you down is what you don't see coming, the one thing you maybe ignored."

"Sir, yes, sir."

"Tillman, let me tell you a story." Sergeant Maddox leans back in his chair. "Few years ago, I had the meanest, baddest, battle-hungry group of soldiers a drill instructor could pray for. I could have served them up blood and guts, and they would have asked for seconds with a smile. All except one."

He leans up, scoots closer to the desk. "Amazing how just one sorry bastard can cause a whole world of shit." Sergeant Maddox shakes his head the way he does when someone in our platoon screws up royal.

"Yes, sir."

"Well, this one soldier jacked up formations, fell behind on runs, snuck food out of the mess hall, and spent more time trying to be Mr. Funny Man than making himself a better soldier. And every time, his platoon had to pay."

"Tillman, that kid got gigged every day. And I PTed his ass until it was dragging in the mud." Sergeant Maddox's face gets red. He stops for a second, takes a couple of breaths.

"The platoon leader came to me because he and a couple of other soldiers wanted to, how should I say, *educate* this kid. You want to know what I did, Cadet?"

Don't answer.

"Made the biggest mistake of my career as an officer. Told them to lay off for a while, when knowing good and well they could have scared his ass into straightening up. Instead, ignored the situation."

"Did they?"

Sergeant Maddox cracks a half-smile. "Cadet, now you know better than to ask that question. What do you think?"

"Right, sir. Sorry."

"No, Tillman. I was the one who was sorry. Two days later this clown was juggling grenades on a training exercise. Caught one of them by the pin, pin came out. He and most of the others ran. Me and two other soldiers I was training turn around to see everybody shitting and getting. But too late for us. I got this." He points to his arm. "One of the soldiers is blind now, and the other lost his left leg from the knee down."

He looks at me hard. "Leaders aren't immune from making mistakes. I wish that wasn't the case. But you got to make sure you learn from them, pass on what you've learned to others. That's what I'm doing for you, Cadet."

"Yes, sir."

"Now look at you, Tillman. Top cadet here. Good grades, for the most part. Up for the Evans Scholarship. Still some hurdles to overcome. But could possibly have a big career ahead. But you got a problem that needs taking care of. Can't ignore it. Get what I'm saying, Cadet?"

Stare straight back at Sergeant Maddox. "Crystal clear, Sergeant."

"Some situations can't be avoided."

"Yes, sir."

"Good then. Can't have another career go down on my watch."

"No way, sir."

Sergeant Maddox smirks like he does when he sees he's getting through. He slaps the desk with his hand. "Go ahead, get to your squad. Got work to do."

"Yes, sir." Get up from the chair and grab my backpack. Open the door to the empty ROTC room. Sergeant Maddox stops me.

"Tillman, figure I don't have to say it, but I will anyway. We didn't have this conversation."

"What conversation?"

"Good, soldier."

alpha-tango

Wednesday, 26 Oct 05, 1657

When a situation can't be avoided, the only choice a soldier has is to adapt and deal. So that's why I took Mr. Coffeen's Old Spice from the bathroom cabinet this morning and stuffed it in my bag. Can't meet Ms. Francis unprepared, not like last time.

In the bathroom at the hardware store, I take the after-shave from my bag, unscrew the top, and put a few drops in my palm. Wipe the cologne across my upper lip and under my chin. The smell shoots up my nose, stings my eyes. Perfect.

Put the bottle back in my bag, sling it over my shoulder. March out of the bathroom.

Mr. Coffeen stands at the cash register counting money from the day. Before I can make it to the counter, he says, "Oh, don't somebody smell nice this evening. This must be serious."

"Sir?"

"J.T., my nose is about the only part of my body still holding up. And I smell somebody trying to impress." He doesn't look up, just keeps counting bills.

"Sir, it's not what you think."

"No?"

"No, sir." Don't feel like lying to him. "It's to keep me from getting distracted."

"What do you mean?"

"Sir, Ms. Francis is helping me with English. But the way she smells makes it hard to concentrate. Figure this ought to cover it up, make it easier to focus."

"Oh, J.T., don't I know it. The smell of a woman is enough to turn you into Play-Doh. Nothing like it." He laughs while he writes numbers down in his ledger.

"Yeah, well, don't have time for that."

Mr. Coffeen licks the end of his thumb and smacks bills down on the counter. "All I can say is you're a better man than me."

"Wouldn't say that, sir."

"Whatever you say, J.T. Whatever you say." He picks up another stack of bills and starts counting.

"See you at home, sir."

"Alrighty."

As soon as the bell rings on the door, Mr. Coffeen stops me. "J.T., now you be careful, that Old Spice will drive the women crazy." He laughs.

Crack half a smile. Shake my head at him. "Keep that in mind, sir." Let go of the door and head across the street.

Ms. Francis is already sitting in the booth when I walk

into Billie's. No ponytail today. Her black hair hangs down the right side of her face, shielding her eyes from the sun that is just about to fall behind the buildings on Main Street. The table is half-covered with a couple books and a three-ring binder. She sips coffee and flips the pages of one of her books. She doesn't see me.

"Sorry I'm late, ma'am."

She looks up from her book. "Hey, J.T." She looks down at her watch. "You're not late. Right on time." She swings her long hair over her shoulder, and the wind it creates fans my face. But the Old Spice blocks any trace of female wrapped in that breeze.

"Here, let me clear off some of this mess." She flips her books closed and slides the binder off the table onto the seat. "I got here a while ago to get some work done. It's quiet, so I thought I'd take advantage."

"Quiet *is* hard to find sometimes, ma'am," I say and slide into the booth.

Ms. Francis finishes stacking her stuff on the bench and turns back to me. Her eyes bounce to the side, then up and down. "What is that?"

"What is what, ma'am?"

"That smell. It's familiar." She sniffs into the air.

Keep my face straight. "Aftershave, ma'am."

"That's what it is. Old Spice maybe. I didn't think they still made that stuff." She says it nice, like it's something she misses.

"Shaved this morning, ma'am. Sergeant Maddox wants

us to keep it clean." I'm sure she knows there's no way after-shave would still be strong after a whole day, but no other way to explain it. Not getting anywhere near the truth.

Ms. Francis smiles big. "Reminds me of my dad. When I was little, I'd sit on the bathroom counter and watch him shave. I'd beg him to put some on me when he was done. Everything he did, I wanted to do." She laughs. "My mother was pretty happy when I grew out of that."

Her laugh trails off. "Anyway, enough of that."

Moving on would be good.

Ms. Billie comes out of nowhere with the coffee pot. She fills Ms. Francis' cup. "Hey, hon, what'll it be?"

"Just water, please, ma'am."

Ms. Billie shakes her head, puts her hands on her hips. "Just water again. Not exactly what a growing boy needs." She looks at me funny, like she's waiting for me to change my mind. But I don't.

"Ma'am, I know. It's just all I want right now," I say, at least hinting that I might order something.

"O.K. Have it your way." She bolts away and comes back in a matter of seconds. She slides the glass in front of me. "So," she says and puts her empty hand on her hip.

Ms. Francis takes the cue. "Whatever the special is."

"One Brunswick stew. And…"

"Nothing for me, ma'am."

"What's the matter? You scared of my cooking?" Her lips do this strange twisted smirk.

"No ma'am, just not hungry."

"Who you think you're fooling? Now honey, I raised

four boys, and the only time they weren't ready to eat was when they were sleeping."

Figure she's not moving until I order something. "I'll just have the same."

"Well, praise the Lord. Two Brunswick stews coming right out." She bolts away.

"She's something else, isn't she?" Ms. Francis shakes her head.

"And then some, ma'am."

She pushes her books closer to the window so she can have room to fold her arms on the table. The muscles in her forearms wave and wiggle when she leans forward. Think of what Sergeant said about how hardworking she used to be. Should have noticed before.

"O.K., so tell me how *The Crucible* is coming."

Pull my eyes away from the lines under her skin. "Better."

I unzip my backpack and get my English notebook. Take out the quiz from yesterday on Act II. Hand it to Ms. Francis.

"Ninety! That's more like it."

"Sergeant Maddox will definitely think so." Have to remember he gives the final command. And if he says this doesn't stop until I get a perfect score, then all the smiles, cheery chirps, and pats on the back won't mean anything.

"Guess I'm pretty good, huh?"

"Looks like it, ma'am."

She rolls her eyes at me. "J.T., I'm joking."

Don't know why. No way that grade would have happened without her input. As far as I'm concerned, she's just as responsible for it as I am.

Ms. Francis scans down the page, mouthing my answers to herself. "Well, can't say you're much for elaboration. That will have to change. But the answers are dead on." She reaches over, grabs my hand, and squeezes it. "Good stuff."

Her soft cool palm feels entirely out of place, like tissue wrapped around a razor blade. Jerk away. "Thank you, ma'am."

She pulls her hand back. "Sorry, J.T.," she says, even though she's not the one who should apologize.

"No, ma'am. My bad. Just not used to … well …" Can't find the words. And Ms. Francis doesn't make me.

"So, you feel like you're getting a handle on it?" She pulls her hair up as she says it.

Wish she wouldn't do that. When her hair is down it's like a door half-opened—you know something is in there but you only get flashes of it from time to time. With it up, the door is wide open and not noticing is useless. Her dark eyes and sharp nose jump out at you. The line of her neck slopes down to a slightly raised trapezius muscle. Her body screams athlete, but at the same time she throws a blanket of softness over a room that makes you relax.

Finally, I say, "Maybe."

"Why maybe?"

Ms. Billie comes nearly running across the restaurant. "Hot stuff coming." She gets to the table and sets the bowls of stew with a side of cornbread down in front of us. "Get you anything else right now?"

"I believe we're fine," Ms. Francis says.

"Just give a holler if you need anything."

"Will do. Thank you." Ms. Francis picks up her spoon and waits for Ms. Billie to get some distance away. "Back to why maybe."

Pull out a slip of paper Ms. Miles gave us in class today. "Essay." Hand the slip across the table. "Words not my thing, ma'am."

"Oh, whatever. You just need to practice more. Force yourself to say more than you think you have to."

"Hear you loud and clear, ma'am. Just not sure if that's possible."

Ms. Francis looks down at the paper. "Oh, it's all possible," she says without expecting me to reply. Then she reads the questions out loud. "How does John Proctor support the theme of individualism versus conformity in Arthur Miller's *The Crucible*? What role does the importance of reputation have in the play and compare that to modern society? Compare and contrast the witch trials in *The Crucible* to our modern judicial system." She raises her eyebrows. "Whoa."

"We select one. Got a week."

"Plenty of time," she blurts out with confidence I wish I could steal. She sets the paper on the table. While dissecting the questions, she takes a bite of stew. After swallowing, she looks over at me. "So, which one do you like?"

"Like, ma'am?"

"O.K., well maybe *like* isn't the word to use. Which one do you feel the most capable of tackling?"

"Ma'am, you pick. Better qualified to make the decision."

She scans the questions again. "Looks to me the first one is the most straightforward. What do you think?"

"Your call. I just follow orders."

"That's right, tough guy." She holds up two fists in a mock boxing pose with a funny smirk across her face.

Smile. She drops her hands, smiles back, and holds her eyes right on me. Turn my head away because it's suddenly weird to look at her. Been doing good keeping this focused on the business at hand, but her soft hand, little jokes, and crippling smile are pushing my head off track. Need the Old Spice in my eyes as well.

"So, where do I start, ma'am?" Just focus on the work.

"Well, let's talk about it first."

No, no talking. Action. Need to move some.

"Tell me what John Proctor does that shows he's not like everyone else?" She takes another bite of stew and waits for me to answer.

Don't know how somebody can look good chewing, but she's doing it like a pro. Rack my brain trying to stop the thoughts spinning around long enough for me to grab one sentence about *The Crucible* and spit it out.

"Ma'am, he just seems to be one of the few who doesn't believe the girls. You know, everybody just buys into their accusations without question, except for him."

"Right." She takes a sip of coffee. "What else?"

She finally puts on her no-bullshit face. Helps.

"I guess he's willing to put his own neck on the line instead of saving himself by doing what everybody else does. He does what has to be done, even when that isn't the easiest or safest thing. He's a leader."

Ms. Francis nods her head because her mouth is full again. When she finally swallows, she says, "See there. You know this stuff."

Shrug at her.

"No sense in waiting. Start there and then we'll see what we have." She nods toward my backpack. "Go ahead."

I take out my book and a pen. Relieved to have something to do besides looking across the table at her. Flip open my notebook to a blank page. Stare at it, all that blank space waiting for me to screw it up.

Ms. Francis pulls her books back in front of her and picks up her binder. She opens them and starts reading one of the books.

I stare at the tiny blue lines, wishing I could run my pen across them as fast as I run a mile. Got nothing, though.

A few seconds later, see her lift her head. "J.T., don't worry about right or wrong. Just get something down on the page."

Nod.

"I can't help you with anything there." She looks at me like she knows this isn't easy, but has to be done anyway.

"Yes, ma'am."

Put the pen to the page. Search my brain for at least one damn sentence. Words scream by like they're on a spinning wheel. Finally get a hold of something. I start. *Being a leader is hardly ever easy...*

alpha-uniform

The two of us sit at the table in silence except for the scratching noise of my pen moving across the page. Ms. Billie comes by a couple of times to fill Ms. Francis' cup. She comes back a third time and picks up the Brunswick stew I didn't touch, but she doesn't say anything. Guess somebody who has worked as hard as she has her whole life recognizes when folks need to be left alone.

I fill the front of the page and turn and start on the back. Don't open my book. Worried if I stop, I won't be able to start again. Trying to do like Ms. Francis said— don't worry about right or wrong.

My brain finally runs out of words. "Done, ma'am."

Ms. Francis looks up from her book. "O.K., let's have a look." She slides her book to the side and reaches across the table to take my notebook.

Pick it up and give it to her.

She clicks her pen and begins to read. For something that has nothing to do with ROTC, this feels just about identical to Thursday inspections—standing there knowing every minute detail is being scrutinized. But this is worse.

What seems like every couple of lines, Ms. Francis stops and makes a mark or writes something on the page. Feels like a blow to my gut every time her pen hits the page. Just sit here, taking my shots. I guess so much for, "Don't worry about right or wrong."

When she finishes, she tears out the paper and folds it in half. "Here's the deal. You can't look at it until tomorrow, at the earliest. Got me?"

"Can I ask why, ma'am?" As soon as I say it I remember that Sergeant Maddox said to do whatever she says. "Ma'am, I mean—"

"That's O.K., J.T. You can ask. I don't want you looking at it now because it is too fresh in your mind. It will be better for you to wait. You'll see it differently tomorrow."

I take the paper from her, place it in my notebook, and shut it. "No problem."

"I wrote as many suggestions as I could think of. You just follow those, and you should do fine."

"Ma'am, can I ask you another question?"

"Certainly," she chirps.

"Did Sergeant Maddox say how long you'd have to help me?"

"He just said until we get you into the clear."

Nod.

"That essay just might do it. It really isn't a bad rough draft."

"Not a good one either, ma'am. Correct?"

Ms. Francis smiles. "No, not yet, but it will be."

Respect her honesty.

Ms. Billie comes up to the table. "I guess we're done here."

"Yep, all done," Ms. Francis says.

"I'll take this when you're ready." Ms. Billie sets the check in the middle of the table and then hands me a Styrofoam container. "Figured you could eat it when you get home." She winks at me and walks away.

I watch her, reminded that some folks *are* nice without needing anything in return. Just not enough of them.

"So tell me about this scholarship."

"Ma'am?"

"Tracy told me you were trying to get some scholarship to go to The Citadel."

"Yes, ma'am."

"Well, tell me about it."

Not really something I want to get into. "Just a scholarship, ma'am."

"Why The Citadel then?"

Catches me off guard. Nobody's ever asked me this question. Guess to everybody else it's obvious—The Citadel only takes the best. Period. Can walk out of school, finish basic training, and immediately be an officer. Could just tell her that. But it would be a lie, or only part of the truth. Can't disrespect my father like that—hide him like he's something to be ashamed of.

"Ma'am"—I straighten my shoulders—"my father attended The Citadel." Know this could open up a whole bag of shit that could get out of control quick. But it's worth the risk.

"Wow, so you're a legacy."

Like that word. Sounds strong, important. "Yes, ma'am. Or least I hope to be." My heart starts to beat faster. Hands get hot.

"How long did he serve?"

"Not absolutely sure, ma'am." Wipe my hands on my pants. "He uh, didn't make it back from Desert Storm."

"J.T., I'm sorry."

Nod.

"No, I really am."

Take a deep breath. "Just hope I can pick up where he left off. People over there need help, protection." The heat in my hands has moved up into my chest.

"That's right, soldier. Keep the blood alive." My father's voice rings loud and clear.

"Well, I hope you do it."

"You don't have a choice, soldier."

He's right.

"No choice, ma'am. Can't lose."

Ms. Francis gives me that same concerned look Mr. Coffeen does. "Do me a favor, J.T., and have a back-up plan. You know, just in case things don't work out with the scholarship."

"Soldier, she doesn't get it, does she?"

Look hard across the table. "Ma'am, with all due respect, you don't get it. J.T. doesn't lose. Not an option." Pictures of Chris Walker flash in front of me. His truck burning down the street. Him laughing, doing his best to humiliate me, break me down.

Ms. Francis gives a nervous smile. She doesn't look so nice anymore.

"O.K.," she says softly.

She gathers her stuff, picks up the check. I let her.

"I'll wish you luck anyway, J.T." Her real smile comes back. Then she looks away and puts her stuff in her bag.

"No luck. Just focus, hard work, dedication."

"Hooah, soldier!"

Ms. Francis gets up from the booth and walks over to my side. "Just take it from me, be careful with that." She pats me on the shoulder and leaves.

As soon as she walks away, the heat evaporates. Head clears, no trace of my father's voice. Hear Ms. Billie ringing up the check. Don't turn to look, though. Can't see Ms. Francis. Know without a doubt. Should be gigged for talking to her that way.

Don't move from the table until she's gone. Then put my stuff in my backpack, sling it over my shoulders, tighten the straps. Pick up the Styrofoam container. Figure three miles with this load will hurt enough.

Walk out the door, and my legs immediately start pounding out my payment.

alpha-victor

The run was supposed to make me feel better, but it got interrupted. Dropped the stew Ms. Billie gave me somewhere around the mile mark. The container busted on the street. Had to stop, break my rhythm. But before I could really feel anything, snatched up the empty container. And ran even harder.

Walk into the house, soaking with sweat, to find nothing but the smell of fried bologna coming from the kitchen. Mr. Coffeen's favorite meal, but only when I'm not at home. He knows I don't eat that stuff.

Drop my backpack in my room. Go to the kitchen and set the Styrofoam container on top of the overflowing trash can that Mr. Coffeen will need me to take out later. Then pull the water bottle out of the refrigerator. The cold air chills the skin under my shirt. Chug half the bottle and put it back. Should go take a shower, but don't feel like being in the house by myself. Not with the guilt of the way I talked to Ms. Francis and slinging Ms. Billie's stew all over the place clinging to me as tight as my wet shirt. Only one place Mr. Coffeen could be.

When I walk into the shop, Mr. Coffeen sits hunched over his workbench holding a paintbrush surrounded by rubber band guns, little wooden tricycles, and little chairs only big enough for a doll. If this was the North Pole, I'd swear he was one of Santa's elves.

"Busy, sir?"

He picks his head up and pulls off his reading glasses. "Oh yeah, got to get this stuff ready for the festival on Saturday. If I don't finish up this painting, I ain't going to make a dime."

"Could help if you need it, sir."

"From the looks of it, you've done enough this evening." He laughs.

"Just a run." I stand still, waiting for him to give me something to do.

He looks at me, thinking I've got more to say. One of his things, giving me time to see if I really want to talk anymore. Finally, he waves me over. "Come on. How good at painting are you?"

"Can't say I really know, sir."

"Well, then sanding it will be. Grab that pack of sandpaper over there." Mr. Coffeen points to the table behind him.

Do like he says.

"Yeah, just get right down there on the floor and go to work on those tricycles. You don't have to kill yourself, just sand them enough so the paint sticks good."

He slides his reading glasses back on his face and goes back to painting the little chair sitting in front of him.

I sit down on the concrete floor. My wet legs sprout goose bumps from the cold floor, but comfort is not something I really deserve right now. Roll one of the tricycles in front of me and start running the sandpaper over it.

"So, how'd it go this evening? That Old Spice work for you?"

"Not as expected, sir." Useless to remind him it's all business.

"Few things ever do, J.T. Just God's way of keeping us on our toes."

I wipe a layer of dust off the tricycle and pick up one end to get the underside.

"Did you eat?"

Answering the question would mean telling him about the stew, which I want to get as far away from as possible. Put it back on him. "Smells like you did."

He laughs. "Bologna sandwiches. Mmm, that stuff might be the death of me, but it just might be worth it."

"Guess I can't be missing any more meals here then, sir." Keep running the paper across the wood and wiping off the dust.

"Now, you just remember when you're off being a big tough cadet up at The Citadel, I'm going to have to make up for all those bologna sandwiches I've missed."

Stop sanding. Rub the rough surface between my fingers, trying to grab on to the idea that I will have to leave one day, out of high school and on my way to The Citadel.

Mr. Coffeen's duty to society will be done. But mine will only be starting. Well, continuing anyway.

Remember leaving Honeywell House. The last good place before here. Stomach turns. Wish it was from being empty.

"J.T., don't you worry about me. A little meat product ain't going to get me."

"Absolutely not, sir."

Start sanding again before my head gets too wrapped up in the ideas Mr. Coffeen is throwing around.

Finish the first tricycle and roll another over. Get a new sheet of sandpaper.

"Why don't you tell me about what happened this evening?"

"Sir?"

"You said it didn't go as expected. How come?"

Look up at him, but he's focused on the pale pink chair he just finished painting. Could go for the door, but something tells me he'd block me like the last time I tried to dodge him. Only choice is to skip all the stuff that doesn't matter. Jump right to it, so we can move on.

"Disrespected my tutor, sir."

"Uh huh," he says as he sets the chair back away from him.

Know he wants me to explain. Only give him, "Just didn't speak to her the way I should."

He stays turned away from me. Pulls an unpainted chair in front of him. Opens a yellow can of paint, grabs a new brush. "Yep, the mouth can be a dangerous weapon. A whole lot easier to do harm with it than good."

"All the more reason I should keep it shut, sir," I shoot back.

"Heck, J.T., if you kept yours shut anymore, we'd have to resort to sign language. Not a person walking God's green earth hasn't said something they wish they could take back."

"But you can't."

"Nope."

I use up another sheet of sandpaper and pull another out of the pack. Dust from the wood cakes on my jeans. No sense in even trying to brush it off.

"So, did you apologize?" Mr. Coffeen chimes back in. He's got his head tilted back so he can glare through his glasses and run a clean line of yellow down the one-inch wooden slats.

"No, sir." As soon as I say it, my stomach jumps. Can't handle making mistakes, and just as bad admitting to them.

"How come?"

"Just didn't, sir." Don't look up. Just keep rubbing the tricycle as hard as I can.

Catch a glance of Mr. Coffeen spinning around on the stool. Pick up my head.

He pulls the glasses off his face. He picks up one of the rubber band guns and shakes it at me. "You see this, J.T. These things have been driving mamas crazy for decades. Still can't think for the life of me why they keep buying them. Hell, common sense should tell them that sooner or later, that boy is going to take this thing and tag his little brother, sister, or the next-door neighbor. Then he's going to have to say he's sorry. Damn hard thing to say. But learning how to say it and mean it can cure a whole lot of heartache—on both sides."

Mr. Coffeen's little speech just raises one question for me. "Sir, what if the person doesn't deserve the apology?"

"You saying she didn't, J.T.?"

"No, sir. Not Ms. Francis. Just in general."

Mr. Coffeen rubs the side of his face, really thinking. "Now that's a hard one there." He rubs a couple more times, then says, "J.T., wish I could say that everybody deserves an apology all the time. But that just ain't human nature. Guess the best thing I could tell you is go with your gut instinct."

Couldn't have said it better.

alpha-whisky

By the time me and Mr. Coffeen finish in the workshop, my body has reached its limit for the day. Arms feel like Silly Putty after all the sanding, and legs ache from running and being curled up on the floor of the shop for so long. Brain almost as tired. Actually look forward to getting in bed. Not the norm. But Mr. Coffeen doesn't realize how battered I feel so he has one more chore.

"J.T., before you get all cleaned up, can you get that trash out? That can ain't going to hold much else."

Could probably ask him if it could wait until morning and he'd be O.K. with it. Mr. Coffeen don't ask for much though, so he doesn't deserve questioning.

"Yes, sir. No problem."

"Thank you, sir. You're a good man," Mr. Coffeen says.

"Sir, it's just the trash."

"Yeah, but doing little things like that says a lot about a person. You'll figure that out, if you haven't already." He sits at the kitchen table and takes off his shoes.

Grab the edges of the trash bag and lift it out of the

can. The container Ms. Billie gave me, the one filled with the Brunswick stew, falls off the top and lands on the floor. Mr. Coffeen sees it.

"Here, let me get that for you." He gets up from the table, shuffles over, and picks it up. "What's this from? You bring home leftovers from Billie's and not tell me?" He says it like a joke.

"Not exactly, sir. Dropped it on the way home." Immediately feel guilty. Ms. Billie did something nice for me when she didn't have to, and I ruined it.

"Oh, that's just a shame. Good food like that wasted." Mr. Coffeen shakes his head and sets the container back in the trash bag. But he's not pissed. Not like Mike.

———

"In this house, we eat everything on our plates. No wasting." Mike sets his fork down and put his hands in his lap. "Now finish up, so you can get to clearing the table."

Stare at my plate. Can't eat the potatoes. They're not Mom's. Always loved her mashed potatoes. Told her, joking one time, I'd never eat anybody else's. Now it's not a joke.

Kevin stops eating. Cindy, Mike's wife and my foster mother, stops too.

"Jason, you hear me? I said we eat everything on our plates. We don't waste food around here."

Don't say anything. Grab my father's dog tags with my right hand. Wish he was here to help me. Mom too, and these were her potatoes.

"Boy, I'm going to count to three, and by the time I get to three, you better be shoveling some food into that mouth. It's got to be good for something."

I'm frozen in the chair.

"One," Mike starts to count.

"Just try, Jason," Cindy pleads.

"Two."

Still can't move.

"Three." Mike barely gets it out of his mouth before he jumps out of his chair. He slams his hand down on my plate, grabbing a handful of mashed potatoes. He grabs the back of my head and crams the potatoes in my face.

Try to jerk my head to the side, but the pressure is too much. Can't breathe.

"I said we finish our plates in this house." He keeps pushing. Nose feels like it'll go through the back of my head. Try to suck in air, but Mike's hand is like a dam. Cough and jerk my head to side. But his hand grips my face.

Potatoes fall into my lap.

"Mike, please," Cindy says.

"Shut up. This boy is going to learn."

Ears buzz. Lungs tighten and stomach lurches trying to find air somewhere. Finally, he lets go. Potatoes all over my face, up my nose, and in my eyes.

"Now finish. All of it." He points to the floor by my chair where some of the potatoes fell.

Let go of my father's dog tags and wipe my face. A soldier would never let something like this happen. He'd be stronger, know how to fight back. Look over to Kevin, but he just hangs his head. Cindy is almost crying.

"I'm waiting." Mike stands over me, knowing I can't do anything to stop all this.

Slide my chair away from the table. Lean over, scoop the potatoes with my hands, and place them back on my plate. Mrs. Hernandez would be upset with me right now. She tried to tell me not to make trouble. Some things I just can't do.

alpha-x-ray

Thursday, 27 Oct 05, 1151

One week and it's become obvious that nothing will happen to Chris Walker for the stunt he pulled last Thursday, even if everyone knows he did it. Sure that's because Mrs. Polk has to be able to prove he did it. Too many rumors and the fact that anyone could have taken the mask out of Ms. Teagan's room just leaves too many gaps that can't be filled. Everybody just remains the same, except for Ms. Teagan.

She doesn't leave the art room for her daily break anymore. Since last Thursday, she's watched the class like she's standing post, waiting for an attack. The free, work-on-whatever-you-want atmosphere is dead and gone. Ms. Teagan now actually tries to teach us something. We all have to work on the same thing, and nobody can even get out of their seat without an interrogation.

"Tyler, why are you getting up?" she barks from her post beside her desk.

"I was just going to the trash can." Tyler Cobb holds up a piece of wadded paper, his face pleading innocence.

"Can't it wait until the end of class?"

Tyler looks at the paper then back at Ms. Teagan. "Yes, ma'am, I guess so." He looks at her waiting for her to tell him to go ahead and throw the paper away, but she doesn't.

"Have a seat, please."

Tyler sits down and puts the paper on the table.

Ms. Teagan's put three containers half-filled with paint on every table—the primary colors red, blue, and yellow. We have to make a color wheel with three circles, one red, one blue, and one yellow. The circles have to overlap to show the colors that are made when the primary colors are mixed. Much rather draw The Citadel logo, but can't argue with Ms. Teagan wanting to keep a tighter rein on the room. She's definitely learned from her mistake.

"Don't you dare get paint on that uniform, Cadet," I whisper to Pickens. The last thing the squad needs two days before competition.

He nods at me and dips his brush into the red paint.

My jacket is tight across the back so it makes moving my arms more difficult. Should have taken it off when I came in, but there's no way I'm getting up and taking it off now. Just have to deal with the situation as it is.

Look up at the board where Ms. Teagan hung a big poster of the color wheel. Everyone's head is down, working, even Chris Walker. He's kept pretty low-key at school the last few days. Guess he knows he could have gotten discharged out of here for good for what he pulled. Then he wouldn't have an audience.

Dip my brush in the blue paint and start a circle on the paper. Move slow, precise, trying to make the circle as perfect as possible. Pickens just slaps paint all over the paper without regard. Guess it fits him. Nothing he does is going to look pretty. Just shake my head at him.

Ten minutes and the room remains silent except for the occasional crumpling of paper. Every time I glance up at the color wheel poster, I see Ms. Teagan still standing her post. Sure this is killing her as much as it's been killing Chris Walker not to act like a dickhead every day.

"Ms. Teagan, we need more red."

Pick my head up to see Chris Walker holding up the plastic container.

Ms. Teagan doesn't move. "I put plenty in there."

"Well, it would have been enough if some people hadn't started over three times." Chris nudges Tyler Cobb.

"Piss off, Chris," Tyler says.

Chris Walker still holds the container up.

Ms. Teagan takes a deep breath and lets it out. "Go ahead, make it fast."

Chris Walker gets up from the table, and Ms. Teagan walks halfway across the room like she's trying to tell Chris he shouldn't try anything funny.

"Heck, I don't need a chaperone," Chris says.

A few people snicker, but Ms. Teagan keeps her eyes on Chris Walker. Her face doesn't change. "Just making sure."

Chris Walker walks past me and kicks my backpack

on the floor. "Jesus, you need to move that thing before it hurts somebody," he says.

Ms. Teagan stays right on top of him. "Chris," she says in that tone that teachers have that means not another word.

Ignore him. He just wants to engage me so he can try to embarrass me again. It's easy for him to take chances in a class where he doesn't get a grade. He forgets that I'm just better than him.

Chris continues to the far side of the room by the sink where the gallon jugs of tempera paint sit. Watch him out of the corner of my eye.

He starts to pour paint into the container. Ms. Teagan tries to rush him along. "Let's get going, Chris."

"Jeez, Ms. Teagan, I can't change the force of gravity."

Nobody laughs.

Keep watching.

He puts the cap back on the bottle and heads back, taking the same route, just faster.

Don't move. Want to be ready, just in case.

Hear Chris Walker's foot slam into my backpack. See a streak of movement. Jerk to the left and swing my body in the seat. But not fast enough.

Red paint hits the arm of my jacket at the same time Chris Walker hits the floor.

"Jesus Christ, I told you to move that thing," he says from the tile.

Look down at the red on my jacket and then at Pickens. His eyes stretch open with fear.

My uniform. It's wounded. Ruined.

287

A blaze of heat shoots up through my chest and head, almost like it's going to set my hair on fire. Don't even think.

Jump out of my chair. Grab Chris Walker's shirt with my right hand and snatch him off the floor.

"J.T.," Ms. Teagan yells.

Don't let go.

Chris smiles at me.

Rear back.

"J.T.," Ms. Teagan yells again.

"Captain," Pickens says right after her. He's out of his seat, standing next to her.

Chris Walker holds his hands up in surrender. "It was an accident. Look." He motions down his shirt. Red paint covers part of the right side. "It's Abercrombie, for God's sake."

"J.T., let go," Ms. Teagan says, softer now.

"Captain, really, let go," Pickens says because he knows if I do this, there won't be a drill competition for us Saturday. And that victory is more important than this one.

Let go of Chris Walker's shirt. "Competition Saturday. You're lucky."

Chris Walker smiles back at me, and we stare at each other for few seconds. Ms. Teagan finally says, "Gentlemen."

Turn our heads toward her.

"Chris, clean this up. NOW."

Bolt over to the sink. Snatch my jacket off and turn on the water. Pump liquid soap into my hand. Scrub the sleeve under the water. Red bleeds out of the fabric.

The bell rings. Everyone leaves except Pickens, who stands next to me watching me try to save my uniform.

Keep pumping soap and scrubbing, over and over, until the fabric starts to tear the skin away from my knuckles. But it's no use. All of it won't come out. The jacket will always have a trace of red. Just like the scar on my face.

alpha-yankee

Friday, 28 Oct 05, 2105

Sometimes an attack has to be made to prevent future damage. Clear as that. Weigh the options, benefits versus costs. Simple equation. Not hard to figure out. And Pickens agrees.

"It's like you said, Captain. Some people don't go away, until you make them."

And we both agree that Chris Walker has to be stopped.

On one side, the people who win: Pickens, Mr. Coffeen, J.T. On the other side, only one loser. And only one result—peace.

Some might say there's no honor in offense. And they could be right. But J.T. is done letting bad people have their way. Like Sergeant Maddox said, got a problem that needs to be taken care of. It would be a disgrace not to do something.

Me and Pickens walk down the sidewalk toward the school so we can run on the track where every cadet starts with Sergeant Maddox. This is the last night before our first drill competition where we'll find out if our training has been good enough, if we're up to the challenge. Tonight we just need a little extra to prime the mind, to get focused on the mission at hand.

"So what do you want to do?" Pickens asks.

"Tomorrow. I'll figure it out after the competition. Got to focus on one mission at a time."

We walk through the gate at the stadium. The football team plays on the road tonight. Clouds cover the sky so the field and track are so dark I can't even see the other side. Quiet. Nice.

We start at an easy pace just to warm up. Pickens' off-rhythm stride bounces off the ground next to me. But he hangs in there, right next to me, right where he's always been.

We don't talk. Just start pushing the pace to find that pain that reminds us that we are stronger than people think.

Two laps and I increase the pace. "This lap under a minute. Count aloud. Go."

Pickens starts to count it out. "One Mississippi, two Mississippi, three Mississippi."

By twenty Mississippi, it's getting hard for him to count so I pick it up. "Twenty-one Mississippi, twenty-two Mississippi, twenty-three Mississippi." The count comes out smooth.

Push down the backside of the track. Counting louder. Hear my voice echo off the bleachers, the voice that will give the commands tomorrow to the squad that will win. No other choice.

Make the last turn, and both of us are pushing the limits. Pickens wheezes behind me, but he's not giving up. He never gives up, no matter how hard I am on him. He wants to be as strong as me, but he can't. There can only be one captain.

"Fifty-four Mississippi, fifty-five Mississippi, fifty-six Mississippi." Cross the line. Pain shoots down my left leg, making me limp a little when we slow down. Don't stop, though. Can't yet.

Me and Pickens make two more laps. Can hear that Pickens is ready to stop, switch it up.

"Halt." Slow to a walk. Pickens lifts his better arm and props it on his head, breathing deep.

"Got some left?" I ask.

"Always, sir."

"Push-ups."

We stop. Before we get down, I take my father's picture out of my pocket. Wanted him here as we prepare for battle. "You see this, Pickens?" Hold the picture in front of him. "That's what we got to live up to, that's what we got to be."

He looks at the picture. Doesn't ask any questions. Guess he knows who it is.

Turn the photo to look at my father's face. Wonder if he had the picture taken after a battle he won—protected his country, defeated the enemy, found some peace.

"Tomorrow." Talk right to the picture. "Tomorrow you'll be proud."

"Damn right," Pickens says.

"Be a winner tomorrow. Taking everybody down. Alpha Squad. Can't be beat. Won't be beat. One squad. One mission. Victory. Ain't that right?"

"Exactly," Pickens says.

"Absolutely, soldier." My father's voice comes in right after Pickens. *"Let me hear some more of that."*

"Got to take control."

"There you go."

"Got to win. No losers."

"No losers," Pickens shouts.

"No losers," my father echoes.

"Losing is for the weak."

"No weak soldiers here, is there?"

"Hard, strong, committed." Punch my chest.

"Say again, soldier."

"Hard." Punch my chest again. "Strong," and again. "Committed," one more time.

"There you go, soldier. Now let's see it. Got to be ready."

Set the picture back on the ground. Drop to the track. Pickens drops down beside me. Start banging out push-ups. Focus.

"No more losing. Winning only."

Don't even slow my body before it slams against the track. Like the feeling.

"No wrong maneuvers. Perfect plan. Perfect execution. No mistakes."

"There you go, soldier." The voice sounds better than ever. *"Right attitude."*

"That's right. Tomorrow." Keep pushing up, down,

slamming my chest into the floor. "Tomorrow is the day. Big win. Victory."

"Defeat the enemy. Take him down," my father yells back.

"Down."

"What do you want, soldier?" he asks.

"Victory."

"Say it again, soldier."

"Victory."

"There you go."

Don't stop until spit and sweat fall off me in buckets. Pickens even almost matches me push-up for push-up. Might be a little stiff tomorrow. A small price to pay for preparation.

Tomorrow. Razor sharp. Victory. Peace.

alpha-zulu

Saturday, 29 Oct 05, 0712 (D-Day)

Heard that lawyers should never ask a question they don't already know the answer to. Just like that with my squad. Know exactly what they are capable of, what to expect. Today is not a day for surprises.

But Mr. Coffeen is not on my squad.

"J.T., that drill competition, where's that happening?" Mr. Coffeen asks as I'm finishing breakfast.

"Central Covington High School, sir."

"And y'all start at what time?"

"0900. How come?"

"Well, I's thinking I'd drive over to take a look."

This is surprise. "Sir, you have the Fall Festival."

"Aw, I don't ever really make any money at that thing. Not even really worth the time."

"But all the stuff you made?" Can't believe he just did all that work for nothing.

"Well, I make that stuff because I like it, not because I

make any profit. Truth be told, I barely break even. Some-times don't."

"But..."

"J.T., it's O.K. if you don't want me there. I'd under-stand."

"Sir, no, it's not that."

"Then you don't mind?"

"No, sir."

"Alright then. I'm going to take all that stuff for the fes-tival down to the store and unload it. Maybe I'll sell some of it to customers. Then I'll head over to Central. Sound good?"

"Yes, sir. I guess so."

Mr. Coffeen swipes his keys off the table. For once he doesn't have to look for them. "See you over there."

He walks out the front door, and I finish the eggs and toast he made for me. Clean the plate and fork.

Walk to my room to get the jacket Sergeant Maddox is letting me borrow. He didn't say much about the ruined jacket. He just found a solution. That's what good leaders do. Don't worry about what caused the situation, just find a solution that will let the mission go forward. But I know he'll have something to say later.

The only hiccup was finding someone who could sew my patches on the new jacket. And true to recent form, Freeman came through. She took the two jackets home and had her mom do the work. Offered to pay, but Freeman wouldn't have any of it. Her mom did a perfect job. The only way I know the new one isn't mine is it doesn't fit as tight.

Take the new jacket off the hanger. Slide it on. Step over to my nightstand. My father's picture leans against the lamp, next to The Citadel brochure. Pick up the picture. "Ready for battle, sir."

Put the picture in my jacket pocket. No way he's going to miss this.

Take my beret off the chest of drawers. Look down at my uniform one more time to make sure every line is perfect. Ready.

Know which squad is mine from a hundred yards away from the school. Not because of their faces. The way they are standing. My squad stands on the sidewalk in a straight line, shoulder to shoulder. Bravo groups together like this is any other day, doesn't mean anything. That's why they're Bravo.

March down the sidewalk, cross the street where just over a week ago a crowd stood waiting to see if the school would blow up. After seeing the mannequin, I know they later wondered what I was capable of doing.

I wonder too. Guess today I'll find out.

Step up onto the sidewalk in front of my squad. My cadets keep their eyes forward, faces blank. "Good morning, cadets."

"Good morning, Captain," they say. O'Malley, Freeman, MacDonald, Pickens, Dixon all pick up their shoulders just a bit, a slight tilt of the chin. They already embarrass Roper's group, and we haven't even left the school yet. That's my squad.

Scan their uniforms. Every crease is like the edge of paper. Shoes reflect the sun. Covers are tight and straight. "Mighty sharp."

They don't say thank you. Just doing what is expected.

"At ease," I tell them.

They all relax but stay in line. "Sergeant Maddox went to get the van. He'll be here in a second," Freeman says.

Nod at her.

Look over at Roper standing with his hands in his pockets. Want to shake my head at him. Tell him stuff like that is why he's never going to beat us. But wouldn't do any good. Just nod at him to show respect. Even though he doesn't take this as seriously as he should, he still deserves respect for doing this at all. Most guys are lying in bed this morning or sitting on the couch flipping channels between cartoons and ESPN pre-game shows.

Roper nods back. "Looks like you got them ready, J.T."

"You expected otherwise?"

He kind of laughs. "No. But we'll still give you a run for your money."

"Good. It'll make victory sweeter." Roper takes it as a joke, which is what I want. He smiles and nods.

Hear one of my cadets chuckle. Snap my head around to see MacDonald trying to force away a smile. "Cadet, better keep it straight."

"Yes, sir," MacDonald says and loses the smile.

Sergeant Maddox pulls up in the van—one of those fifteen passenger jobs with *North Covington High School* painted on the side. He steps out and immediately puts on his cover. "Cadets, attention."

My cadets slap their heels together while I step over in line with them. Sergeant Maddox waits for Bravo Squad to get themselves together.

He walks in front of my squad, barely looking at them. He stops in front of Bravo Squad, checks them over, and then walks behind them. He knows his name might as well be on the side of that van with *North Covington High School*, so he's double-checking.

Back in front of us, he says, "Cadets, today is your first real test of the year. Get to find out if you can take the pressure, execute when it matters." He steps over in front of me. Looks me in the eyes. "Got a lot riding on today. And I'm not talking about points or trophies. Talking about pride, reputation, respect." He steps away from me, looks down the line of cadets. "Are you hearing me, cadets?"

"Yes, Sergeant," we all say in unison.

"Good." He moves closer, slowly walks in front of each cadet, the brim of his cover almost slicing against their foreheads. "You know what I'm looking for?" Everybody knows it is one of his questions he really doesn't want answered. "The crack," he says. "Bound to have one here. Sometimes it is so small you can barely make it out. But it's there. And as soon as you add a little pressure—boom, disaster." Sergeant Maddox stops at Roper at the other end of the line. He snaps back around. "Well, cadets, let's just hope my eyes are not deceiving me. Load up."

We break out of line and walk around to the other side of the van. I'll sit in the front with Sergeant Maddox—we sit according to rank and position. Not a rule or anything, just one of those things that gets passed down from squad to squad without anyone ever really saying it. I know it because I waited a year to be standing by this van. Trained harder than anyone, watched practices, listened when no one thought I was. Practiced maneuvers on my own, even though I wasn't part of a drill squad. Sergeant Maddox said if I trained hard enough, maybe he'd give me a chance. Today is proof that training works.

My squad sits on the first row of seats, and Bravo goes in the back. Wait for my cadets to load up before I get in. Pickens is last. He steps up to the van and takes off his cover. His hair is virtually gone, cut down as close as mine. Must have done it this morning.

Pickens sees me checking him over. "High and tight, right, Captain?"

"Tight as ever."

Close the door, slide my cover off and get in the front seat. Sergeant Maddox cranks the van, pulls his seat belt on with his good arm, and looks in the rear-view mirror. "Alright, cadets, let's go kick some ass."

The back of the van hoots and hollers. Look over my shoulder at my cadets. They stop immediately. Trained them better than that. They know better. No emotion. Just focus and execution. Can't have Roper and his squad of slackers distract us. Made too much progress for that.

The twenty minute ride over to Central gets quieter and quieter the closer we get, like somebody slowly turning down the volume on a TV. Hear cadets in the backseat shifting around, fidgeting. The importance of today starts settling in. The air tingles with excitement. No more play time. Today is for real.

Sergeant Maddox flips on the turn signal and eases over to take the ramp off the highway. As soon as he flips off the signal, a flash of yellow jerks over in front of us. "Some drivers," Sergeant Maddox says, "just need to be shot." The way he says it, nobody knows just how much of a joke it really is.

The flash of yellow comes into focus. Seen the tailgate of the truck before—when I was running down the street having eggs and laughter hurled at me. Don't say a word.

Sergeant Maddox continues down the ramp and into the merge lane on Lee Parkway. The yellow truck in front of us travels halfway down the merge lane. Slams on its brakes.

Sergeant Maddox locks it up.

The tires screech, van lunges forward. Seat belt catches and yanks against my chest and waist. Body folds like a rag doll. Dixon slams against the back of my seat.

Tires still screeching. Grab the dash. Truck rushing closer.

Like a wall dropped out of the sky, the van stops inches from the back of the truck. Smoke from the tires blows by the windshield. That smell of burning brakes and rubber fills the van. Get dizzy.

"Son of a bitch," Sergeant Maddox yells at the windshield and blows the horn. He grabs the door handle to get out, but the truck pulls away into traffic. Just like Chris Walker to pull away like nothing happened. But something is happening.

My chest gets tight. The echo of the horn rings in my ears. Hurts, but not the good kind. Daggers stab into my head. Dizzy.

J.T., tell him not to blow the horn anymore.

Sergeant Maddox turns to the backseat. "Anybody broken?"

"No, sirs" bounce around. Dixon pushes against the back of my seat to get himself off the floorboard. Feel like I'm tumbling upside down. Place my hands on the dash, trying to get some balance, keep Jason away.

"Alright Dixon? Didn't mess up that uniform?" Sergeant Maddox asks.

Don't hear Dixon respond. Can't hear him over the tires.

Don't move my head, my eyes, nothing. Those tires scream in my head. Hands stay on the dash. A bead of sweat races down the side of my face, over the scar. Shake my head to get rid of the dizziness, but it's not going anywhere.

———

"Son, can you tell us what happened, what you saw?" Two policemen stand at the end of the hospital bed. The one asking the question moves and sits on the edge of the bed.

"Not sure." Pull the covers up on my chest.

"Not sure you remember or not sure you saw anything?"

Just stare down at the white blanket, the sheets on the bed. Can't see anything, just the white.

"Son, I know this is hard, but try to tell us something." He pats my leg. Jerk it away.

"Stop saying that. Stop calling me 'son.'"

"O.K., sorry uh...sorry Jason."

Keep looking to find something to say so they'll go away. Then there's something. "Mom was listening to the radio."

"Good. What else?" The policeman leans in closer.

"She was singing. She always sings with the radio." Pull the covers up close to my chin.

"O.K." He says it quiet.

"I didn't like the song." Feel the knot grab my throat, but remember what the nurse said. Can't cry. Swallow hard to push it away. "So I...I reached over and changed the station. Just wanted to hear something else." Stop and breathe deep. Swallow again. "She turned to look at me. It was only for a couple of seconds. She just wanted it back on that station." Stop to catch my breath.

"And then?" the cop asks, just loud enough to hear.

"A horn, heard a horn blow. Then...then she looked back up at the road. Her face got scared. And then the screeching. I grabbed the dash." Put my hands out in front like I did in the car.

"After that?"

"It hurt."

bravo-alpha

"You hurt, J.T.? Cadet, you alright?" Sergeant Maddox's voice is almost yelling.

Turn my head toward him. He looks at me like he's never seen me before. "Sir?"

"You O.K.?"

Chest heaves up and down. Look at my hands. They still clench the dash. Let go and sit back in the seat. Run my hands down the front of my uniform to smooth it out. Press my palms against my eyes.

"Cadet, you going to make it?"

"One second, sir." Keep my eyes closed and palms pressed tight, waiting for the world to stop spinning.

Nobody in the van makes a sound.

Take a deep breath and hold it. Let it out, working my way back to the present. The back of my throat aches like it does right before tears come. Not today, though. Swallow twice to keep them back.

A few more slow breaths and I can remove my hands

and open my eyes. Wipe sweat off my forehead. Heart slows down. Finally make it back.

"O.K., let's go." Nod at Sergeant Maddox.

He doesn't move or say anything, like he's thinking it over. Finally, he shifts the van into drive, checks his mirror, and pulls out into traffic.

The van doesn't feel the same as it did. Everybody's still quiet, but the air has lost the tingle, the feeling of anticipation. Maybe the near accident. Maybe me.

Have to do something to get back on track. Only one thing to do—go over the squad's maneuvers in my head. Got to get focused and ready. No excuses today. Jason can't have any part of it. J.T. has to win, take the first step. Good soldiers don't let anything get in the way of victory.

See every turn, every step. Hear every order. Perfect. Crisp. Like Sergeant Maddox says. Got to see it before it can happen. If you don't visualize victory, you guarantee defeat.

Make it through our whole routine before we get to Central. Hear Sergeant Maddox roll down the window and ask somebody where to park. Open my eyes. He talks to a cop. The cop points to the side of the school. "Just follow this around to the back. You'll see where the other vans and buses are parked."

"Thank you, sir," Sergeant Maddox says and tips his head.

The cop tips his back to him and says, "Good luck to you guys today."

Sergeant Maddox rolls up the window and pulls away. "Freeman, he meant you, too."

Freeman waits a few seconds, then says, "Sir, all due respect, but I'm not a guy." And before Sergeant Maddox can say anything, she adds, "None of us are. We're cadets."

Sergeant Maddox actually smiles. "Damn right, Freeman."

Everybody in the van but me chuckles. Look over my shoulder to see a couple of Bravos slap hands. Tension gone.

Sergeant Maddox parks at the end of a line of vans just like ours except for the names on the side. He shifts the van into park. We all get out. Sergeant Maddox says, "Quick inspection, squad leaders."

Both Alpha and Bravo Squads fall in line behind the van. Start at the end with O'Malley. Glance at Dixon who is using the holes in his pockets, although he doesn't need them as much anymore. O'Malley is straight. MacDonald has to shift his belt buckle to get the perfect line. Dixon is clear. Pickens has never been cleaner. And Freeman looks like her uniform is made out of cardboard.

Finish and ask Freeman to look me over. She takes a quick glance up and down. "Perfect as always, Captain."

Not perfect. Head still splitting, hands sweating. Off balance. Can't let it stop me, though.

Nod at her. Look at my cadets. "Alright, cadets. One Squad. One Mission."

"Victory," they finish.

"Nothing else."

bravo-bravo

Nobody stares. No whispers, snickers, or spit insults. Nothing like school. Almost everybody is a cadet, and if they're not, they're here supporting one. It feels safe. But I've learned safety is often just an illusion.

Sergeant Maddox gets us checked in with the sergeant that runs Central's program. He's a lot older than Sergeant Maddox. Retired Army, like most who have the job of dealing with cadets. He asks Sergeant Maddox about us. "So, how your fellas looking?"

Can't believe he called us fellas.

Sergeant Maddox corrects him. "Cadets looking razor sharp, sir."

"Got them ready to go, then?"

Sergeant Maddox doesn't reply right away. He signs a piece of paper on a clipboard on the table. He looks up and says, "Just expect the best."

The sergeant from Central smiles and gives a lazy salute, sitting down. Sergeant Maddox salutes back. But as soon as we walk away from the table, Sergeant Maddox says,

"Cadets, if we lose to Central, it's going to make me lose my mind, so make sure we don't."

We all fall in behind Sergeant Maddox and march toward the field that would normally be used for soccer. Not today. Today it's a battlefield.

Two sets of bleachers are set up on the near side. One is half-filled with moms, dads, grandparents, and siblings that got dragged out of the house at 0800 on a Saturday morning. The other is just a blotch of green, cadets sitting shoulder to shoulder. The only thing different about them is the patch on the shoulder with the school colors.

Scan the spectators when we walk by. Remember that Mr. Marsh said he heard Mrs. Evans is supposed to be here today. Can't make her out, though. Must be twenty old ladies in the stands.

Keep marching down the sidelines right past the table where the judges will sit. Sergeant Maddox stops in front of the green bleachers, snaps around. "Here, cadets."

Let my cadets sit first. Take a look up in the bleachers. Cadets sit straight and still like they've been nailed down. They're trying to look hard. Looks are one thing, performance is another.

Step over to the bleachers, turn sharp, and sit. A couple of conversations start behind us, but can't hear what they're saying.

Sergeant Maddox doesn't sit, just stands facing away from us like he's on guard watch. He glances at his watch. "0845. Fifteen minutes, cadets. Get your heads on straight."

Nobody responds. All the talk is over.

Not nervous. Nervous is for those not prepared, not trained. Just look out at the field, see it all happening right there. Hitting every turn, maneuver. Judges writing down our scores. Close my eyes and run through our maneuvers one more time. Some people think you can prepare too much. But like Sergeant Maddox says, too much is never enough.

About halfway through the routine, hear my name. But not the one I'm used to.

"Jason Tillman?"

Open my eyes. Standing in front of me blocking the sun is a man, looks to be about thirty-five, black hair parted and gelled, Polo sweatshirt and jeans.

"Just J.T."

He sticks out his hand, "Chad Evans."

Evans. Better stand. Get up. Shake his hand. Nod. "Sir."

"Just wanted to come over and speak to you a second before this whole show gets started." He smiles big like a car salesman.

Show? Bad vibe. But stand straight, chin up. Look like a soldier. "Yes, sir. Big day."

"I guess it is." He looks into the stands, then left and right. Laughs a fake, short laugh.

Stare back at him, wondering if this guy is for real.

"Guess you were expecting someone a lot older and shorter. My grandmother wanted me to come out and meet the candidates for the scholarship since they're all here today."

"So, Mrs. Evans isn't here today?"

"No, she doesn't get out much anymore. She's near

ninety, so the family elected me to help her screen the candidates."

Has to be a joke. This guy shouldn't be screening anything but waitresses for Hooters. "I see."

"Mind if I ask you a couple of questions?" He steps away like he wants me to walk with him. Good thing. Don't want my cadets hearing what I have to say. The less they know about this whole thing, the better. Don't want them to think I am putting any more pressure on them than they're putting on themselves.

Step along side of him, and we walk away from the green bleachers. "Watch the time, Tillman," Sergeant Maddox says as we pass him.

"Yes, sir."

We take a few steps. Glance up into the bleachers. See Mr. Coffeen making his way up the bleachers to find a seat. Guess he was serious about being here. Nice to have the support.

We take a few more steps, and this Chad Evans guy says, "So J.T., why do you want to attend The Citadel?"

Big question. Mr. Marsh said this one would come. Had the answer prepared for a couple of months. "Well, sir, you only get better, smarter, stronger if you're challenged. Figure The Citadel would offer the biggest challenge, give me the best training. Plus, my father went there. Want to continue the legacy," I say, using Ms. Francis' word. "Just like your grandmother wants to continue your uncle's legacy with the scholarship."

He doesn't say anything for a few seconds, just nods

his head, thinking about my answer. "So, your dad is a military man."

"Was. His service ended with the price some are willing to pay to defend this country."

"Oh, sorry about that." He says it like I told him I stepped in gum.

"Sometimes it happens to soldiers. Part of the deal."

He nods again. "So what about your mom?"

"What about her?" I say back too quickly.

"Well, how does she feel about her son going to a place like The Citadel, becoming a soldier, knowing her husband died because he was in the military?"

Stop walking. Turn to face him. Only somebody who has never put on a uniform could say something like that. Had this guy pegged from the get-go. Want to let him have it. Ask him what his grandmother would think. But keep it straight. Got to score points with this guy. Lift my chin and say, "Nothing would make her more proud."

"Good to hear." He smiles like he's ready to hand me the keys to a new BMW. He turns to walk back toward the green bleachers. "Just one more question."

"Go ahead."

"So, why do you think you are the best candidate for the scholarship?"

Now some weak-ass punk might tell this guy about my mom being gone and living with foster families and not having any money and not many options. But sympathy is the last thing I want, especially from a guy like this.

Force my lips to say, "Sir," and then pause for a second.

"My squad here today. Sergeant Maddox gave them to me because they were the worst in the program. Told me to make something of them. That's what I did. Turned them into the best squad in North Covington's ROTC. That's what I can do. Make something from nothing. Be a leader. Lead by example and never back down. Not everybody can do that every day. I can."

He nods his head a few times and says, "Good answer, J.T." He sticks out his hand. "Good luck to your squad today. But it almost sounds like you don't think you need it." He laughs a little.

"Thank you."

"Maybe I'll see you again."

"Hope so." Only if it means him giving me the scholarship.

He turns and walks around the end of the bleachers. He's not staying to watch. Not surprised.

Turn and walk back to my squad. Sergeant Maddox stops me before I can sit. "How'd it go?"

"Guess as good as it could."

"On your way, Tillman. On your way." Sergeant Maddox tips his head. "Now strap it up tight."

He's right. Things falling into place—cadets ready, solid interview, all my grades coming around. Couldn't be more battle-ready. Ms. Francis thinks I need a back-up plan. Nope. Just the right mind, motivation, and know-how. One thing I know how to do is perform, overcome.

bravo-charlie

B efore Trent takes the field, the judges are introduced—two captains from the Army, one corporal from the Air Force, and one lieutenant from the Navy. Navy four hours away from the Atlantic? Not much sense in that.

Each judge waves, sits down, and then nods to the announcer who happens to be the old sergeant from Central. Guess if you're hosting the competition, you get the mic.

"Alright, folks, the first squad taking the field this morning represents Trent High School, led by cadet Bradley Henderson." He stops to let the crowd clap. In the middle of the crowd clapping, a horn blows. At the other end of the field, the yellow truck is parked with the doors open. Chris Walker stands on the driver's side, reaching in and blowing the horn, and another guy I don't know stands on the hood hooting and hollering—not like he's excited, but like he's mocking.

The sergeant tries to make a joke. "Looks like Trent brought their own cheering section this morning." He laughs. Nobody else does.

The horn keeps blowing. Try to ignore it. Not the time for this.

They finally stop, and the sergeant announces, "Cadets, you may take the field."

As soon as Trent's squad takes their first steps, Sergeant Maddox says over his shoulder, "Cadets." That's our order.

We all close our eyes. Sergeant Maddox doesn't want us to watch the other squads. Says either way it won't do us good. If a squad does well, he thinks we'll wonder if we're as good. If one bombs, then we'll think we've got it easy. This way, we won't know. Can only worry about what we do. Some might think it's disrespectful. But respect has nothing to do with it. Some tactics are just necessary.

Even though my eyes are closed, can still tell how Trent is doing. Claps are light and polite. Hear one cadet drop his rifle during rifle maneuvers. Hear Trent's squad leader give the order to start the last section. They're in trouble. Know it because each squad has five minutes. Feel five minutes coming up. We've practiced so much I know five minutes just by feel. Can always guess it within about ten seconds. And Trent just passed it.

Trent's squad leader barks another order, but he's followed by one of those hand-held air horns that signals time's up. Trent has to stop before finishing.

Shortly after the air horn, the sergeant from Central comes on the mic. "Thank you, cadets. Folks, let's hear it for Trent High School."

The crowd claps but no horn this time.

We can look now, so we open our eyes and clap with the rest of the crowd. We're one squad closer to our turn.

Heart starts racing. Sweating.

Trent's squad makes it back to the bleachers. Got to move, do something that will make me forget the horn.

Stand up from the bench and turn to face Trent's squad. "Good job, cadets."

They say thank you with about as much believability as when MacDonald told Freeman it didn't hurt when she accidentally hit him in the nuts. They say it anyway— except for one. Sure it's the guy who dropped his rifle. Really sucks for him. He's got to walk around with that on him until he can prove himself at the next competition.

The first squad from South is called. They go through the same routine. Nothing major happens. No big claps. Don't hear any catastrophes. Solid routine.

The second squad from South is called, and it seems like a blink before they're finished. Now Bravo is up.

Alpha stands with Bravo when they're called. Even though we're competing against each other, show support and respect to the other. Only way to maintain unity within the program. Sergeant Maddox often reminds us we're not kids, we're cadets. And cadets support each other, no matter what.

We keep standing until the announcement is made for them to take the field. Alpha sits in unison. Shut eyes.

Roper gives the first order. Listen hard, to hear any missteps or miscues. But there are none. Hear a couple of mistakes with timing during the rifle section and a couple of other places. Overall, sounds like a good performance. Not better than us, though. Seen Bravo's routine. Too simple. Even if they nailed it perfect, they'd still be behind on technical skill.

Alpha stands when Bravo comes off the field. Check their faces. They're satisfied, not thrilled. Door wide open.

"Solid effort," Sergeant Maddox says to Bravo when they walk by. That's code for "Could have done better." And Bravo knows it.

Roper says, "Making it easy on you today."

"Never easy, Roper. Good job," tell him even though he knows I didn't see. Unity. Support. Better than honesty sometimes.

Bravo doesn't sit. They just get in line to wait for Alpha to be called. When the sergeant calls us, my cadets jump up like they were set on fire. Snap to the left and before they take a step, they salute me. Not required. Not planned. Sure it was Freeman's idea. Salute back.

When Pickens walks past me, he says, "Here we go, Captain."

Look at each face when they pass me. Stone. Focused.

Fall in behind them. Sergeant Maddox doesn't say a word when we walk by. Nothing left to say.

Alpha takes its place on the sideline and waits for the order to take the field. The sergeant announces the squad and says my name as the squad leader—the right name. Then comes the order for us to take the field. As soon as I hear it, bark, "Cadets, forward march."

Cadets march in a straight line toward the middle of the field. Except for Pickens' slight limp, their steps are identical. Without having to give an order, MacDonald, Freeman, and O'Malley stop and let Pickens and Dixon take two more steps to make our two lines. When they stop, the whole squad smacks their heels together.

"Cadets, about face."

The squad jerks around so fast, almost worry that one of them will fall over. But they stick to the ground like they've been drilled into the earth. They slap the forearm of their rifles hard enough to echo off the bleachers, and they jam the butts of the rifles into the ground next to their right feet with a thud. Chins up, chests out. They're as tight as a guitar string.

Let's see how they play.

Most squads start with marching and formations. Get the squad warmed up, get rid of the butterflies. And that was my plan too, until three days ago. Changed it to rifles first. Mistakes happen with rifle maneuvers because the cadets start to get tired. Putting rifles first eliminates that element. Brings nerves a bit more into the picture. Not worried about nerves, though.

Call out, "Right shoulder, huh."

Rifles bolt off the ground, hands slap the forearms with timing so perfect it makes a cracking sound across the field. Just about have to break your hand to make that sound. Their bodies remain solid while the rifle moves around their heads, just like I taught them, and settles into place on their right shoulders.

Now let's blow their minds.

"Cadets, rifle maneuvers, huh!" Most squad leaders give multiple orders during the rifle section, but want to show my cadets are trained better than that. Give one order. That's it. Let them do the rest from memory.

Rifles come off their shoulders, grab the forearm, flip the rifle over on their right hands, catching it in their left on every spin. After three spins, they let go of one end of the rifle. Front row lets go of the forearm, back row lets go of the butts. Front row hands their rifles to the right, back row to the left. They have to do this while catching the rifle that is coming to them at the same time, in unison. Three times.

They nail it.

As soon as the third pass is made, cadets go to the present position, grab the barrels. Shoot the butt of the rifle to the ground. A perfect second after the rifle hits the ground, kick the stock with their right foot. Rifle flips around, catch it with their hand. Return to the present position. Three more spins. Back to the ground next to their right leg.

Cadets yell, "HUH!"

Crowd roars. And Chris Walker blows the horn. That horn, deep, rumbling, old, just like the one in the truck that hit us.

See Pickens' face. He doesn't like it either.

Ignore him. Stay focused.

"Right, face."

Rifles come up to present position.

Call out, "Transition, huh."

Front row turns an about face. Back row left face. Two steps each line. Dixon and Pickens turn left face again and fall right in step with the rest. Straight line. And I'm centered perfect, marching with them. Ten yards back.

We turn right. March straight at the judges.

Ten feet in front of the table, we turn about face. Dixon and Pickens go right. MacDonald, Freeman, and O'Malley go left. Five steps.

Walk past them. Stop, wait.

MacDonald, Freeman, and O'Malley square left at the same time Dixon and Pickens square right. The two lines make another turn and fall in in front of me at our starting position. I'd swear they were standing in their own footsteps.

The crowd claps and whistles. And the horn blows in a solid stretch without interruption.

Pickens looks like he's going to lose it.

Wish I could get my hands on Chris Walker. Make him stop. Just one more section, though.

Focus. Make everybody proud.

But Pickens starts to crack.

———

The nurse comes rushing in. Cop still sitting on my bed. "What did you do? I told you to take it easy on him."

"Just asked him a couple of questions. He was doing fine. Said something about hearing a car horn and then broke apart."

The nurse screams, "Get out."

She grabs my wrists. My hands are plastered to my face.

"Jason, you got to let go, sweetie. You got to let me see. Please."

Let her pull my hands away.

Look at my hands. They're covered.

"Oh, Jason. You tore the stitches, honey."

Blood runs down my face. Whole head throbs. Don't care. Deserve it.

The nurse runs to get some help. Should tell her. Don't need it.

bravo-delta

Freeman grunts.

Look at my cadets. Their eyes wide, begging me for the next order.

Inhale deeply to bark out the next order. Never get it out.

The air horn blows. Time's up.

"Thank you, cadets. Let's hear it for North Covington."

The crowd doesn't roar. Nobody whistles. The truck's horn doesn't blow.

My cadets square to the right and take a step.

"NO," I yell.

They stop.

"Alpha Squad, fall in."

They just look at me.

"I said fall in."

Pickens tries to speak. "But Captain, the sergeant—"

"Cadet, who gives the orders around here? Fall in."

They do it.

Look hard at each of them. "We're not done here."

The sergeant from Central comes back on the mic. "Thanks, cadets. You can exit the field now." He laughs like something is funny.

Give the order. "Left, face."

They turn, not sharp like they're supposed to.

"Forward, march."

Five steps. Give the next order. "Left, face."

As soon as they turn, another announcement. "Cadets, please exit the field." No laugh this time.

Keep marching my cadets in the opposite direction. Turn them again. "Right, face." Two steps, then again. "About, face."

They make the turn. Looking better now. Have to finish. They cut our time. Know it. Didn't go five minutes. Win. Victory. Only way.

"TILLMAN!"

My cadets stop.

Look toward the bleachers. Sergeant Maddox stands halfway on the field with his hands on his hips and fire blazing from his face. Glance toward the bleachers to see only one person standing—Mr. Coffeen.

Turn to look at my cadets, Alpha Squad. Their faces tell me. Not anymore.

bravo-echo

Sergeant Maddox doesn't even look at us when we come off the field empty-handed after awards. And Mr. Coffeen is nowhere to be found either. Guess he knew it was best to leave this one alone.

With his back to us, Sergeant Maddox says, "Load up, cadets." No emotion.

Guess he's saving up.

The cadets walk past him, heading toward the parking lot. Me and Pickens don't.

"Sergeant, the head."

He doesn't even look over his shoulder. "Go."

Enemy actions can't go unpunished. Keeps shit in line. Like gigs for soldiers, enemies have to pay the price, too.

Me and Pickens turn to make it look like we're going toward the head. About fifty feet away, slip into the flow of people heading for their cars and SUVs with their happy faces, and Central with their trophy. Pull off my cover.

The crowd thins the farther into the parking lot we move, looking for Chris Walker's truck. Scan the lot. Don't see the truck. Walk over a couple of rows, eyes searching. And finally they find Chris Walker's truck, pulling out of the parking lot.

"What now, Captain?"

"The battle's not over, Cadet. Not until I say so."

————

Sergeant Maddox grips and ungrips the steering wheel, blowing up the veins in his one good arm, all the way home. He pulls the van up to the front of the school. He speaks to the group for the first time since he said to load up in the van. "Exit, cadets."

Dixon opens the back door, climbs out. The rest file out behind him.

Grab the door handle. Sergeant Maddox has something else to say.

"Tillman, hold it."

Let go of the handle. This is where he tells me what kind of gig I got coming. Keep my head forward, make no attempt to look in his direction.

"Four gigs."

Don't move. "Yes, sir."

"Four gigs and one week to get your shit together."

"Yes, sir."

"Don't know what the hell got into you. But you need to focus. You're too good to make that kind of mistake." He pauses for a few seconds. "Do I need to be worried?"

"No, sir. I'll be straight Monday. Straight now."

"You'll have a chance to prove it. But only one chance. Screw up like that again and The Citadel won't be an option." He stops to let that sink in. "Tillman, everything in me knows you should be the one they pick. But you know I can't let any cadet ruin the reputation of the program, even my best one. Got me?"

"Affirmative, sir."

"We're good then?"

"Absolutely, sir."

"I'm trusting you, Tillman. And not many cadets get that."

"Won't let you down, sir."

Sergeant Maddox shifts the van into gear, signaling me to get out.

Open the door and step out of the van. Sergeant Maddox drives away. My squad stands there staring at me, looking for an explanation. But they're afraid to ask. Everyone except Freeman.

"Captain, what happened?" she asks.

"I failed you, cadets." Have to accept responsibility. I'm the leader. Blame goes on me.

"But Captain—"

"No buts. Just didn't get it done." Think of what Mr. Coffeen said about learning to apologize. Know they deserve it. But can't seem to find it in my gut.

Freeman closes her mouth. Her face is unsatisfied.

"No excuses, cadets. Better next time."

They all just nod slightly, turn and leave. Only Pickens

left there. Not surprised. Lost trust, respect today. Won't be gone for long, though. Make sure of that.

"Sucks, Captain," Pickens says.

No reply. Can't disagree. Don't want to affirm.

"We still should have won. No way did anybody perform like we did. They had to get the time wrong. It ain't fair." Pickens kicks a rock off the sidewalk. "Just ain't damn fair," he says again and drops his head.

He stands there wanting to feel sorry for himself, but I'm not going to let him.

"One battle doesn't lose the war, Cadet. We'll fight back."

Pickens needs to learn—replace failure with success. Even everything out.

"You got it?"

"Got it, sir." Pickens doesn't sound committed, though.

We start marching toward the house. "We still have one more mission today."

bravo-foxtrot

Have no one to blame but myself. Made a serious tactical error. Told Chris Walker we had a competition. Should have known he would try to sabotage me. Been his goal all along. But I have a goal, too. Not going to let anyone get in the way.

Pickens and I storm through the front door. Head toward my room. Mr. Coffeen sits on the couch watching a football game on TV. He tries to stop us. "J.T., just a minute."

"Not now, sir." Don't even look in his direction.

Pickens follows me into my bedroom. Take my father's picture out of my pocket and put him back on the nightstand. Know he's disgraced.

"You lost control of your squad, soldier. No excuse for that."

"No, sir. Never happen again."

"I've trained you better than that, soldier. Correct?"

Hear his disappointment ringing loud and clear.

"Yes, sir."

Pickens sees and hears me, but he knows who I'm talking to. He understands. Doesn't ask any questions.

"So what are you going to do about it?"

"Make the enemy pay, sir."

"That's right, soldier. But you got to pay too. Both of you. Your mistake. Your gig. Nothing free."

"Know, sir." Look over at Pickens. "Down, Cadet."

"O.K., Captain."

Mr. Coffeen knocks on the door. "J.T.? Who you talking to?"

"Pickens, sir." Guess he didn't notice both of us walk in.

He waits a few seconds. "You got a minute?" he says through the door.

"Not now, sir."

Mr. Coffeen pauses again. "Well, you let me know. Got to talk."

Know he wants to talk about the competition. He's probably disappointed, too. Can't face him right now. Have to get gigged first. "After awhile, sir."

Mr. Coffeen doesn't reply. Hear him walk away.

Look back at Pickens. Motion toward the floor. We get down. Put palms on the floor and shoot our feet back into the push-up position. Ready.

"No, soldiers. Too easy. On your feet."

Stand up. "Just give the order, sir."

"Make fists with both hands."

Do as ordered. Look at Pickens to let him know he needs to do the same.

"Face. Three shots."

Turn toward Pickens. He faces me. "Just a gig, Cadet. You know we deserve it."

Pickens is scared, but he doesn't say anything. He's learned some things are just necessary.

Clench my fists tight, dig fingertips into my palms. Eyes straight ahead.

"Let's go, soldier. Now."

Stare at Pickens. He nods. Ready.

Swing right hand and plant it into his jaw.

Pickens stumbles a bit, but holds his ground. He comes back hard, slamming his fist into my left cheek.

"That's one."

Pickens is ready for the next shot. We swing almost in unison, catching each other at the same time.

"There you go."

Head rings. Beating ears. That metallic taste of blood fills my mouth.

"Don't stop now, soldiers. Let's go."

Swing fast and hard before Pickens is ready. The third shot almost takes him down. But he's got enough left to give me everything he's got.

His fist lands on the corner of mouth and chin, snapping my head back. He's stronger than anyone would think.

"That's what I'm talking about. No holding back."

Blood pools under the tongue. Don't spit. Swallow it down. Heat radiates off my face. The pain beats inside like a sledge hammer. Just what we needed.

"No sir, no holding back."

"Never, sir," Pickens says. His face is red and swollen a little. Feel a drop of blood at the corner of my mouth. For once, Pickens got the best of me.

Wipe the blood with the back of my hand.

"You're ready now, soldiers. Ready for battle. You know what you have to do."

Pickens has already caught his breath. His face is stone, waiting for the next order.

"Alright, Cadet. Now it's Chris Walker's turn."

"Absolutely, Captain."

Don't change out of my uniform. Chris Walker disrespected the uniform so it has to get it back.

Yank open the bedroom door, and Pickens follows behind me. Mr. Coffeen is standing in the living room, instead of sitting.

He grabs my arm before we can make it to the front door. "Whoa, hang on there a minute."

Stop and stare back at him. "Sir, let go. Please."

He looks at my face, probably a trace of blood still on my mouth. "Know where you're headed. And that ain't a good idea." Mr. Coffeen doesn't even acknowledge Pickens. He just looks straight at me.

"Don't know what you're talking about, sir." Pickens stands to my left, waiting. Can't even hear him breathe.

"J.T., now don't play dumb with me. There's a few things I know." He still holds my arm.

"Sir, due respect, but you wouldn't know about this."

Mr. Coffeen looks straight into my eyes. Can see the wheels turning in his head. "Martin Jorge Hernandez." He lets the last name sink in. "Mrs. Hernandez's husband."

My eyes widen. "Sir?"

"I was young, in my twenties, I guess. They lived next

door." He stops for me to get the picture in my head. "He was drunk and beating on her all the time. Should have called the cops, but I thought I could stop him on my own. Just too hot-headed for my own good."

Mr. Coffeen lets go of my arm because he knows he's got my attention. "Met him in the front yard one evening and told him I wasn't letting him go in that house. We fought. He pulled a knife. I got it away from him." He pauses. "And it ended up in his chest."

He stops. Looks down at the floor. Shakes his head like he is still trying to believe it.

"Self-defense, they said. Mrs. Hernandez wasn't but eighteen." Mr. Coffeen looks back up at me. "When it was over, she came up to me, took both my hands, and said, 'Mister, thank you for protecting me.'"

Look at Mr. Coffeen, trying as hard as I can to believe what he's telling me. But it doesn't make any sense.

He keeps talking. "That's why she brought you to me all those years later. She never forgot. Said she knew I would protect you. And I thought maybe if I could help, make things better for you, then I could feel right again."

His last words erase his story and refocus my head on the mission. "Well, sir, that's all I'm trying to do, too."

Make a move toward the front door. Mr. Coffeen tries to grab my arm again, but I'm too quick this time. Snatch my arm away before he can get a hold.

"Let's go, Pickens."

We get out the front door before Mr. Coffeen can catch me.

"J.T.," Mr. Coffeen yells from the front door. "Come back here. Think about what you're doing, son."

"That's all I do, sir." Take a few steps down the sidewalk, then yell back, "Enemies have to be stopped."

Me and Pickens start jogging toward downtown. Not too fast. This will be over before Mr. Coffeen even finds the keys to his truck.

———————

Mom sings loud with the radio. She waves her arms and points at me like she's performing on stage.

I shake my head because I hate this song.

Mom shakes her shoulders and bounces, dancing in her seat. She doesn't have her seat belt on so her whole body comes off the seat. She is so goofy. It makes me crazy.

I reach over and turn the station because I can't take too much of this.

She punches the button to go back to the song, picking up the lyrics without missing a beat.

Her voice reaches the top of her lungs. She keeps pointing and shaking. Mom smiles at me because she knows this is agony.

"Mom, give me a break."

She just smiles even bigger and keeps on singing. If I ignored her the way she is me, she'd have a fit.

Way past enough of this. Reach over and change the station again.

Mom takes her eyes off the road. She looks at me like I've

gotten on her last nerve, then at the radio. She reaches for it.
But she doesn't get a chance to go back to her song. She hears
the truck's horn.

And I don't get a chance to hear her sing.

bravo-golf

Downtown Covington is only really alive for one day a year—the day of the Fall Festival. It is the one event that brings out all the people who normally drive past the few shops and the square like they're obstacles while headed for the strip malls and huge stores out by the interstate. But today Main Street is lined with cars and the square is covered with tents and tables. Some sell crafts and peach preserves. Others try to unload fall vegetables grown in backyard gardens. The North Covington Marching Band even has a dunking booth set up to raise money. The whole place crawls with people like an anthill. And Chris Walker is one of them.

His yellow truck sticks halfway out into the street in front of Billie's Café. No way he would be bothered to park it right. Typical. Always in the way.

Watch the crowd, trying to figure out if we should stand post closer to the square or not. Don't have to wonder long. Chris Walker and the same guy from the competition come walking out of the mob of people. He walks with that swagger that says he doesn't care about anything or anyone.

Pickens and me are lucky. They don't get into his truck. They go into Ms. Billie's instead.

"Last chance to bail," I tell Pickens. Want to throw him the bait to see if he'll take it, find out if he's really ready for this or not. Once we cross the street, that's it. Won't turn back. Forward is the only direction to go.

"Not a chance, Captain." Pickens does his best to look tough and ready. Guess he is compared to what he used to be—weak, stumbling, scared.

We step off the sidewalk in unison, not even bothering to look for cars coming. March across the street with heels popping against the asphalt like gunshots. Slide by a few people standing in front of the café, swing the door open and step in. The place is packed.

Scan the room. Ms. Billie runs around trying to handle the crowd that is too much for her. Two girls from school sit in the booth where Ms. Francis helped me with the essay. Jerk my eyes away before I can think of how much she probably wouldn't approve of this. Would tell her just like John Proctor, I have to stand up to the enemy.

Stop my eyes on every face at each table until I find him.

"I thought the pickles were just on the hamburgers." He laughs, and I know the enemy has been found.

Engage.

Snap my eyes to the right to see Chris Walker, sitting

on one of the stools at the counter, his big grin plastered across his face. He gets up, and so does the guy with him.

Shift my feet into position, ready for attack, like Sergeant Maddox showed me. Can't see Pickens to my side so he must be just behind me.

Chris Walker steps over and claps his hands lightly. "Beautiful performance this morning. Didn't you think so?" He nudges the huge guy standing next to him.

The guy laughs. "Perfection." He claps the way Chris did. Notice his hands are thick, rough. Like Mike's.

"Pickle Freak, this is my buddy Carter. Just joined one of my dad's crews. Used to play baseball for the Braves."

Stare right at this guy who is so big he blocks the view of the entire room behind him. His face is covered with a half-grown beard.

"You must have sucked then." Not going to let this guy think he scares me. That's what Chris Walker wants. But today is about what J.T. wants.

Carter's face changes. He's not smiling anymore. Can see his brain is too slow to reply.

"Not any more than your little band of idiots did out on that field," Chris Walker says.

Take my eyes off Carter and turn them to Chris.

"Guess you can't win them all. Well, some of us can." He laughs.

"Yeah, little man," Carter says, sounding just like Mike used to. His thick hand hits me in the side of the arm—the one that will never be as good as it should be.

Mike bangs on the door so hard it sounds like the door frame will bust. I crouch down on the floor between the toilet and the wall, hands trying to stop the blood pouring out of my nose. Head rings like a siren.

"How'd you like that, little man? That's what you get for having a smart mouth," he yells. "Don't hear you laughing now, little man."

It didn't matter that Kevin was the one who said the macaroni and cheese tasted like shit. I was the one who laughed. Then the back of Mike's hand shut me up.

Mike keeps pounding the door with his fist. "You better come out of there. That's an order." He pounds a few more times.

Can't move.

"One, two," Mike yells. "Three."

He doesn't pound the door again. Hear Mike walk down the hall. Stay wedged against the wall. Pull toilet paper off the roll. Close my eyes so I don't have to see the blood on the white paper. Press the wad against my nose. The ringing in my head has dissolved into pounding.

Push my shoulders forward enough to get my weight over my feet and dislodge myself from the corner. Need to turn the light off so I will be safe.

Reach for the switch, but the door crashes into my hand before I can get to it. The force throws me back toward the bathtub.

Mike fills up the doorway, his calloused hands wrapped

around a baseball bat. "Little man, I warned you." He grabs a handful of my shirt.

Can smell the beer he spilled when he hit me.

Mike snatches me out of the bathroom into the hallway. Reach and grab the doorknob to the closet, but he is too strong. Turn and start beating his arm with both hands. His grip doesn't loosen, even a little. Start swinging at his body, but my hands might as well be hitting a brick wall.

Mike throws me down on the living room floor, my bloody nose skidding against the rug. "Guess they didn't teach you no manners up in Pickens County. Now you're going to learn some."

He stops yelling. The next sound I hear is the bones crushing in my knee when Mike plants the bat into my leg.

Put my hands up to stop him. He just knocks them away. Can't fight back. Too weak. Curl up into a ball. Close my eyes to make it dark, but it's only dark to me.

Mike swings the bat down again, slamming it into my left bicep. It sounds like a line drive.

Tears pour out of my face. Body shakes. Don't move. Just wait to die.

"Come on, little man, can't fight back?" Mike taunts. "Come on, show me what you got."

bravo-hotel

Jason from Pickens County couldn't fight back. But J.T. can.

Strike Chris Walker dead in the face before he can even wipe away his grin. Jump toward Carter and slam both hands into his chest, knocking him over the chair behind him. So much stronger now.

The whole café comes to a screeching halt.

Body on fire. Perfect. The heat of battle. Look around. Pickens has disappeared. Doesn't matter. This is my battle.

Turn toward Chris Walker. He takes a swing, but I catch it the way Sergeant Maddox showed, like a good soldier. Good soldiers win.

Twist his arm, bending him over, and kick him in the stomach. Finally getting what he deserves. He's always just been in the way too much.

What feels like a truck slams into the side of my head, turning the room into blurry thick liquid. Let go of Chris Walker's wrist. Try to get my bearings.

Carter kicks my bad leg, dropping me to one knee. Chris

Walker tries to punch me again, but knock it away with my left arm and plant another strike in his gut. Jason could have never done this. J.T. is strong, a soldier, a machine.

Then the truck comes back and sends me to the floor.

What feels like a stampede pummels my back, stomach, sides, and face. That familiar metallic taste wraps around my teeth. A spike drives into the top of my skull. But I don't curl up. Swing my arms and kick my feet to fight them off, to make them pay. Enemies have to pay. My father fought the enemy. Mom was proud of him. Now she'll be proud of me.

Kick and swing enough to get to my knees. I'm not going to be beat. Feel warm wetness on my face. Not stopping.

Chris Walker lands a shot against my ear. Sirens go off. Hate sirens like horns.

Carter kicks me again, but the body has already found that nice place where the pain transforms into nothingness. The kick doesn't even phase me.

Put my right foot on the ground to get up, to make one more charge.

Chairs squeak on the floor as people shove them, trying to get out of the way, get out the door. Chris Walker grabs one. He swings.

Perfect execution.

———

"Come on, Jason, just two more." Danny, my physical therapist, pushes me to curl the five-pound dumbbell.

I strain as hard as I can, but my left arm just doesn't want to cooperate. Needles shoot up my arm. The muscles shake as the dumbbell comes up a centimeter at a time.

"That's it, don't give up, soldier." Danny gets way too excited about something so small. He's called me soldier ever since the first time I came in here after the casts were taken off four weeks ago. He saw my father's dog tags and decided it was appropriate.

"So you want to be a soldier, huh?" Danny asked that first day.

I looked down at my father's dog tags hanging around my neck. "Yes, sir."

"Well, alright then. Got to start with the right PT."

Danny looked at me like I was supposed to reply, but I didn't have anything to say. So he just clapped his hands one time. "Ready to go, soldier?"

I liked the way the word sounded coming out of his mouth, so I let him keep calling me that.

Sweating and straining, I get the two more reps Danny wants and drop the weight on the blue mat.

"There we go. No problem. Too easy." He smiles big at me. He waves his arm. "Now come over here." Danny walks toward the other side of the room with a slightly spastic motion that he's had his whole life. He has cerebral palsy. But he said he never let that stop him from doing anything.

I follow him, limping as well, but I wasn't born with it. Mike gave it to me.

"Stand against the wall," Danny instructs.

Do like he says.

"Now move your feet a little in front of you. Keep your back flat against the wall. And squat down as close to getting the back of your legs parallel with the floor as you can, and then push back up. Got me?"

Nod at him. Squat slowly, letting the wall support most of my weight. The pain in my left leg makes me want to drop to the floor. Squeeze my eyes shut and fight my way back up to the standing position.

"Nine more of those."

"Nine?"

"Hey." Danny points at me, his hand in the shape of a gun. "Soldiers have to be strong." Nod.

Keep my eyes shut for all of them because the pain seems lighter when I don't see anything.

Finish, let out a big breath, and open my eyes. Mrs. Hernandez sits across the room in a chair with her purse in her lap. She smiles like she is proud of me. Don't know how she could be. Ruined things. She had to take me back to Honeywell House, and now she has to find me a new place to go.

Look at her for a few seconds and then ask Danny the question that Mrs. Hernandez has refused to answer.

"Danny, when will my arm and leg get back to normal?" Wipe the sweat off my forehead.

"Oh, Jason, don't worry about that right now." Danny doesn't look at me when he says it. And he didn't call me soldier.

"No, tell me. How long?" Look over at Mrs. Hernandez.

She's still smiling because she doesn't know I'm getting information she won't give me.

Danny looks at me with the wrong kind of eyes. They're not bright and happy like they normally are. Stare hard back at him. "Just say it."

He shrugs. "There's some bad nerve damage," he says, in a serious tone that he has never used with me.

"So what does that mean?"

"The right PT will definitely make your arm and leg stronger."

"How long?" Bark at him. "When will they be back to normal, full strength?"

"Maybe," he says, and pauses. He looks at the floor then back at me. "Probably, never."

Drop my eyes. See my father's dog tags resting against my chest. This isn't possible. Have to be a soldier like him. Strong, brave. Not weak and scared. That's what gets you hurt.

Look back up at Danny. "No. I can train. You said the right PT. That's what you said."

"Yes, I know what I said, Jason. But the reality is—"

"Forget reality. I can train, right? That can make me strong. I can focus, work hard. Right?"

"Yeah, but Jason, you have to accept—"

"No, I don't have to accept anything." Push my body off the wall. Pain stabs into my bicep and knee. Stumble forward. "What do we do next?" Limp around in a circle. "Come on Danny, what's next? Got to train. Come on, PT me." I'm almost yelling.

Look at all the machines and mats around the room. Keep stumbling in circles, waiting for Danny to tell me what exercise is next. See Mrs. Hernandez get out of her chair and walk toward me.

"Jason, what's wrong?" *Mrs. Hernandez asks.*

"Don't talk to me. Have to train." *Look at Danny.* "Come on. We can't stop now."

"Jason, slow down just a second," *he says.*

"No. Can't. Got to PT." *Limp over to the bench press machine. Almost fall into the seat. Grab the handles. Push as hard as I can, ignoring the hurt that seems to take over my whole left side. The pain don't matter. Just being strong matters. Not weak. Not Jason.*

Danny and Mrs. Hernandez walk over in front of me.

"Jasonito, please," *Mrs. Hernandez says in that voice that is supposed to make me feel better.*

"Jason, just hang on. Stop for a minute."

"No. No more talking. Have to be strong. Got to be able to fight back—like a soldier." *Look at Danny.* "Right? PT will make me stronger?"

Danny reaches over to stop me from exercising. "Jason, this isn't doing you any good."

"Stop. Don't call me that." *Yelling now.* "I'm not Jason. I'm a soldier. I'm...I'm...I'm J.T."

Keep pushing the weight until I can't feel Jason anymore.

bravo-india

Climbing out of the dark isn't easy. Eyes won't snap open like they're supposed to do. They crack open to let in blurred colors for just a few seconds before fighting their way closed again. Have to get them open to see what is coming at me.

Keep forcing my eyes open, grabbing a few images at a time—the TV mounted high on the wall, a picture hanging next to a mirror, blue curtains on a dark window, a yellow chair, Mr. Coffeen sleeping with a magazine on his chest.

Finally, the whole room comes into focus. Hospital room.

Failed again.

Move my arms and feel a plastic tube graze my forearm. It runs down my arm and into my wrist. Try to scoot up. My body feels like it's been run over. The skin on my face is tight. No doubt from swelling. Not the first time it's been messed up.

Push harder to sit up and a ton of weight comes down on my head. The tube running into my arm tugs the metal stand with the IV bag, and the wheels on the bottom squeak.

Mr. Coffeen stirs in the yellow chair. His magazine falls to the floor. He wakes and shoots up in the chair. He takes a few seconds to get his head clear from sleeping, then looks over at me. "How you feeling?"

Think for a few seconds to get some real awareness of my body. Some of the weight lifts off my head. "Shredded, sir."

Mr. Coffeen nods. "Well, that would be about right." He gets up out of the chair and walks over to the bed. He looks at my face, eyes darting around, taking in the damage.

"How bad, sir?"

"Let's just say I'm glad you don't have to enter no beauty contest in the next few days." He tries to chuckle, but it doesn't come out like it normally does.

"No," I say, and then immediately think of our next drill competition. "Just as long as I'm ready for next weekend." The words come out slow. Hard to speak.

"Next weekend?"

"Another drill competition. Got to ..." A wave of dizziness swims through my head. "Got to be ready to lead my squad."

Mr. Coffeen looks at me with sad eyes that don't look right on his face. "J.T., I think it's going to be a bit longer than that. You're banged up pretty good. Got a broken nose, a couple of cracked ribs, probably a concussion. But your cadets will still be there when you're well." He forces a smile to say everything will be just fine, but Mr. Coffeen's not very good at lying. "Nurse been coming in here waking you up every hour."

I give him a strange look.

"You don't remember?"

"No, sir." Stop to try to grab the last thing I do remember. "The café—"

"Now, we don't have to talk about that right now." For once, Mr. Coffeen doesn't feel like talking about something. But I do.

"Who told you, sir?"

"Nobody. Heard the sirens and just knew in my gut. Got there just as they were loading you up." Mr. Coffeen shakes his head. "J.T., you just about gave this old man a heart attack."

"Had to do it, sir."

"You think so?"

"Yes, sir. Enemies have to be stopped. And nobody was going to stop Chris Walker, so me and Pickens had to."

"Who?"

"Pickens, sir. My cadet. The one with me at the house. Pickens."

"J.T., son, nobody was with you today."

"Yeah, you know. He's a little shorter than me. Walks with a bit of limp. He was standing right next to me in the living room."

"J.T., you must be confused. It's probably the concussion. Pickens is the county you used to live in before you came to live with me. Where Honeywell House is. You're just getting mixed up."

"Sir, I'm not mixed up." Sit up more. Pain stabs my side. Ignore it. "I'm the Captain of *five* cadets—MacDonald, O'Malley, Dixon, Freeman, and Pickens. You're wrong."

"Yeah, I saw the others at the competition. But there were only four."

"No, FIVE."

"O.K., hang on. You getting all wound up." Mr. Coffeen puts a hand on my shoulder. "We'll have a chance to think all this through, later."

"No, no thinking. Later I have to train, get ready for next weekend. Competition. My squad. Chris Walker can't stop me. He can't win, sir." Pull the sheets back off my legs.

"J.T., what are you doing?" Mr. Coffeen puts his hands on my legs. "You got to stay in bed. You're hurt now."

"No, I'm not. Never going to be hurt again. Got to win—the competition, the scholarship. Going to The Citadel." Try to force my way out of bed, but Mr. Coffeen presses his weight down.

"Now J.T., listen to me. That's all good to try for. But the truth is, son, in the condition you're in, it...it ain't likely." He looks at me like he's ashamed of what he's saying. "Somebody has to say it."

Shake my head. "No. Go get Pickens. Go get him. We have to train. Get ready."

He doesn't move.

"GO GET PICKENS."

Mr. Coffeen has half his body down on my legs. My bad leg twitches and pulses.

"J.T., there's no Pickens. There's only you. Look at me."

Try to push him off me. If my left arm was stronger then maybe I could.

"Look at me," Mr. Coffeen says again.

Stop pushing. Do like he says and stare straight into his eyes.

"There's just you, J.T. Understand?"

Look at him for a few seconds, then lift my head and rest back on the pillow.

Mr. Coffeen stands up, pulls the covers back over my legs. He stands at the side of the bed for a while without talking. Eventually, he says, "You alright now?"

"Absolutely, sir." Turn my head so I can't see him standing over me. See my wallet and my father's dog tags on the stand by the bed. "I understand."

Mr. Coffeen waits a while longer. I just keep staring at my dog tags.

"Well, I'll be right back. I'm just going to talk to one of the nurses, get somebody in here to check on you."

"I understand."

Mr. Coffeen walks away from the bed. He stops at the doorway. "Be right back."

Hear his steps going down the hallway.

Throw back the covers. Roll out of bed, plant my feet on the ground. "I understand…" Grab the metal stand with the IV bag. Pick it up, kneel down, and lay the stand on the floor beside me.

"I understand J.T. has to be gigged."

Lean over and put my palms on the floor. Lift my head to see in front of me.

"And you too," I say to Pickens, still in his uniform.

"Yes, Captain." He gets in the push-up position.

Stretch my legs out behind me. Hold the up position, my left arm shaking a little. The pain in my ribs feels like I've been cut in half. But that still isn't enough to stop me. Nothing is ever enough.

Look at Pickens to make sure he's ready.

"One mission. Victory."